COLLATERAL DAMAGE

BY

Austin S. Camacho

Copyright © 2002 by Austin S. Camacho

ISBN 1-890158-62-3

Cover design by Cathi A. Wong
Published by:

Intrigue Books

Intrigue Books are published by:
PublishingGold.com, Inc.
An affiliate of Small Business Advisors, Inc.
P.O. Box 436
Woodmere, New York 11598-0436 USA
Telephone: 516-374-1387
Facsimile: 516-374-1175
Mail to: Letters@publishinggold.com

Printed in the United States of America
Published October 2002

COLLATERAL DAMAGE

-1-
SATURDAY

Isaac sent Anna into the corner with one last backhand slap before responding to the pounding behind him. "If this is one of your nosy neighbor friends, they'll get the same as you," he said. He shuffled his broad frame to the door to stare through the small pane just below his eye level. Somebody was there but it was too dark to see them. Arrogance rumbling in his throat, he flung the door wide.

His visitor offered more than a few surprises. First, he was dressed rather formally, in a black suit and tie. He wore black leather driving gloves and dark sunglasses, despite the fact that the moon was out behind him. He must have been black too, but he was awfully light for a black man, more like the color of coffee if you used real cream. And his hair was wavy, but not kinky like all the black guys at Redskins camp before they threw him out. For his temper, they said. As if having a temper was bad for a lineman.

"You know, a woman screaming like that will attract people's attention," the black guy said. Isaac figured the most surprising thing about this guy was that he was smiling. He looked so relaxed, Isaac was tempted to relax too. Some of the rage was seeping out of him. He glanced down at his bruised left knuckles, then back up at the man at the door. Well not up, really. The black guy was a good four inches shorter, which would make him just about six feet tall.

The newcomer also looked at Isaac's big knuckles, and his smile dimmed just a bit. He kept one hand wrapped around the other in front of him. When he looked up, his gaze focused past Isaac for a moment, then he looked up into Isaac's face. "My name is Hannibal Jones. My little friend back there called me because he thought you folks might be having some trouble. "Mind if I come in?"

Isaac looked behind himself to see a scrawny black kid, maybe twelve years old, crouching at the back of the room. As he did, his new visitor slid past him. None of the other busy bodies who came to the door ever tried to come in, not even the cops. Not until they asked Anna if they should, and she was always smart enough to say no. Not that this guy was any threat. Isaac had maintained his training weight, almost three hundred twenty-five pounds, a good hundred fifty pound advantage over the intruder from the look of him.

Hannibal walked to the center of the room, and seemed to anchor himself there. The boy stood frozen against the far wall. Hannibal stared hard at the woman in the corner, petite, cowering, waving him away. Her mouth formed the words "go now" without sound. He resumed that damned arrogant smile and returned his attention to Isaac.

"So, er...where's your boy?" Not a question Isaac expected. Usually the intruders started with "why are you doing this" or "what did she do to make you do this" or some such idiocy, as if they really cared. This guy didn't seem concerned about why. Isaac wasn't sure if that was good or bad.

"In his room," Isaac growled, flipping his head menacingly, his dirty blond hair dancing across his face. "What's it to you?"

Hannibal pointed to the boy leaning against the wall and said "Monty, please." The boy ran back into the house. Isaac stepped toward him, but Hannibal stepped into his path.

"Monty goes to school with Nicky. He might just want to tell his friend goodnight, eh?"

Isaac hesitated for a moment, then his eyes flared as he realized for the first time that he was losing control of the situation. "Get out of my house!" he roared, his teeth bared like a cornered animal. "Get out now!"

Hannibal stood his ground, his nose wrinkling as he stared up into Isaac's big face. Was that some kind of subtle insult to

Isaac's breath? And so what if it was? Wasn't a man entitled to a few beers on the weekend in his own house? Isaac could feel the blood pumping back into his face, knew he would be getting red as he always did just before the explosion. At least, that's what Anna always said. His fists shook at his sides. The smaller man slowly raised his left hand to chest height, his palm facing Isaac.

"How about we clear the field first? Doesn't it seem crowded in here to you?"

Isaac watched his son and the black kid run past behind Hannibal, and out the door. Isaac was surprised Nicky left without even looking up, not a backward glance at his old man. Something like regret flitted through his mind, and the rage dimmed just a bit.

"My boy..."

"Yes," Hannibal said quietly. "And now the lady, okay?"

The black kid was back in the house, taking Anna's hand, helping her to her feet. They were walking behind the smaller man. She walked slowly, limping. Isaac was aware then of his power. And while he watched her, she turned her face to him. A red trail led down from her nose. Purple patches stood under her deep blue eyes, almost like the paint he used to put on before a game. But her eyes still cut into him, as they had earlier this evening, before it all started.

"No!" Isaac screamed in his guttural voice, his right arm reaching out for her. Two gloved hands wrapped around his arm, at the wrist and just below the elbow.

"Can't we talk about this?" Hannibal said, his voice still calm but more urgent now.

Isaac swung his arm outward and around. Hannibal lifted off the floor and sailed across the room to crash into a wall. Isaac centered his attention on his wife, so close to the door, about to leave him. "Get back here right now, you bitch!" he shouted. The woman stopped, and if not for the boy with her, may well have turned around.

But then Isaac felt a thump in his ribs on his right side, and staggered to the left. Hannibal recovered from delivering the stamp kick and raised his arms as a guard. Now his posture was familiar. He was ready to fight.

3

"Let her go, Isaac," Hannibal said softly. "You don't really want to hurt her. Or anyone else."

What the hell did he know? Isaac could feel the rage building again as he watched his woman vanish through the door. He would teach her to desert him. He would settle with her as soon as he was done with this intruder. He turned to square off against the other man. Hannibal stood with fists raised, feet spread apart like a boxer. Probably thought he was some kind of fighter. He would never know what hit him.

Isaac dropped his shoulders and charged as if breaking through the line to sack the quarterback. Hannibal appeared frozen in fear at first. It would be easy. But then, just as Isaac reached him Hannibal's body shifted to the right. One foot did not move, and Isaac tripped over that outstretched right leg. A gloved fist thumped hard against the back of Isaac's head. Momentum sent him crashing into the sofa, forcing it back into the wall with enough force to create a long crease in the plaster. Hannibal was on Isaac's back in an instant, wrapping his right arm around Isaac's throat. His voice was close in Isaac's ear.

"How about we calm down a bit now?" Hannibal said. "No point in hurting each other..."

Isaac wouldn't let him finish. He stood easily with the man on his back, and ran backward as quickly as he could across the small room. He knew he had run out of space when the wall stopped him. He heard the breath burst out of the little man on his back. He raised his arms to reach behind himself, clamping thick fingers around Hannibal's neck. Hannibal's left arm swung under Isaac's arm and his left hand clapped onto the back of Isaac's head. Hannibal's right, still across Isaac's throat, gripped his own left arm. A simple but effective choke hold. Isaac pulled his own arms down, but it only increased the pressure on his throat.

This little man wasn't going to bring him down. He moved forward just far enough to smash backward into the wall again, crushing Hannibal between the cracking plaster and his own massive bulk. Again Isaac's huge legs propelled him back into the wall. A third time. The intruder cried out in pain each time. He would have to give it up soon.

But then the room began to spin and darken. Isaac's head ached and the little breath he was getting rasped in his throat. Then pain shot through his knees. That's how he knew they had hit the bare tiles of the floor. Then his hands slapped the floor, supporting him and the burden on his back.

The last thing he remembered thinking was that he could have beaten the black guy easily if he had fought fair.

*   *   *

Hannibal freed his arms from Isaac's unconscious form and pulled himself to his knees, swallowing and panting a bit. Pain pulsed from the center of his back outward in all directions. His arms ached from sustaining pressure long enough to knock Isaac out. And his throat was a little raw from Isaac's thumbs digging into it. But at least he had managed to end this conflict without either of them getting badly hurt. He suspected that would answer the first question he'd hear when he got outside.

Anna Ingersoll watched him close her front door and step slowly toward her. She leaned against his white Volvo 850 GLT, her arms wrapped very tightly around her son. Hannibal did not avoid her eyes, but explored them under the street lamp for what they could tell him. He saw desperate fear there, but relief and curiosity hung close behind that. He opened the passenger door and waved her inside. She only held her boy tighter.

"He'll be after us," Anna said.

"No he won't. Not for a while. Get in the car."

"Is he okay?" Now her face showed more concern. She still loved him.

"He's asleep, but not hurt. Please get in the car."

"You're not the police," Anna said. "Police don't act like that. Who are you?"

"I'll tell you in the car." Hannibal said. When Anna didn't move, Monty squeezed past Hannibal and squirmed into the back seat. He pulled Nicky in behind him, out of Anna's embrace. She looked more confused now, as if her son was her touchstone with reality. Eyes darting left and right, she finally dropped into the front seat. Hannibal closed her door, quickly walked around the car and got behind the wheel. His eyes clamped briefly as he sat back, and he swallowed a gasp of pain.

"You're hurt." Anna said.

Hannibal nodded and started the car. "Not bad. This really went better than I expected from what Monty told me when he called me from your kitchen."

"What now?" Anna asked as Hannibal guided his car away from the curb and down the darkened streets of Southeast Washington, DC. "I can't just leave." She turned in her seat and Hannibal wished he could see what passed between mother and son. Then she turned back to Hannibal and her voice was different.

"I didn't say thank you," she said, wiping the wetness from her blackened eyes. "Thank you. Now, who are you and why did you become involved with us?" She didn't attack him for interfering in her personal life. That meant Monty had been right. She was ready for the torture to end.

"My name is Hannibal Jones and I'm a professional troubleshooter."

Anna ran her fingers through her short-cropped blonde hair, momentarily scratching at its darker brown roots. "Troubleshooter? Like a private eye or something?"

"Well, I do have a private investigator's license, but I don't do much P.I. work. I make my living helping people in trouble, whatever kind of trouble they can't get help with otherwise. And sometimes," he glanced back at Monty, "sometimes I do it as a favor to a special friend."

Anna sat silent for a moment, as if considering his words and how she might qualify as a person in trouble. And as each block passed separating her more and more from her husband, Hannibal could see her shoulders rise and straighten a little more. He wasn't sure what had kept her in that house with that dangerous man, but he began to believe she would not be going back. When she seemed to have it all neatly in order in her mind, she looked at him again.

"Okay, back to my original question. What now? Where are we going? Some halfway house or something?"

"For now I'll take you to the safest place I know. Monty's house. Actually the home of his grandmother, Mother Washington. I imagine you'll come to the barbecue I'm giving tomorrow, and then we can decide what you want to do from there. The important thing is for you to be in a safe environment for a little while and have time to think."

Hannibal's explanation brought the first word he heard from Nicky, who leaned forward between the front seats and said, "Barbecue?"

-2-
SUNDAY

Hannibal loved the smell of a charcoal fire. And there in his building's backyard, behind the three story brick he called home, he hovered close enough to his round Weber kettle grill to absorb the smoke of the coals and mesquite chips into his pores. He leaned back, filling his lungs with the sweet scent of steaks and ribs dripping with Mother Washington's dark red sauce, and stared up at the clear blue sky. Nature had sent him a perfect crisp autumn day and he was enjoying it to the fullest.

For most folks, the middle of Columbus Day weekend was a bit late in the season for cooking out, but this was Hannibal's idea of a good time, and the neighbors who wandered in and out seemed to agree. He scanned the yard, an almost square patch of green marginally wider than the building. A dozen or so of his closest friends and neighbors occupied folding chairs, lawn chairs, and the occasional kitchen chair dragged outside for the event. Three picnic tables groaned under the contributions so many guests had brought: potato, macaroni, green and cold pasta salads. Cole slaw. Baked beans.

Everyone who lived in Hannibal's building had turned out. Virgil, Quaker and Sarge had even invited ladies. Ray was hunkered down over a big plate of ribs across the table from his daughter Cindy. While Hannibal watched, she looked up, apparently decided she had spent enough time on family, and headed for Hannibal over at the grill.

Cindy's form still made Hannibal's breath catch in his throat. She was tall and svelte, with eyes the color of dark sweet chocolate and a broad inviting smile. She wrapped an arm around his waist, pressed her ample bosom into his chest, and brushed her lips across his.

"Why don't you grab a plate and come enjoy some of this party? All work and no play you know."

Hannibal had long since given up trying to resist Cindy's suggestions. He laid the last of the meat on a serving plate and covered the grill, but hung behind a few inches so he could watch her hips sway seductively as they headed for the tables. He waited for her to sit to make sure he was facing her. Virgil poked at the boom box two tables away, and the Crusaders filled the yard with their unique smooth jazz sound. That music and friendly laughter filled Hannibal's mind as he stared deep into Cindy's eyes and filled his mouth with sweet, tender rib meat. A soft breeze flipped the collar of his knit shirt against his cheek. Hannibal silently prayed that when he got to heaven it would be just like this.

Anna Ingersoll stood out painfully when she stepped through Hannibal's back door into the yard. Not because she and her son were white. After all, Quaker and his date were also, not that anyone present cared. In fact, as Monty led them in, he and Nicky darted for the food and instantly became part of the festivities. Nor was it because she wore a conservative skirt and low heels. All the men were in jeans, but some of the ladies had recently returned from church and hadn't bothered to change. No, Anna stood out because Hannibal was swimming in a sea of smiles, and hers was the only face in the place not lightened by the joy of the moment.

Hannibal waved Anna over to his table, and Cindy slid aside to make space for her facing Hannibal. Anna seemed overwhelmed by this small kindness shown by a stranger, as if it were something she was not used to. Hannibal stood momentarily as Anna sat.

"Cindy, this is Anna Ingersoll, the lady I drove over to Mother Washington's last night. Mrs. Ingersoll, I want you to meet Cindy Santiago, the only attorney foolish enough to hang around with the likes of me."

Anna shook the tips of Cindy's fingers and nodded. When she turned to Hannibal he noticed how different she looked from the night before. Her face and hair glowed from scrubbing. She had done her nails and applied light but attractive makeup, almost concealing her bruises. When she spoke she flashed small, even, perfect teeth. The fact that one of her incisors was chipped was a jarring reminder of the night before.

"I realized this morning that I hadn't thanked you properly, Mister Jones. What you did last night...the way you did it. I mean, I know you could have really hurt Isaac, and I remembered today that when you got in your car I could see you were carrying a gun. Thank you for helping us, and for not hurting him."

"Mrs. Ingersoll..." Hannibal began.

"Anna. Please."

"Well then, Anna, when Monty comes banging on my door on a Saturday night screaming that it's a matter of life and death I don't hesitate."

"But, you usually get paid for this kind of thing, right?" she asked. "I must owe you..."

Hannibal chuckled. "Actually, Monty was my client last night, and we'll work something out. But how are you doing in that area anyway? I mean, do you have money?"

Anna's shoulders seemed to lower a bit, as if talking relaxed her. Nicky was sitting beside Monty chewing on a burger. Her eyes followed his movements for a moment, then returned to Hannibal. "We'll be all right. I'm not exactly pulling in millions down at the DMV, but I think I can feed the two of us if we can find a place to live."

"I might be able to help with that part," Cindy said. "My firm's senior partner owns quite a bit of investment property. I'll bet he has a vacancy for anyone I vouch for."

"You'd do that?"

"For a friend of Hannibal's?" Cindy said. "Any time. But I'm curious. How did you end up living in Southeast to begin with? MOST of the folks in this part of the city are only here because they can't be anywhere else." Her eyes cut to Hannibal with cold sarcasm.

"Isaac moved us here from North Dakota because he was to be a right guard for the Redskins," Anna said. "We left everything behind to chase his dream. But some things happened at the training camp. Isaac didn't fit in with the team. He has a temper, as Mister Jones knows too well. Other team members just didn't want to work with him."

Hannibal put his rib down on his plate. "Okay, so you were in Washington and didn't know anyone, but why..."

"For a very long time Isaac refused to believe he couldn't play football," Anna said, her hand raised as if to goad her audience into understanding. "He kept thinking they'd call him back. We had no money, no friends, nothing. I eventually found work, but we were so broke. One of the other players owned that building we live in and he had a vacancy. Anyway, it was the first apartment that looked like we might be able to afford. It sounded like he was doing us a favor at the time, but now I think maybe it was all a big joke on Isaac. We don't belong there. Still, I tried so hard to keep our family together, for little Nicky's sake. But Isaac just sat all day, stewing in his anger, and the longer he sat, the angrier he got until he had to lash out at something and...."

As she spoke Anna's eyes slowly squeezed shut, her head lowered, and her outstretched hand gradually curled into a tightly balled fist. Hannibal looked at Cindy, but neither had any idea what to do or how to help.

Then a white-gloved hand rested gently on Anna's shoulder. Hannibal looked up to see Mother Washington standing behind Anna, her round dark face aglow from the rapture of recent Pentecostal church service. That loving glow softened the worry lines covering her kindly face, but Hannibal could still see them, even shadowed by her broad brimmed black church hat. She was a big woman, and her black dress reached nearly to her ankles, but no kinder person lived in Hannibal's world. When she spoke to him, it was the voice of everyone's grandmother.

"This child needs me right now, and the help the Lord can give when we go to Him in prayer," Mother Washington said softly, looking down at Anna. Then she pointed back toward the house. "That child needs you, and what you can do. Go help her."

Hannibal looked past Mother Washington to find another black woman standing in his kitchen doorway. This one was no one's grandmother, judging by her apparent age. She was in fact as petite as Anna, nicely rounded and attractive without being aggressive about it. She wore a conservatively cut navy blue skirt suit and heels, which added a couple of artificial inches to her height. Her black hair was straightened and hung to shoulder length. Long artistic fingers clung to a small clutch purse as if for dear life.

"Well, go on," Cindy said. "Can't you see she's got trouble?"

Yes, Hannibal could see that plainly on her face and in her body language. And as he stood, he saw his perfect Sunday afternoon fading in the distance. He considered that for a self-employed man he certainly seemed to take orders from a lot of people. Partially in revenge and partially in self-defense, he reached down to capture Cindy's hand.

"I'll go, but not alone."

At the door, Hannibal held out his hand and introduced himself and Cindy. The woman took his hand solidly, then Cindy's.

"Very pleased to meet you. I'm Bea Collins. Mrs. Washington tells me you're very good at helping people. And I'm afraid I need some help today."

"Let's not talk out here," Hannibal said. "There's a party going on and I hate to ruin it. My office is right next door."

Mother Washington had escorted Bea through Hannibal's unlocked front door and through his kitchen to the backyard. He took her to the door on the other side, just a few feet away. The kitchen they entered was never used.

*   *   *

Hannibal didn't like to do business this way: in jeans and sneakers, with barbecue sauce under his nails. He escorted Bea through the flat he used for business, past the spare guest bedroom, the storage room, the room with weights and the hanging bag he sometimes used, to the big front room that was his office. He settled behind his desk and waved his visitor into the facing chair. Cindy sat at the smaller desk by the door. Thick shafts of sunshine poured in through the two big windows on Hannibal's left, splashing the room with brightness and calling his mind away from work. With an effort he ignored the light and focused on the nervous woman in front of him. She was staring at his eyes, but they often did at first. He ignored it unless they actually asked about them. Her own eyes were a soft fawn brown, and very vulnerable.

"All right, Miss Collins, you seem to know a bit about me from Mother Washington. Why don't you tell me a little bit about yourself and what kind of trouble you've found yourself in?"

"Myself?" Bea asked as if the question were a surprise. "Well, I'm an interior design architect with offices in Georgetown. The trouble is that Dean, that's my fiancé, Dean Edwards, he disappeared yesterday. I think he might be in danger." It sounded to Hannibal like a response on the Dating Game. But while she spoke, Bea sat leaning forward on the edge of her chair, knees clamped together, fingers wrapped around the top of her purse in her lap. Her posture reminded Hannibal of a dog sitting up to beg. Her eyes were begging too.

"Disappeared?" Hannibal asked. He had learned to ask open, general questions if he wanted full answers.

"Yesterday, Mister Jones. I went out shopping early. When I got home he was, well, just gone."

"So, you live together." That implied a degree of commitment, but no diamond ring adorned her hand.

Bea was about to answer when Mother Washington and Anna entered the room. Her eyes cut to Mother Washington and she briefly hesitated. "Yes," she finally said. "He lives at my place now. For the last couple weeks. Three, actually."

"I see. And what makes you think he's in danger?" Hannibal asked.

Bea's face said that was a stupid question. "Well, why else would he be gone? Without a word, without even a note?"

Hannibal could think of several possibilities, but none this woman was likely interested in hearing. Instead he asked "Is Dean in with a bad crowd? Involved with drugs or some sort of illegal activity?" When Bea's eyes cut to Cindy, Hannibal added, "Ms. Santiago is an attorney and anything said in her presence will be kept in strictest confidence."

"It hardly matters. My Dean would never use drugs or do anything illegal."

Hannibal nodded, leaned back, crossed his legs. "You've filed a police report, of course."

"Yes, this morning, but those people don't care. They won't twitch a muscle until a body turns up dripping blood."

An exaggeration of course, but Hannibal knew the police would not invest resources into a search for an adult missing less than twenty-four hours, and to his way of thinking there was good reason for that. He leaned forward slowly, wanting to soften his answer as much as possible. "Miss Collins, I'm sorry but this isn't really my type of case. Maybe you don't understand what it is I do."

Before pain could even register on Bea's face, Mother Washington said, "She understands, Hannibal. You help people, just like this little girl here." She patted Anna's hand as she said it. "And I just know you're going to help her."

"Mother Washington," Hannibal said, standing, "We don't have any reason to believe this woman's fiancé is in any kind of trouble."

Mother Washington stepped heavily to the desk and placed a big soft hand on Hannibal's shoulder. "Look at her son. It's Bea Collins who's troubled right now. A woman who sits in my church every Sunday and sings out so you can hear her on every hymn and I bring her to you for help. I know you won't let her down."

Hannibal shoved his hands in his pockets and stared at the floor. Mother Washington had helped him move in and become part of the neighborhood. She had a heart as big as the Capitol dome and, besides that, she was the unofficial mayor of this block and everybody's surrogate grandmother. Why did she work so hard when she must know he hadn't the strength to say no to her?

"Look, maybe he's visiting family."

"Dean hasn't any living relatives," Bea said. "I'm all he's got."

"Maybe a coworker," Hannibal said. "Sometimes guys get cold feet and want to hang with the fellows for a bit. Why not call his job tomorrow morning? If he's at work you know he's okay, right."

At this point Bea sniffled. Mother Washington's eyes bored into Hannibal. Cindy's eyes rolled toward the ceiling. Bea managed to look up at Hannibal with damp eyes. "I went to his job yesterday afternoon. Sometimes he goes on the weekend for a while. At least I thought so."

"Excuse me?"

"Please, Mister Jones. He told me he was working on a programming project for a marketing company over in Alexandria. And there were people there, working on the weekend. But, they had never heard of him. Oh, Mister Jones...."

The picture was morphing before Hannibal's eyes. Mother Washington's face told him he was getting her view of the situation at last. Another woman being abused by a man, but more subtly than what Anna Ingersoll's husband did. More subtle, but perhaps no less damaging. When Cindy stood, Hannibal knew she saw the same picture. She stepped closer to Bea, looking down at her as if she were a witness on the stand.

"Sounds like you don't know this man very well. Maybe it would be better if you just never saw him again, eh?"

Bea's eyes slid up Cindy's body, past the jeans clinging so tightly to her rounded form, past the tee shirt her breasts threatened to burst through, past the wavy hair cascading wantonly onto her shoulders, and stared deep into her dark Latin eyes. Hannibal would never have believed any woman could make Cindy look cheap, but the tiny curve at the edge of Bea's lips spoke volumes.

"That," Bea said slowly, "is not the nature of my love." Then her eyes returned to Hannibal. He could see then that this Dean had wormed his way all the way down into her soul.

"Will you find him for me Mister Jones?"

"You understand this isn't a free service, Miss Collins."

Now Bea's cutting smile settled on Hannibal. "This isn't about money for me, Mister Jones. I will pay you whatever it takes if you're the man who can do the job. Business has been good for me. I already have enough saved for the down payment on our.." the sentence tripped her, but only for a moment, "our first home. Picked out a nice little brownstone in Georgetown, near my office. But without Dean, that's an empty dream, isn't it? Will you help me? I may not be your usual client, whatever that may be, but Mother Washington told me that you help those who have no place else to turn. I have no place else to turn."

Would he help her? Help a woman being taken in by a swindler, a swindler who had perhaps had a change of heart or moved on to bigger things? Would he take her money to find the con artist and show her his true face? Perhaps Mother Washington was right and it was the only way to free this woman's heart to love again. Not the kind of trouble he usually helped people out of, but perhaps as valid as any.

Besides, even if he could say no to this petite stranger sitting in his office on Sunday morning in her church clothes, he could never say no to Mother Washington. He pulled a drawer open, pulled out a contract and slid it across the desk to Bea. She signed without reading it while he was talking.

"Five hundred dollars a day. Plus unusual expenses. And another two fifty if I need to subcontract other professionals on the case. No way to know how long a trace like this can take. If he's lied about his work, he's probably lied about a lot more. Are you sure you want to see this fellow again that badly?"

Bea's signature was small and precise. When she finished, she returned Hannibal's pen to its stand and asked, "When can you get started?"

Hannibal looked at Mother Washington who smiled warmly. "It's a fine yard party, son, but it's running itself just fine. And I think all your friends would understand." He continued to glare at her. "I'll clean up and make sure everything gets put away proper."

He walked around the desk to lean against it just to the side of Bea's chair. His office seemed stifling just then, but maybe it was just the mix of four different women's perfumes.

"Truth is, with missing persons, the sooner you start the more likely success is. Do you have a recent photo of the missing man, Miss Collins?"

"Well, not a still picture," she said, fumbling her purse open. "Never really had time to take any. But I've something even better!" She gave him her first genuine smile and handed up a tape cassette.

*   *   *

Hannibal managed to leave Mother Washington and Anna behind when he shifted to his own apartment across the hall. His front door entered the fourth room back, just before the kitchen. Cindy dropped onto his sofa but Bea stood while he pushed the tape into his VCR. The image soon resolved itself into a news broadcast, and a second later the sound kicked in. An anchor was setting up the next story, a fluff piece, but Bea narrated right over her.

"This is from Monday's news. It's about last Sunday's event at the Mall. You remember, the international food thing? Dean and I were there."

The story was the kind of light fare beginning reporters are often assigned and composed mostly of man on the scene interviews. The reporter, a trim redhead, was too perky by half. She interviewed couple after couple, child after child, about what a fun time they were having getting a "Taste of DC" as the event was called. The annual event took place on The National Mall. Not a collection of stores but rather a flat park sitting in the middle of the city, anchored at one end by the Washington Monument.

The National Mall is as perfect a gathering place today as it was a hundred years ago, big enough to give the revelers the illusion of being separated from the traffic and the grime of government at work, surrounded as they are by this nation's repositories of knowledge and culture, the various buildings of the Smithsonian Institute.

The screen presented a collage of revelers biting into sausages and baklava and meat pies with unpronounceable names. Less than a minute into the story, the camera zoomed in on the happy couple. Hannibal was focused on the twenty-six inch screen, but he heard Bea drag in a ragged breath as the cameraman zoomed in with that jerky movement now popular, and framed up Dean's face.

Hannibal didn't react, but he was surprised. He was briefly displeased with himself for making assumptions. He expected a slick looking, dapper brother of the Taye Diggs school. Instead, he was staring into a rounded, clean-shaven Caucasian face, with straw-colored hair falling into eyes that crinkled almost shut when he smiled. He was a little on the heavy side, clearly not athletic, in stonewashed jeans and a flannel shirt. He had rolled the sleeves halfway up his arms. And when he slipped his arm around Bea's waist, her face lit with new love.

He babbled something about "having a stone blast out here, like Epcot Center in Disney World," and the whole time he was speaking into the camera, Bea's eyes were on him, watching his precious words being formed by thin lips and pushed out between white, even teeth. Yep, he had her.

Hannibal rewound to the closest shot of Dean and froze the picture. Perfect con artist looks, he thought. Average height, weight, hair and eye color, common haircut, no facial hair, nothing to make him stand out in a crowd, or a lineup.

"This is all you've got?" Hannibal asked.

Bea was startled. "Surely you'd recognize him from this. I've just never taken any pictures or anything."

Hannibal stopped and ejected the tape. "I don't need pictures for myself, Miss Collins. I need to distribute pictures if we're going to find this guy. I need to be able to leave them in as many hands as possible in places he might go: airports, train stations, bus stations. If he told you the truth about his profession, maybe computer companies. Does he have a car?"

"No. No car. Is that important?"

"Well it means we add taxi stands and rental car agencies to our distribution list," Hannibal said. He glanced at Cindy who nodded slightly. No car meant mobility, a man who probably didn't plan on staying in one place too long. A bad sign.

Cindy stood, one hand to her chin. "Hannibal, can't you get a still made from the video? I'm sure we've had that done at the office."

"I can," he said, handing the tape back to Bea. She handled it like a precious artifact, gently guiding it back into her purse. "The image quality will be crap if I take it from VHS though.

What I will do, is trot on down to Channel 8 and see if I can talk somebody down there into printing a still frame from the original broadcast quality Betacam tape. That might be clear enough. Then we run off fifty glossies and then the legwork begins. Now, would you be kind enough to escort Miss Collins back to the party?"

Bea stood, her spine as straight as a reed, and at that moment looking just as fragile. "That's it? Is that all you're going to do?"

Hannibal sighed, thinking how much this woman really didn't want what he was sure to find if his hunt was successful. "No, Miss Collins it isn't. I'm going to change my clothes. Then you and I are going to take a ride over to your apartment so I can look around, maybe learn a little more about this Dean Edwards."

-3-

Half an hour later, Hannibal followed Bea down his front steps to the Washington DC street. The sunshine was still bright, but the world looked different to him. Out here, in front of his three-story tenement, poverty blew in on him like the hot breath from a panting engine. Boys traveled in gangs and older people moved quickly, not looking left or right. Even the few trees on his block struggled to maintain their lives at the edge of the sidewalk. And he was no longer on vacation. He was at work, and his work was always grim.

Hannibal looked different too. Now in his black suit and tie, wearing his signature Oakley sunglasses, he felt more businesslike. Black driving gloves did not impede his pushing the button on his remote control to unlock the white Volvo. He held the door for Bea to get into what was the only new car on the block. Once behind the wheel, he started the CD player, filling the car with the sound of Wynton Marsalis' unique interpretations of movement and sound, melody and rhythm. With an easy smile he pulled away from the curb, headed for the Fourteenth Street Bridge.

Relaxing back into the white leather, Hannibal asked, "Just what is a professional woman like you doing in this neighborhood, Miss Collins?"

"My mother and Mother Washington were very close, Mister Jones," Bea said. She sat very straight and looked forward at the crumbling inner city beyond the windshield. "I still attend her church. Every Sunday. The Lord has brought me everything, Mister Jones with never a trial, until..."

Hannibal nodded. "Until now. Well, maybe we can make this a short trial. And please, call me Hannibal okay?"

Bea nodded and sat quietly for a while. Hannibal drove them across the Potomac River and onto the George Washington Parkway. Past Reagan National Airport the park on their left was overrun with joggers, picnickers, and the occasional fisherman trying to make the river give up its rockfish. Three small sailboats seemed to be playing tag against the background of the well-wooded Maryland shore.

"And what about you, er, Hannibal?" Bea asked. "I understand you are a successful businessman. What takes you to that neighborhood?"

"Long story. I'm surprised Mother Washington hasn't told you." Hannibal turned left at the second light into the part of Alexandria locals called old town, then right on Fairfax, the street closest to the river. As other streets moved closer to the river, he turned to keep the open water on his left. "So tell me, how long have you known this Dean Edwards?"

Two blocks of expensive townhouses passed. Bea watched Hannibal's face until she was ready to answer but when she did she turned to stare into her own lap. "Three months. You think I'm being a crazy woman, don't you? You won't find him. You don't think I should even be looking."

Hannibal parked in the numbered space designated for Bea's home. The new bank of colorful townhouses called Ford's Landing hung at the edge of the Potomac shore. All brick homes, with private garages, private patios facing the water, and price tags reaching almost a million dollars. Hannibal gained a new appreciation for the value of interior design. Or at least, for the value some wealthy people must put on interior design.

Bea's home was almost in the shadow of the Woodrow Wilson Bridge, which carried a couple hundred thousand commuters from Maryland to Virginia and back every day. Today the bridge was quiet but Hannibal could imagine the din of the traffic she must hear every weekday. The coarse smell of the Potomac splashed across his face as he opened his car door. Actually the smell would mostly be from the waste treatment plant across the river, not far down on his left. He wondered briefly how this could be one of the most sought after addresses in the city.

Bea gripped his hand before he could quite get out of the car. When he looked back she said, "Will you find him, Mister Jones?"

"Hannibal," he repeated, smiling into her soft eyes. "And if I don't find the man, it won't be for lack of trying. You hired me to do a job, not to judge anyone. You'll have to trust me. Can you trust me?"

Bea smiled, and looked even more vulnerable for it. "I handed the keys to my Lexus to your girlfriend, didn't I? Yes, I trust you. You, and Mother Washington, and the Lord who brought us together."

*   *   *

Bea's three level home told Hannibal volumes about her, but there was scant evidence of a male resident. Bea explained that she had spent most of Saturday in a slowly growing panic, and when she was upset, she cleaned. He noticed a copy of Architectural Digest on a glass end table, open to the picture of what looked like a huge, rambling hotel.

"My work," Bea said. He saw Bea cited as interior designer, and read part of the description under the heading "Best Rental Development."

This 262-unit rental community features an upscale appearance and quality finishes in apartments designed to appeal to employees of local high-tech companies. The development features two distinct building styles: high density, 1- and 2-bedroom"atrium" units that range in size from 717 to 1208 square feet and feature subterranean parking; and low-density, 1-, 2- and 3-bedroom "villa" units that form the perimeter of the development and have direct-access garages and private entries. Units feature such desirable amenities as ceramic tile counters, custom cabinets and flooring, marble fireplaces, crown molding, and upgraded lighting...

Hannibal whistled aloud. "You did this? I imagined you picking the drapes in rich people's houses."

"All my work," Bea said, "and not just the residence areas. I designed the interiors of the 10,000-square-foot resident pavilion, the business center, gourmet commercial kitchen, billiards room and even the fitness center."

Hannibal dropped the magazine and moved to the kitchen. "Not many start in the hood and fly so high. Is that what Sidwell Friends School does for you?"

Bea stopped mid-step. "How did you..."

"Lucky guess," Hannibal said, opening an extremely orderly cabinet filled with glassware. "You don't talk like public school. Your folks must have worked their butts off to get you into that place."

Hannibal closed the cabinet and continued to explore Bea's home. She was proud when he went through her kitchen, and clearly embarrassed when he entered her bedroom, despite the fact that it looked like a showroom. At Hannibal's insistence Bea checked her jewelry case and quite arrogantly announced that nothing was missing.

"Good," Hannibal said, exploring the dresser she had assigned to Dean. "Did you have any cash in the house?"

Pause. "Maybe a couple of hundred dollars I guess."

"And where is that?"

"Well I figure he must have needed some expense money, after all."

The big walk-in closet was clearly divided. Her clothes very orderly on the left, his on the right. Dean had left most of his clothes behind, but they were in no way remarkable. Hannibal found what would be a set of luggage on the overhead racks, but the second largest piece was missing.

Hannibal found British Sterling cologne in the bathroom. Otherwise he used her toothpaste, soap and shampoo, no brand of his own. And Hannibal doubted a fingerprint team could have proved that a second person ever lived there after Bea's cleaning binge. His toothbrush and comb were gone, so not even a stray sample of the man's hair remained.

Yes, Dean was remarkable for the footprint he did not leave behind. Bea confirmed he had brought no pictures when he moved in, no music, no games, and only a handful of books, which he took when he left. After forty-five minutes in her apartment, Hannibal knew no more about Dean Edwards than when he arrived.

On Bea's front landing the afternoon sun made the world seem a lot cleaner than it was. They moved slowly on their way to the car, floating through an idyllic setting that had nothing to do with the ache on Bea's face. She waved sullenly to a middle aged white man who was lovingly paste waxing a maroon Jaguar XJ6 of indeterminate age.

"If he keeps at it, that car will shine as bright as his scalp," Hannibal said.

"Oh, Murray's okay," Bea said. "No crime against being chubby, white and bald. He's a good neighbor, and he's out here doing something on that car every Saturday and Sunday."

"Really? Did he see Dean leave?"

"Maybe," she said, reaching for the Volvo's door handle.

"Maybe? You mean you haven't asked him?"

Hannibal turned and headed back toward the Jaguar. Murray kept his head down and his arm moving in a smooth circular motion. Hannibal understood. He was an unknown and Murray didn't want any trouble with his neighbor. So Hannibal stood, watching his own reflection in the maroon hood until Bea reached his side. Then he took Bea's hand and broadened his smile to its limit.

"Excuse me. Got a minute?"

Murray looked up, his eyes flicking from Hannibal to Bea and back. Then Murray smiled in return, nodded and muttered, "Much better" under his breath. His expression said he approved of the new man more than the last one. "What can I do for you?"

"That car's a beauty. Must take a lot of work, eh?"

Murray grinned bigger. "Sorry sport, she's not for sale if that's what you're thinking."

"Actually, Bea tells me you were working on her yesterday too. Thought you might have seen Dean go out."

"Maybe," Murray said. His eyes grew wary and his focus shifted to Bea. "Why? You after him?"

Hannibal patted Bea's hand in his. "Well he hasn't been back since yesterday morning and, well, Bea's a bit worried about him. I thought you might have noticed what time it was or which way he went."

Conflict contorted Murray's face. Hannibal thought he might not want to get involved with a neighbor's personal life. Or maybe he just didn't want to hurt her feelings. Or maybe he knew something he wasn't sure hc should share. Hannibal reevaluated the man's age and probable social background, and decided how he should proceed. He turned to Bea and his smile became condescending.

"Honey, why don't you go ahead and get in the car and let the men talk for a minute, okay?"

Bea looked confused but obeyed. Hannibal resisted slapping her fanny for effect, but he did pick up a chamois and start slowly rubbing the Jaguar's fender. Murray was silent for a moment, then seemed to realize he had control of the conversation. Some people are comfortable with silence. Hannibal had judged correctly that Murray was not.

"You going to take care of her? Instead of her taking care of you?"

"I'm not Dean, if that's what you mean," Hannibal said softly.

Murray worked the chrome of the door handle with more concentration than necessary. "He left around ten thirty. Right behind the woman."

"Woman?" Hannibal asked. "Are you saying he had another woman here?" He did not have to fake his indignation. Bea deserved better.

"White woman," Murray said, as if that was significant. "Skinny blonde dame, older than him by a ways. She hit that door as soon as Miss Collins rounded the corner."

Murray glanced around as if he was looking for someplace to spit. Hannibal nodded in agreement with his sentiments. "How long was she in there?"

"Maybe half an hour. Just about long enough, if you know what I mean."

"And Dean came out five or ten minutes later," Hannibal said aloud but to himself. Time enough to quickly pack. So who was the woman? Certainly not a lover as Murray clearly assumed.

"He was carrying a suitcase. Did he leave on foot? Which way did he head?"

Murray sat back on his haunches. "What are you, some kind of a detective?"

"Something like that. Just trying to help Bea out. Which way?"

"He was walking when he left," Murray said, glancing over at Bea in Hannibal's car. "Never looked left or right, just headed up toward Washington Street. Looked like he was in an awful hurry to get away from here. Can't understand it myself. She's a peach, that girl."

Hannibal nodded again. "Thanks for the help, mister. I think maybe the only way for her to understand what this guy was, is to face him again. If I can find him, then maybe..."

-4-

Hannibal shook Murray's hand just as Bea's silver Lexus pulled into the parking lot beside Hannibal's car. He reached it in time to see Cindy hand Bea her keys.

"That was fun," Cindy said. "Might have to get myself a car one of these days."

"You don't own a car?" Bea asked, as if Cindy had just revealed she didn't wear underwear.

"She prefers to hand her money to cab drivers," Hannibal said, "or ride around with me."

Cindy slipped a possessive arm around Hannibal's waist. "Yep, this is my favorite cabby right here. So, did you get anywhere, honey?"

Honey was what Cindy called Hannibal in the presence of unattached women. He considered it only marginally more subtle than the method dogs use to mark their territory. "I was just getting the lay of the land here, Cindy. The work will start after I get some pictures to distribute."

"When can we get started with that?" Bea asked.

"If the reporter or cameraman who covered the event you and Dean attended is at work today I should get them pretty quickly," Hannibal said. "I, not we."

"I want to come with you."

"Bea," Hannibal said as gently as he could, "I'm sorry but we can't do this together. I can do this. Or you can do this. The choice, of course, is up to you."

The woman actually pouted. "But I want to do something."

"Then stay by the phone," Hannibal said. "He might call or send a message. But let me do the searching, all right?"

*   *   *

News Channel 8 was all local and all news and, predictably, a twenty-four hour operation. But despite what Hannibal told Bea, he was surprised to find the reporter he needed to talk to at work on a Sunday evening. Yet there she stood, not so perky as she appeared on screen, standing over the young man at the controls in a darkened editing room, directing the construction of another video story.

Hannibal had called the station soon after driving away from Bea's house. He had learned that the girl in question, Irma Andrews, was the newest television reporter on staff. That being the case, it was no surprise that she drew many of the weekend fluff assignments. He also learned that she would be in-house on that Sunday evening, helping a videotape editor turn her latest script into two or three minutes of video news.

After placing that call, he had joined Cindy for dinner at the Blue Pointe Grill, a seafood haven on Washington Street, Alexandria's main thoroughfare. It had become Cindy's favorite eating spot since the day they found themselves two tables away from John Ashcroft. As far as lawyers go, this was a celebrity just short of a Supreme Court justice. Hannibal's only memory of that night was that for an Attorney General, he seemed to be a pretty poor tipper.

Hannibal told Cindy what he learned from Murray over swordfish marinated with rosemary.

"A woman?" she asked between bites. "How terrible for Bea. Another lover you think?"

"Actually, I'm thinking an accomplice. Maybe his partner come to tell him it was time to move on to the next vulnerable mark."

"Hannibal, if you think this Dean guy is a con man just getting close to her to get into her bank account, then why'd he run?"

Hannibal chewed thoughtfully. "Who knows? Maybe the woman's a spotter who has an even better mark set up for him. Or maybe the police are on his trail and getting a little too close for comfort. He might need to just disappear for while. Lots of possible reasons."

"Okay," she said, not willing to let it go and just enjoy dinner. "Suppose you're right. He's just a con man. She's in love with him, and he's gone for good. In that case, why find him at all?"

"Because, Cindy dear, that is what I'm being paid to do."

*   *   *

Less than a thirty-minute drive took Hannibal to the offices of NWS8 in Springfield, Virginia. And five minutes of friendly chat with several members of the skeleton staff on duty got him to what they called the edit tank where Irma Andrews was working. When she turned to face him, her piercing eyes moved over his entire body, from top to bottom, scanning him into her memory banks. The soft, open persona she projected on television was totally absent. In this woman's out-thrust jaw and pointed nose he read the kind of dogged determination that so often makes a good detective. And he supposed that, in a way, that was what a good reporter was.

"And you're Hannibal Jones," Irma said, "and you need my help and it has to do with the feature I made last weekend which first aired Monday morning. You're not police. I don't think a lawyer. Maybe related to someone I interviewed but.... no. A private detective?"

Her stately frame leaned naturally forward and her eyes didn't blink as often as they should. It was a rare person who could put Hannibal off balance, but here stood one of them. "Private, yes," he said. "I can see you're busy, but I'm hoping you'll take a minute to print me out a still photo from that video."

Irma looked over her shoulder at her editor, who waved her on. She tossed her scarlet locks and motioned for Hannibal to follow her. Her strut seemed exaggerated to him, and accented by the tightness of her jeans, but her walk was so forceful and aggressive it lost all sensuousness. Under her breath she mumbled, "I wish you guys would all get together on these things."

They entered another edit cell, smaller than eight by ten feet, the two long walls lined with what looked to Hannibal like the controls of the Starship Enterprise. Irma handed Hannibal a pad of preprinted forms and a pen.

"You'll have to fill that out when I give you the picture," she said. Then she pulled a videotape from a wall rack and dropped into a chair. She pushed the tape, thinner but longer and wider than a VHS cassette, into a machine and her fingers began to play over a bank of controls, shuttling around the tape, looking for the right story.

"You shoot in Beta format?" Hannibal asked.

"Right," Irma said. "Beta SP actually. The boys shoot on little twenty-minute cassettes, but each reporter can archive their stories on one of these sixties. You know something about this stuff?"

"Not really," Hannibal said, watching the blurred images fly past on a small monitor. "Do people ask you to do this all the time?"

The images slowed and an anchor came into view, introducing the story. "Actually it's pretty rare," Irma said. "Not many people even know we can do this. But I had to print out a still for somebody else from this particular story a few days ago. In fact it was Monday night, not long after we aired it. The usual thing, they wanted a clear picture of a relative. I assume that's not your purpose."

"No, I need copies to distribute. The person we're looking for has come up missing."

"Oh, well in that case you want more than a print." Servomotors whined as Irma put the tape player into normal speed. She pushed her wheeled chair a few feet to the side and punched a button, starting a computer. "Once you pick out the image I'll copy it to a floppy. You can get as many copies of that digital image as you want from lots of places."

"Appreciate it," Hannibal said, watching the action move along, watching Bea come into view, and the zoom he'd seen before, to lock onto Dean's face. "That's our boy."

"Really," Irma said slowly. She was moving the tape forward and back. Seen a frame at a time, it looked very much like a piece of motion picture film going past.

"A lot to choose from," Hannibal said. "I thought the sequence was shorter."

"At thirty frames a second, there are a lot of images to choose from. But this is the best one." She pushed more buttons, and a variety of hums and clicks started. "So what's up with this fellow? He in some kind of trouble or something?"

"Like I said, he's missing," Hannibal said. "If there's more to the story, I don't know it yet."

Irma lapsed into silence while she gathered the print of Dean's face and the floppy disc she had loaded the image onto. Then she left the room. Hannibal followed her into a cubicle barely big enough to stand and turn around in. The desk she sat at was covered with papers, most of them bearing a small precise handwriting he assumed was hers. She gestured to a chair in the next cubicle, and Hannibal dragged it over. He sat, crossed his legs, flipped the top page on the forms pad over and began to fill in the requested information.

"Not yet," Irma repeated. "Well, the woman who came Monday wanted a shot of the same boy." Direct and to the point. Hannibal liked that. "She said she was related, but now I have to wonder."

Hannibal kept writing. He wasn't sure yet how he should handle this. What was this young reporter after?

Irma moved a bit closer. Not the kind of closeness that implies intimacy, but rather the kind that applies a subtle pressure. "Look, just tell me if there's a story here, huh? I don't want to do festivals in the park the rest of my life."

Now he knew. He didn't think he had anything newsworthy, but this woman might be helpful if she thought there could be something in it for her. He considered his answer carefully, because lying would be counterproductive. "Miss Andrews, I've been on this case only a few hours. Right now it's a man who's run away without telling his fiancé e. Not much there, but it could be anything. What if he's running from the law? Or from the mob? Or the woman you met earlier in the week could be his sister, separated at birth, searching for him."

"Not likely," Irma said. "This woman looked a couple decades older than your boy there."

"Really?" Hannibal said. He sat quite still, his hands on the arms of his chair, but the middle finger of his left hand began to tap up and down. "Blonde woman, on the thin side?"

"That's right, bottle blonde. Brown eyes. Long, conservative cut flowered dress. Makeup carefully applied. And there is something going on here."

"Won't know until I find him will I?" Hannibal asked, handing over the completed form. Irma scanned the form the same way she had scanned Hannibal. He braced to stand, but her upraised hand stopped him.

"Just two questions. Please. First, is Jones your real name?" In response Hannibal handed her one of his simple white cards. There wasn't much there: His name, address, telephone number and the word "Troubleshooter" in bold block letters.

"I think I may have heard something about you," Irma said. "All right. If. If this turns out to be a story that could be of general interest. If it does, will you call me?"

Hannibal stood and removed his glasses. She stared at his eyes, the way they often did. "If this ends up on the news in any way, I'll do what I can to make sure you're the reporter who breaks it, okay?"

"Fair enough," Irma said rising and extending her hand. Hannibal accepted it and the strong handshake that came with it. "And you're a story in yourself, aren't you? A black man with blue eyes. Or are they?"

*   *   *

Hannibal drove just two blocks away from the television station before he pulled to the curb again. His instincts told him that Irma was a good reporter, and right now that was a bad thing. He had gotten lucky and tripped over a clue to Dean's location. But she had the clue as well, and if she got involved she might chase it all away.

He flipped on the interior light and unfolded the form he had pocketed on his way to Irma's desk. It had been on top of the pad of forms he had filled out. Feeling a bit childish, Hannibal pulled a pencil from his glove compartment and began rubbing the side of the point across the form. Of course there was no way to be sure the woman who wanted Dean's picture was the last person to fill one of these out. But it seemed a pretty secure guess.

A woman's flowery script slowly came into view. The name was Mary Irons. The address looked to be a hotel room on Richmond Highway, just south of Alexandria. That fit Hannibal's theory nicely. He turned off the light and put his car into gear. He knew Irma could find the same address in Channel 8's files in the morning. She might be tempted to go looking for the thin blonde woman and chase her away. With luck, he could pin Dean down tonight, before Irma went looking for the mystery woman tomorrow.

On his way through the darkened streets, Hannibal popped an old Elton John CD into his player and began to rethink his position. Why would Dean's accomplice need his picture from the news? Perhaps just to prove to him he wasn't keeping a low enough profile. A good reason to tell him to move on. Maybe, but the idea wasn't hanging together as well as it once had.

It made even less sense as Hannibal pulled into the Alexandria Motel's parking area. The motel was one long building, one story tall and one room wide, sitting with its short end facing the street but at an off angle. Its front doors faced the back of a brick building, a Chinese restaurant judging from the smell of the dumpsters. Peeling white paint covered the structure, and a row of narrow pillars supported a short overhang in front of the dozen or so doors. In the dying sunlight the place almost looked haunted, but he figured the only spirit around there was the ghost of disuse. Hannibal drove past the target door and parked at the far end of the drive. When he shut his car door the sound echoed ominously between the motel and the back of the restaurant.

Hannibal knocked on the door of the room registered to Mary Irons, then stepped back from it. He had no idea what to expect but he was sure of one thing. No successful confidence man or woman would stay here. This was not the motel room of anyone fleecing wealthy marks.

When the door opened inward Hannibal was faced with another surprise, a man wearing only jeans and a belligerent expression.

"Yeah?" is all the man said. He was Hannibal's height but a bit bulkier. Steel gray hair topped a swarthy Mediterranean face. Ink black eyebrows formed a pitched roof above dark eyes that were always looking for trouble. Hannibal guessed they had seen a lot of it. A mass of steel wool cluttered the man's chest. A tattoo of a rose covered his left shoulder, and a chain tattoo wrapped his right biceps.

"You must be Mister Irons," Hannibal said with a small smile.

"So?"

Friendly sort, Hannibal thought. "I need to speak to Mary if you don't mind."

The man squared his shoulders, sending a universal message. "She ain't here. Beat it." His breath threw the odor of stale beer into Hannibal's face.

"Look, this is a matter of some importance." Hannibal held his hands out in a gesture of peace, while subtly bracing for an attack.

"I said get lost," Irons said, his voice low. His right foot moved forward and the heel of his right hand slammed out for Hannibal's chest. Hannibal stood his ground and clamped both his hands over Irons'. By twisting slightly he locked Irons' elbow. Then Hannibal leaned forward slightly. Startled, the bigger man found himself driven to his knees.

"Who's there, Harry?" A woman's voice called from inside.

Harry looked up at Hannibal and shook his head slightly from side to side. He was ready to concede rather than have his woman see him in this position. Well, no point in embarrassing him. Besides, Hannibal wondered how much he knew. He released Harry's hand and raised his voice. "I'm Hannibal Jones and I'd like just a moment of your time, ma'am. It's about your photography order."

Harry got quickly to his feet. Hannibal stood on the other side of the portal in the outside world and watched Harry's eyes, as Harry watched his. The standoff lasted forever. Then, three minutes later, the woman spoke again very close behind Harry.

"Honey, would you excuse us for a minute? Please?" Harry turned and although Hannibal couldn't see his face, he could imagine what was there. The woman raised a hand to his cheek, smiled and whispered, "It's all right. I promise."

Harry walked back into the shabby room and the woman stepped forward across the threshold.

"Mary Irons?" Hannibal asked.

"Who are you and why are you here? No one knows me here."

Hannibal handed her his card, and waited for her to read it and try to imagine his purpose. If she did, she was not about to let him know.

"What's this about, Mister Jones?" she asked, easing the door closed behind her.

"I think you know. You wanted a photo of Dean Edwards. Then you went and visited him. I'd like to know why."

She took a minute to appear to be searching her memory. "Dean Edwards? I'm not sure I know him. Friend of yours?"

The harsh shadows of twilight didn't help her one bit. Dark roots held her thin yellow hair in place. Makeup could not conceal the lines of worry, of fear, of living etched into her face. Not a hard woman, he decided, not a criminal. Yet there was a steel rod at her center, deep down. And much of her surface tenderness had been worn away somehow. All that aside, she was certainly no confidence woman. She was, in fact, an abysmal liar.

"I'm not accusing you of a crime, ma'am. But I have an eyewitness who says you were at his house Saturday morning from about ten-thirty to maybe eleven a.m. You waited until his fiancé e had left for a shopping trip. Shall I describe what you were wearing?"

She was jumpy as a caged hamster, and she reacted to his words as if they were a series of blows. Her china blue eyes appeared chipped. "No, that won't be necessary. I guess you must mean that boy I saw Saturday. He wasn't who I thought he was."

"Really? And who did you think he was?" Hannibal turned away and took a small step away to ease the pressure on her. She followed, maintaining a constant two-foot distance. Then they were walking together.

"Someone else," she said. "Someone I knew a long time ago. I've been away a long time, Mister Jones. People change over the course of a decade."

Now that she was talking, Hannibal decided to be quiet for a minute to see what fell out. Most people hate silence. It is often the interrogator's best weapon. While he waited, he examined her body language and posture. She had been a hellcat once, he decided, but something had squeezed that out of her. From what little he knew of Dean Edwards, this woman was more likely to be one of his old victims than his old partner. Someone had hurt her deeply, and it could well have been Dean.

Just as he was about to give up on quiet, she said, "Look, Mister, I don't want any trouble and I hope you won't tell that young man where I am. Harry and me, we're trying to keep a low profile here, okay?"

She didn't know. She probably thought Dean sent him looking for her. They turned and headed back toward the door. It was open a crack and Hannibal saw one of Harry's eyes in the dark space. When they reached the end of their little stroll, Hannibal positioned himself so that the woman's body blocked Harry's view of him. He handed her one of his cards.

"If you think of anything you think someone ought to know, give me a call, okay?" he said. "I don't know what this Dean Edwards might be involved in, but it could reach out and touch you too."

*   *   *

Sitting in his car in the gathering gloom, Hannibal took a moment to wonder why on earth he had felt the need for that burst of honesty. He had no idea who Mary and Harry were or how they tied into Dean's story. He didn't think they could be hiding him, but they must be part of his past. Unless of course she was telling him the truth.

Hannibal turned the key. His engine purred smoothly but before he could put the car into gear, a pair of hands slapped down on the hood. Harry Irons stood in front of him, as if suicide were his only option to prove his superiority. The woman was nowhere in sight. Hannibal turned off the engine, tugged his gloves on tighter, and opened the door.

"Do we have unfinished business?" he asked, stepping out of the car.

"Not like you think," Harry said. He leaned back against the car and pulled out a Zippo lighter. He dragged hard and deep on a Winston, letting the smoke escape his nose. Hannibal saw Harry as a man of traditions. This was a ritual to set up a conversation. Man to man talk. Hannibal leaned against the door, his arms crossed.

"You ever done time, Jones?"

"Can't say I have, Harry," Hannibal replied. "But some close friends have told me what it does to you."

Harry's face clouded over and he stared at his feet. He held his cigarette like Sinatra. "You got a woman, Jones?"

"Yes, I have a woman."

"Love her?" Harry asked, looking at Hannibal out the corner of his eye.

Hannibal grinned. "As a matter of fact I do."

"He could have any young chippy he wants, you know," Harry said, his eyes on a cloud in the night sky. "Don't bring him around here to take mine. I been taking care of Mary for almost a year now. It hasn't been easy for her. But she's got what she needs."

"Then he's out of her past," Hannibal said.

Harry nodded and shifted his feet uneasily. "She's crazy about him, you know. I mean, whatever he did to her, he makes her crazy. But he's too young for her. I could see that."

Hannibal sighed in sympathy. Harry nodded, and sucked hard on his cigarette. "So you've met Edwards?"

"We saw him from across the street," Harry said through clenched teeth. "She was following him like a lovesick puppy. Him and his designer damn suit and his candy apple red fucking Corvette with its faggot vanity plates."

Hannibal fought to control his breathing. Instead of surprise, he forced a smile onto his face and released a little chuckle. "Faggot vanity plates," he repeated, as if it was the funniest thing he'd heard that day.

Harry joined in the laughter. "Yeah buddy. Unless the other girl's name is Kitty. Is that it?"

Hannibal never had to answer. The natural tunnel formed by the motel and the restaurant it faced carried one soft word to them. "Harry?" He stood faster than he would have liked, then effected a relaxed attitude Hannibal recognized.

"I'm going to get back there. She needs me."

"I think she does," Hannibal said, extending a hand. "Go take care of her. And take care of yourself."

-5-
MONDAY

The telephone waited until almost nine-thirty to ring. Not bad for a Monday morning. By then Hannibal had run his five miles, showered, eaten his Cheerios and pulled on his working clothes. Now he sat at his desk dealing with the paperwork the government uses to keep the small businessman in his place. Fortunately these days, most of those papers are really streams of electrons and he was finally becoming pretty comfortable maintaining his records on his computer. Steam curled from his second cup of coffee and a Quincy Jones album sprinkled the room with soft but pulsing background music. Hannibal smiled at the phone for waiting until he was ready for it.

"Mister Jones? It's Anna. Can you come out here? I need some help. Can I hire you?" The words poured out of her mouth like water from a burst dam, jolting Hannibal into rigid attention.

"Slow down a bit and tell me what's wrong."

"He's here," she said. Keeping her voice low didn't cover the panic. "Ike is here. He showed up here at work not much after I arrived. I'm afraid he'll do something."

"Where are you exactly?"

Anna was having trouble catching her breath. "I'm at the Springfield DMV office, over on Franconia. He keeps coming in and going out again. Now he's just standing there by the door, staring at my cage. I just know he'll do something crazy."

Hannibal thought about facing that giant again. It was not a fun thought. "What about the police, Anna? Has your office called them?"

"He hasn't really done anything. And I'm afraid he might go crazy if some uniformed stranger was to push him. He knows you."

Hannibal was about to protest again. Then an image came to him, an image of Isaac Ingersoll on a rampage in a crowded government building. Somebody was sure to get hurt if the police handled the situation, maybe Isaac worst of all. And clearly Anna didn't want that, despite all her husband had done to her. He was not there out of hate, but out of a confused love. If Hannibal might be able to defuse the situation, he really had no choice but to go. He might be able to end the situation with a little talk.

Still, before he slipped his jacket on and pushed his Oakley sunglasses into place, he shoved his Sig Sauer P229 into the holster under his right shoulder.

*   *   *

Hannibal slipped between the glass doors of the Department of Motor Vehicles. The ambient noise level was enervating, but he couldn't pick out any words in any conversations. The counter had to be thirty feet long with maybe a dozen people standing behind it. The line of customers stretched the length of the counter then curled on itself, once, twice, six times. Almost every person in that line was talking, in one of four languages, not counting the small children who have a language all their own. The tone of that mass of indecipherable chatter was negative. It was a room full of frustration, and Isaac Ingersoll stood at the back of it, against the wall counter littered with forms to fill out. Match and powder keg in easy reach of one another.

But what Hannibal saw in Isaac's face was helplessness. He stared across the wide room at Anna who stood behind the eye test machine, working hard at working. When she spotted Hannibal, a huge breath escaped her, as if she were inflated with tension and his presence allowed some of it to leak out. Then her eyes went to her husband, the worry lines crowding her face. Hannibal followed her line of sight to Isaac who seemed to receive her psychic wave because he turned his head and saw

Hannibal for the first time. His jaw set and his hands curled into fists.

Hannibal kept his hands in front of him, one holding the other, and walked toward Isaac. Watching the bigger man's eyes, Hannibal pushed himself closer, inside the danger area, less than arms' length away. His neck craned and he stared up into that big Nordic face, showing no tension.

"Could we just talk a minute?" Hannibal asked softly. "Maybe outside? All these people don't need to be involved in this." Then he turned his back to Isaac and eased away toward the door. A part of him anticipated a fist at the back of his head but he could not look back, could not offer Isaac an option.

He pushed through the door and dim fluorescence was replaced by the scorching fireball hanging in the eastern sky. Hannibal walked a few steps toward it. When he turned, he stood in a corner of the parking lot. Isaac was no more than five feet away, raising his fists. But the sun was stabbing his eyes. Hannibal kept his hands and his voice low.

"Isaac, I think you're ready for a serious fight," Hannibal said. "And you know what else? I think you could beat my face in."

Isaac shifted his feet into a more aggressive fighting stance. "You got that right, asshole."

Hannibal's first goal was accomplished. He had the man talking. The next step was to get him thinking. "You know, your wife could have called the police and told them you were harassing her. Why do you suppose she didn't do that?"

While he talked, Hannibal floated lightly on his feet, keeping himself turned in such a way as to never offer Isaac a perfect target. Anger tightened Isaac's face as he moved to try to reach the right position to land a solid punch. "You her new man," Isaac said. "You tell me."

"You're know it's not like that," Hannibal said with a smile. "Your wife is my client and nothing more. She asked me to come here because she's scared, Isaac, and trouble is my business." Could Hannibal establish a token amount of trust? His Secret Service training told him that was the next step. He stopped moving and extended his right hand. "Hannibal Jones is my name."

"Fuck you!"

No rapport, perhaps, but Isaac didn't sucker punch him while his hand was out. The anger was under some sort of control. "Okay. But I can assure you of this much. Your wife doesn't have another man. In fact, I'm sure she never has."

"Bullshit!" Isaac's fists were shaking with rage now. "Why would she leave me if she didn't have another man?"

It was time to commit. Hannibal rooted his feet and let Isaac get close enough to crush him. "Look at me Isaac, I'm six feet tall and I've been kick-boxing since high school. Years of police training. And if you really wanted to you could kill me with your hands. Your wife is five foot two. Maybe, what, a hundred ten pounds? Think about what happens to her body when you hit her."

Isaac's fist actually whistled through the air, down toward Hannibal's head like a hammer. A sidestep allowed it to blow past, slamming down on the fender of a Taurus. He turned away from the impressive dent, following Hannibal with his eyes.

"If she was scared of me, she would have called the police!"

"You still don't get it," Hannibal said, beginning to dance around a bit, still working to keep the sun in Isaac's eyes. "She's more scared for you. She knew if you tried this crap with the cops they'd just as likely shoot your big dumb ass. And she doesn't want you to get hurt. The woman loves you!"

Hannibal stopped to see what effect his words were having. Isaac bellowed "No!" and swung faster than expected. A fist as big as a twelve-pound ham raked across Hannibal's jaw, lifting him off his feet. He rolled across the asphalt to give himself distance and sprang up ready for action, bouncing on the balls of his feet like a boxer.

"All right you get that one for free. Maybe you owed me one for the other night. Now you've got to call the next play, big man. You come in on me and you mash my face and the police come and throw you in jail. Or, you come in on me and I'm as fast as you know I am and I break your knee and put your face through a car windshield because I can't go easy with a guy your size. Or, you go home and I promise Anna will call you tonight and talk about what's wrong and how maybe you two can fix it."

Isaac looked startled for a moment. Maybe he didn't expect Hannibal to be up so quickly. Or perhaps the sound of Anna's name had an effect on him. His fists lowered a few inches.

"Tonight?"

"My word on it," Hannibal said quickly. When he pulled a card from an inside jacket pocket he watched Isaac's eyes and saw him register the presence of Hannibal's pistol. Now he knew Hannibal didn't have to take that punch.

"My address is right there," Hannibal said, slapping the card on a car hood. "If Anna doesn't call you before the night's over, you can come to me and we can pick this up where we left off if that's what you want to do. Right now, you need to go home and relax a while."

Isaac's big fist closed on Hannibal's card, but his eyes turned back toward the double doors into the motor vehicle building. Hannibal moved into his line of sight. "You can't take her back, Ike. You have to let her come back. I'm sorry, that's just the way it works."

*   *   *

When Hannibal walked into the motor vehicle office, Anna deserted her post and rushed to him. She hustled him into the back offices and ran to the ladies' room for a wet cloth to press against his face.

"God, thank you thank you thank you." The words poured out of Anna, tripping over each other. "Are you all right? What about Ike, did you have to hurt him? You didn't have to involve the police did you? Is he gone, really gone?"

"Not gone from your life, Anna," Hannibal said, stopping her hand's movement over his face and holding the cloth lightly himself. "I'll be fine and he's fine physically, but he's a man in torment. If this is going to go on, I need to know how you feel about this guy. Do you still love him?"

Her answer was very, very quiet. "I don't know."

"What do you want, Anna?"

Anna turned and walked to the closed door. When she turned back, her face was composed again. Her strength was returning with her distance from Isaac. "I want to be safe."

"I understand," Hannibal said, "but it won't be free."

"I'll figure a way to pay you," she said quickly. "I know this is business for you."

Hannibal stood, dropping the cloth on her narrow desk. "That's not what I meant. You can't just avoid him. You've got to make peace with him one way or another. I told him you'd call tonight and talk to him. The two of you need to figure out what you want and how to make it happen. Counseling is probably a good idea."

"I'll call him if you think it's important. But I meant what I said about paying you."

Hannibal considered the inherent strength hidden in this woman and wondered how she ever came to a place where she would let a man beat her. "Anna, you can hardly afford my rates. But we might be able to handle this another way. Take it out in trade. Tell me, how hard is it to find a person if you know their license plate number?"

This brought Anna's first smile of the day. "You kidding? I'm the shift supervisor. Why don't you give me the number and a description of the car and let me see what I can do?"

*   *   *

When Hannibal pulled up in front of the palatial rambling home at the edge of Arlington he was mentally replaying his last conversation with Anna. He was barely a mile from her office, stopped at a red light when she called, sounding chipper and in control again.

"You said a red Chevrolet Corvette with Kitty as the vanity plate? No such vehicle."

"Damn," Hannibal had muttered.

"But," she added with an annoying dramatic pause, "I do show a 1997 'Vette with a plate reading KITTYCAR. Think that could be it?"

Hannibal pulled away from the light a bit faster than he should have. "Very likely, kid. Whose ride is that?"

"Vehicle is registered to one Langford Kitteridge. And if you've got a pad and pencil I can give you his Arlington address."

Instead, he had memorized the address and driven straight there. Now he sat in the colonial's extensive driveway, behind a low-slung midnight blue Lexus, gathering his official attitude. This was certainly the right place. The license plate on the Lexus read KITYCAR1. So the owners had wit and ego to spare. He didn't know anything about the residents except their obvious financial security. Was this Dean's last victim? If so, he might be no closer to tracking him down, but he accepted that as the way the job worked. You tracked down every lead. Detective work, unlike the romance of the movies, was really all about legwork.

The door's chimes echoed like bells in a church steeple. Hannibal imagined house workers scurrying like bats at the summons, but it was soon clear his image was mistaken. A minute is a long time to stand at a door. In that time he decided no one was home. The parked Lexus didn't mean anything. Owners of a house like this might well have a third vehicle, an SUV probably, and the owners would be off in that one. Oh, well, it was still good to have seen the place. He'd return later.

But he was only two steps away from the door when he heard it open, and a voice said, "Can I help you?" It was an older man's voice, commanding but very disciplined. A butler's voice, Hannibal thought.

When he turned, that image dissolved. The tall man at the door wore sweat pants and running shoes. A towel hung around his neck, and his body shone with drying perspiration. His bare chest displayed solid muscles and very low body fat. If not for some telltale sagging skin around his waist, it could have been the body of a thirty-year old, onto which someone had spliced a deeply cleft face with a full shock of white hair. Hannibal recalled actors like Charlton Heston and Charles Bronson whose faces looked ugly to him, but were always described by women as having character. This man's face had character to spare, and charisma and the kind of energy that almost pushed you over.

45

"I was just finishing my workout," the man said. "What can I do for you?"

"Sorry to disturb you," Hannibal said, pulling out a card. "My name is Hannibal Jones, and I was looking for Langford Kitteridge."

"You selling something?"

Hannibal smiled. "No sir, I..."

"Then come on in. Looking for Langford Kitteridge, eh? Well, you found him."

Hannibal followed Kitteridge across a living room he normally wouldn't try to navigate without a map and a guide, into a kitchen many restaurants would be proud of. Kitteridge pulled down a skillet from among the collection hanging above the center island. He carried the pan to the refrigerator and dropped a chicken breast into it.

"Some lunch?"

"No thank you," Hannibal said from the doorway. "I won't take up much of your time."

"I look busy to you?" Kitteridge asked. He covered the chicken breast with a cooking spray and turned it over. Then he lit the gas stove under the skillet. It was early for lunch to Hannibal, but the buttery smell and the crackle of frying called out to his stomach. Kitteridge turned to him, smiling with artificially even teeth. "Well, now that you've found me, what are you planning to do with me?"

Hannibal liked this lively old man immediately, the way he always liked people who chose living over existing. He wished he had encountered the lady of the house instead, though. If his theory was right, there might be a hurt in store for Mister Kitteridge. "Sir, I'm trying to locate a Dean Edwards. Does that name mean anything to you? Young fellow, blonde hair, kind of a round face..."

"Yes, yes I know the boy," Kitteridge said, flipping his chicken breast with a fork. The new top side was blackened, the way Cajun chefs do catfish. "One of Joanie's foundlings. Hangs around here from time to time. Crashes in the guest apartment over the garage from time to time. In fact, I think he's been staying there the last couple of days. She even lets him drive her car sometimes. He in some kind of trouble?"

"You expect him to be?"

"Hey, you're the one come looking for him, eh?"

Smoke began to fill the room, clouding Hannibal's path to the answers he needed. "My client just needs to talk to him about some plans they made. Do you have any idea how I might find him? Or perhaps your wife might know."

Kitteridge looked confused as he slid his steaming prize onto a plate and turned to stand at the island. Then, as if a new thought had struck him he said, "Oh. Yes, I see. Joanie. Sorry, son, there is no Mrs. Kitteridge. At least not yet, heh heh. Joanie's my niece. She's lived with me since I lost my brother in Vietnam. And yep, it's a pretty sure bet she knows where he is. She hired him over at KCS."

"I'm sorry. KCS?"

Kitteridge dumped salsa on his chicken and attacked it with a knife and fork. "Kitteridge Computer Systems. Guess I assumed you knew who I was. I started the company, but Joanie runs it these days. In those damn towers in Falls Church. Sure you won't split this with me?"

-6-

The comfortable but sterile waiting room was at the top floor of the tower, the ninth. The air tasted canned. The door to the hall, like the door into the inner offices, was a wide pane of glass. Both bore the company logo, a stylized letter "K" with lines for whiskers and balls at the top of the two upward lines imitating cat's eyes. The receptionist reminded Hannibal of an old movie called The Stepford Wives. After exchanging the usual greetings and information with her, he sat in an ergonomically correct chair staring out wide panoramic windows and thinking how often what looked like the end of a journey turned out to be the first step.

The man rushing into the room was tall and tanned, with high cheekbones and carefully styled brown hair. In his polo shirt, Dockers and running shoes he looked like a model who had stepped out of the pages of Esquire just long enough to find out what was on Hannibal's mind. As he came within reach, he seemed to take Hannibal in around his perimeter: curly brown hair, Oakley shades, black gloves, highly shined black shoes, and finally back to Hannibal's face. Only then did he offer his hand.

"Mister Jones? I'm Mark Norton, senior systems management analyst here at KCS. We're just coming back from our lunch jog and Ms. Kitteridge isn't quite back from the health club yet. I understand you have business with her?"

Hannibal noticed Norton did his lunch jogging in the same Reebok DMX Run shoes he himself worked out in. "Actually, I asked for her only because her uncle Langford said I should." Norton's eyes flared at the name. It was the right entree. "My business is really with one of your employees, a Dean Edwards."

"Dean?" Norton's face showed chagrin too easily. Hannibal couldn't tell how much of it was fake. "He's one of my systems programmers. Designs and develops accounting and financial applications for our clients. Real whiz with FOCUS and SQL." When Hannibal didn't react he added, "Standard Query Language," as if that would explain it all.

"I'm sure he's a real whiz," Hannibal said, "and I assure you what I need to see him about won't affect his job performance in any way."

"Gee, this is tough," Norton said in the same tone men in commercials say, "this one gives me a close comfortable shave." Then his voice lowered a bit. "I'm afraid Dean didn't show up for work today. But I'm sure Ms. Kitteridge will be happy to give you any information you need. Are you with the SEC?" Hannibal shook his head. "Treasury? Surely not the FBI."

"Not law enforcement at all," Hannibal said. "Really, just trying to help somebody out." "Oh. Well." Norton ran his fingers through his hair, exactly the way men do in dandruff ads. "Tell you what. Why don't you come down to my office? It's a little more comfortable, and you can check CNN while I try to track Joan down. Shouldn't be more than a couple minutes."

Norton's office was indeed comfortable. In fact, it reminded Hannibal of a suburbanite's den, right down to the miniature basketball hoop over the window. Hannibal was sure he'd find a Nerf ball on the desk, but if it was there it was hidden among the tiny wire sculptures of golfers and tennis players. The bookshelf was jammed with volumes whose titles were beyond Hannibal's understanding, so looking in them would be pointless. And the television mounted in the corner was indeed tuned to CNN. If that didn't suit him he could always turn on the bookshelf stereo and see what kind of CD's Norton had loaded. A very comfortable waiting room indeed. If you were the type who didn't mind waiting.

Hannibal gave him a very generous six minutes before stepping out into the hall again. Norton had headed to the left, so he did the same. The carpet was unusually springy, and Hannibal got the feeling that Kitteridge Computer Systems went the distance to make sure its nerd population was as comfortable as possible in every way. He also imagined the aforementioned nerds put in twelve to sixteen-hour days on a regular basis. It had been that way at AOL in the early 90's when it got its start not far from where Hannibal was standing. Its headquarters over near Dulles Airport was a much larger version of KCS in terms of style. It seemed to Hannibal that the design of sweatshops had advanced dramatically in the last century.

Hannibal stopped when he heard Norton's voice. It was coming from the corner office next to Norton's. That would figure. As Hannibal inched closer he detected two other voices. The man's voice was higher than Norton's and contrite. The woman, on the other hand, spoke in commanding tones. The door was not quite closed and Hannibal inched forward until he was within view. He could only see one person from his vantage point, but it was the right one. Despite what Norton had told him, Dean Edwards was in the office today.

"Can I help you?"

Hannibal spun to stare into a pair of thick glasses wedged between a bulbous nose and a thatch of straw colored flyaway hair. The man was three inches shorter than Hannibal and seemed to be stooping even lower, as if he was cringing away from an expected attack.

"I was just waiting for..."

"Ms. Kitteridge?" The newcomer asked. "Get in line there, pizo. It's always a trial getting in to see the boss."

"Pizo?" Hannibal held out his hand. "I've hardly heard that since I left the base in Germany. Hannibal Jones, and really I'm waiting for a chance to talk to Dean Edwards."

"Oscar Peters," the shorter man said, shaking Hannibal's hand vigorously. He wore jeans with a dress shirt and tie, and a pair of expensive Adidas Salvations. "As a matter of fact, Dean works for me. Good man. You another Army brat?"

"Afraid so," Hannibal said. "How long has Dean been with you?"

"Dean's pretty new," Oscar said. "Why are you looking for him? You're not an old friend, are you?"

"Afraid not." Hannibal handed Oscar a card and Oscar, unlike most people, read it closely before slipping it into his shirt pocket. "I see. And is Dean in some sort of trouble?"

From behind Hannibal a strong female voice said "Nothing to worry about." Hannibal turned and was suddenly thankful for his sunglasses. No one could see his eyes widen as he took in the woman facing him. She was a tall woman of flawless detail. Her hair wasn't red, it was a deep, blood-tinged auburn. Her skin wasn't just fair, but creamy clear and so light as to be near translucent. Her nose and cheekbones had been carved by Michelangelo, and her eyes weren't just brown, they were polished onyx. Her perfectly tailored Donna Karan suit covered a shape seldom seen away from a fashion runway. And she wore a pair of heels that added three inches to her height, bringing her nearly to Hannibal's eye level.

"Mister Jones, I'm Joan Kitteridge. Would you mind telling me what this is all about?"

"Actually I would," Hannibal said. "It's a private matter and I think Mister Edwards would like it to stay that way. If I could just have five minutes with him."

Joan nodded, her face clouded with a very convincing veil of concern. As she looked at Hannibal her whole attention seemed focused on him. "Of course. Dean will take you down to the conference room. But afterwards, would you be kind enough to stop by my office?" Then the spotlight of her attention turned to Oscar Peters, and Hannibal felt left in shadows. "Were you waiting to speak to me Oscar? Come on in."

*   *   *

The door shut out all sound when Hannibal closed it behind himself. Comfortable armed swivel chairs surrounded the long conference table, with lesser chairs lined up around three walls of the room. The front of the room was dominated by a projection screen and a flat television screen. If Hannibal stretched his arms out as far as he could, his fingertips might touch the opposite edges of the TV. Dean never even looked at the table, but went straight to a chair near the far corner. His usual seat, Hannibal assumed. Dean wore the company uniform du jour: dress shirt and tie, designer jeans and a pair of exotic Brooks Radius SC running shoes. He sat as he must at company meetings, waiting for someone to tell him what he should know. So Hannibal did, as succinctly as possible.

"Bea Collins cares about you. She doesn't know why you walked out of her life without warning. Bea is a good woman and, in my estimation, deserves better. Now, I don't have any evidence of you having committed any crimes at this time..."

"Crimes?"

Hannibal rounded the table and zoomed in on Dean like a telescopic rifle site. "I stopped digging but I can pick that shovel back up again. Right now, that's not my job. So here are your choices. You can disappear again, abandon your lucrative job and the life you've got started here and start over someplace else. Or, you can do the right thing."

Dean had trouble keeping his eyes on Hannibal's through the sunglasses. In fact, he glanced around nervously looking at everything but Hannibal. "The right thing. And you think you know what the right thing is, is that it? I won't go back to her Mister Jones."

"Lucky for her," Hannibal said, standing over Dean as if he were on the witness stand in a courtroom drama. "But you need to meet with Bea and give her some sort of explanation for disappearing. You might even consider the truth."

Hannibal pressed ahead, even as all his instincts were shouting this was wrong. Dean Edwards was soft in the middle, no hidden core. This man didn't have what it took to run a confidence game. He barely had the confidence to run his own life. His hands were locked together, his thumbs rubbing each other nervously. Yet he had the strength to stick to his intentions this time.

"You don't understand. I care about Bea. Very much. But I had to go. I won't get her involved in. in my life." Then Dean stared at the platter sized triangular device at the center of the table. Hannibal glanced at it as well, realizing belatedly that it was a microphone of some type, designed to pick up comments from around the room. Good for meetings. Bad for confidentiality. And it occurred to Hannibal that whatever Dean's problem was, it could have something to do with his work. And it could catch up to Bea whether he wanted it to or not. He nodded his understanding to Dean, slipped him one of his cards, and backed off a bit.

"Why don't I pick you up from work tonight and we can work out the details. Five o'clock okay?"

Dean nodded and Hannibal turned to leave. He figured he could open Dean up more later, possibly in Bea's presence. He planned to take some time to slowly explain what he learned today and all it might imply. But as he stepped out of the room Oscar took his arm.

"Ms. Kitteridge would like a word with you," Oscar said, steering Hannibal toward the corner office. "She says it's pretty important."

*   *   *

Joan Kitteridge's three-sided desk was a cockpit pinning her against the wall. Between her computer keyboard and monitor, her intercom, television remote control, her mouse, her joystick, her surge protector lined with lighted switches and a control panel for her peripherals, it looked as if she could control the planet from her seat.

Oscar had stopped at the door. Mark Norton waved Hannibal in and toward the leather sofa along the far wall, below the windows. Hannibal lowered himself slowly onto it. Mark stood at the door, not as relaxed as he was trying to appear. Joan leaned forward, hooking titian locks out of her eye with a thumb as she spoke.

"Mister Jones, I'll come to the point. Dean Edwards is a valued employee here. Talented and hard working. It appears he's in some sort of trouble, and I want to know if you're part of it. If you represent a problem that can be solved with money, we may be able to help make it go away."

Hannibal looked hard at the Chief Executive Officer of Kitteridge Computer Systems. Behind her husky voice, this woman was a world away from Dean Edwards. Layer behind layer, like a steel-skinned onion. The kind of woman who could run a multimillion-dollar company.

"Let me make a few things clear," Hannibal said. "First, I'm not here to cause trouble. I was asked to find Mister Edwards and I have. And I have no intention of trying to make him do anything he doesn't want to do. But I think he may have made a bad mistake and I could help him correct it. Now, what makes you think he's in trouble?"

While Hannibal spoke, Joan sat still as a wax figure, absorbing his words. Mark didn't watch Hannibal. His eyes were drawn to his boss' magnetism. He fidgeted a bit.

When Hannibal finished, Joan sat for another ten seconds, then said, "I see." She stood to lean toward him, unwilling to leave the enclosure of her control center. "I think it was pretty obvious to all of us who know him, that Dean was scared when he came in to work this morning. Scared of something. From what I've seen, it doesn't seem to be you. But when I questioned him, he wouldn't tell me anything. I worry about my people, Mister Jones."

"Isn't that a little maternal?"

"Some of these people need a little looking after," she answered, not smiling at all. "They don't live much in this world where you and I function, Mister Jones. That's why they're so good at dealing with the imaginary universe they're in."

-7-

Hannibal was contemplating these people who needed Joan Kitteridge's looking after on his way out. One of them intercepted Hannibal in the reception area and followed him out to the elevators. It was Oscar Peters, who trailed behind Hannibal like a fearful puppy, afraid to get too close for fear that Hannibal might decide to kick him.

"I'm just heading for lunch," Oscar said, stepping into the elevator car with Hannibal and moving to the farthest corner. "I live right by here and just usually go home to eat. Why don't you join me? I think we should talk."

"What about?"

"Well, Dean and I have become pretty good friends," Oscar said, pushing his glasses up. "I might be able to help you help him."

"I imagine I'll find out all I need to know when I pick him up after work tonight," Hannibal said.

The doors slid back and the two men stepped out into the building's marble lobby. "Tonight?" Oscar asked. "I don't think so, pizo. Dean left work for the day right after that meeting with you."

*　　　　*　　　　*

Oscar Peters lived in an antique house a couple of blocks off Route 7 back toward Alexandria. Its entrance was defended by a stone porch, but to stand on it one had to climb a set of rotting wooden steps. The house's small wallpapered living room retained its original hardwood floors, left over from a time when someone boasted about owning the place. An archway led to a formal dining room where Hannibal sat while Oscar heated clam chowder and fried grilled cheese sandwiches on the gas stove. The cooking aromas barely overpowered the lilac air freshener. He delivered the food to the table without a touch of embarrassment. Hannibal pulled off his gloves to eat, but chose to leave his sunglasses on, even in the dim house.

"I used to date Joan Kitteridge you know," Oscar said, biting into his sandwich. Hannibal wondered if it was true. This was clearly a lonely man, and lonely people will often say whatever they think will hold another person's attention.

"So how did you and Dean become friends? He been here long?"

Oscar nodded, accepting Hannibal's question as the price of keeping him interested. "Dean turned up about six months ago I guess. Not long after I joined the company. He crashed here a couple of times in those days. He and I became, well, close."

"Really?" Hannibal said, wiping his hands on the napkin Oscar offered. "And when he stopped crashing here? Did he start crashing at Kitteridge's right after that?"

Oscar looked surprised to find anyone knew that. "Um, yeah I guess so. She kind of took a liking to him."

Hannibal considered what Joan had told him. "Oscar, what is Dean so afraid of?"

Oscar's eyes flashed up at Hannibal, his smile twitching. "Dean? Don't know what he might be scared of. Never know what's going on with that guy."

"What about you?" Hannibal laced his fingers on the table, keeping his face open. "Seen anything around that company that might make employees nervous? Or something about Joan Kitteridge?"

"Well, I see everything that goes on up there," Oscar said, "but I have to get back to work pretty soon. I'd be happy to give you all the dirty little details later." His nervous little hand moved out to cover Hannibal's. "You could stay all night."

Hannibal felt his stomach jump as his body clenched. He pulled his hand away as if burned and jumped to his feet.

"I think I've got enough."

But as Hannibal marched toward the door, Oscar spun in his chair, his eyes widening behind his thick lenses. "I'm sorry. Please don't run off. I'm the one who's scared. Don't leave me alone here."

Hannibal opened the door and stood with his hand on the outside knob. "Just what are you afraid of?"

"I'm afraid for my life," Oscar said, his voice begging. "My life has been threatened. There's trouble on my tail, followed me all the way from Europe."

"Sounds like a job for the police," Hannibal said, pulling his gloves back on.

"The police never believe you until it's too late," Oscar said. "If you're helping Dean you should be helping me." Then, almost as an afterthought, "I can pay you."

"I don't think so," Hannibal said, harder than he intended. "I've already got two clients. Look, after I talk to Dean, I'll check back with you on that."

Hannibal was in his car before he realized that Oscar had not followed. He sat still for a moment, breathing deeply. He didn't like to think of himself as phobic. He didn't like to think he was afraid of anything, there were just some things he didn't like. Like men touching him. Besides, that could have been a genuine cry for help Oscar was sounding. If Oscar was in trouble, it could lead to an explanation for Dean's running off.

Or it could have simply been the cry of loneliness, Hannibal decided as he started his car. And besides, he had done what he was being paid to do. He had found Dean Edwards. He jabbed at the buttons on his car phone while he steered himself back to Route 7 pointed toward Alexandria. After five rings, Cindy's hello pushed into the car, effortlessly blowing away the cloud that had filled his mind a moment earlier.

"Hey baby," Hannibal said. "What you doing for dinner?"

"I'm making it," she said. He could feel her smile through the ether. "Right now I'm standing in your kitchen, holding the phone with my shoulder, cooking the chicken for my arroz imperial. You feel like chicken and rice?"

"Let's see how many speed laws I can break between here and there," Hannibal said. "Then you'll see."

"You done with business for the day?"

"Almost," Hannibal said. "One more phone call to make. Believe it or not, I found Dean Edwards. He ducked out, and he thinks I don't know where he is, but I do. I think I'll just give Bea the boy's location and let her go confront him herself."

-8-

Hannibal loved all types of food except, perhaps, that group of dishes traditionally referred to as American. And he loved to have a woman cook for him. When Cindy carried the large serving dish from the oven to the table, the smile she wore told him she knew how close to heaven she had carried him.

Cindy was not domestic by nature. This tough-minded woman felt more at home in a courtroom than a kitchen. But every once in a while, she felt the need to release her creative side, and her preferred medium for artistic expression was the traditional dishes of her father's homeland. And Hannibal appreciated the hours invested in this art. Tonight's feature creation required hours of preparation, but the imperial rice was worth the effort. Hannibal had dropped his jacket, gloves and glasses, and rolled up the sleeves of his white shirt to dig in.

"So did you tell Bea everything you learned about her man?" Cindy asked as she settled into her chair facing Hannibal.

Smile-inducing aromas were swimming around Hannibal's flat: onions, garlic, peppers, scallions. Those warm homey aromas made him too happy and relaxed to want to talk business. "Well no, not everything babe. Why set her up for that kind of pain? I did my job. I found him. End of the trail. From there, it's between them."

"What if he's telling the truth? What if he really is keeping secrets because he loves her and doesn't want her involved?"

His fork dug into the baked layers of rice and chicken and cheese that stretched out as he lifted the food. Monterey jack, he thought, and maybe Parmesan. "Is that how it works when it's love? If you were in trouble, would you keep it from me, babe?"

Cindy's answer was disrupted by a knock on the door. Actually, the knock was across the hall. Chewing slowly, Hannibal looked up at Cindy. They were quiet for a moment, then she sighed and shook her head sadly.

"If they're at your office door at this hour, they could be in real trouble. No point pretending you don't need to see who it is."

"Better be life and death!" Hannibal wiped his mouth on a napkin and went out into the hall. His living room door was near the back of the building, so he walked past the basement door under the wide staircase to the other side before he could see who was standing at the front of the building, worrying his office door with their knuckles.

"I can't believe he's gone this early," Irma Andrews muttered, staring at the door as if she could open it with the power of her stare.

"How the hell did you find me?" Hannibal asked from the other end of the building. She jumped but recovered quickly and stalked toward him, her heels clicking like gunshots in the hallway.

"Backtracked your phone number. Reporters have to be resourceful, or didn't they tell you? And once I saw the address, I figured it must be your residence as well."

"Actually, I live across the hall," Hannibal said. "Why don't you come in and tell me what's so important you came all the way into The District...."

"You broke your word, Jones," she said, moving past him toward his front door. One foot inside, her eyes met Cindy's. Irma stopped in her tracks, taking in the food on the table and Hannibal's half finished meal. "Oh, sorry. Didn't realize."

Cindy recovered quickly, standing and offering her hand for Irma's reluctant shake. "No bother, come on in. I'm Cindy Santiago, and I didn't realize Hannibal's acquaintances included famous TV news reporters. Won't you join us?"

"Oh no, I couldn't. I mean..."

"What do you mean by that?" Hannibal asked, closing the door behind himself. "I keep my word with everybody, even pushy reporters."

The three of them stood there for a moment, Irma's eyes bouncing from Cindy to Hannibal and back. Then Cindy turned to the cabinet over the sink.

"I'm getting another plate. You can speak plainly to Hannibal, Ms. Andrews. I promise not to get involved."

"Well, that does smell delicious, and I love Mexican food," Irma said, pulling a chair out but still standing. "But I hate to intrude. I just wanted to ask Mister Jones about a story. A story that he assured me he'd call me about if anything came of it."

Hannibal returned to his chair and under Cindy's stare Irma joined them at the table. "I haven't eaten, as a matter of fact," Irma said, pushing her fork into the rice mixture.

"Actually, this is Cuban," Hannibal said. Then to Cindy, "Irma helped me with that video of Dean Edwards, Cindy. I told her if it looked like news I'd give her a call. But so far it looks pretty tame."

Irma was about to launch an outburst, but her taste buds short-circuited that. "Oh my, this is delicious! Now, Mister Jones, do you expect me to believe you didn't know that family's tragic history?"

"History?" Hannibal asked. "I know almost nothing about this guy. Enlighten me."

Irma looked to Cindy who smiled broadly. "Aside from his cook, I'm also Hannibal's lawyer. I understand confidentiality, if that's a concern for you, Ms. Andrews."

"Please call me Irma," the reporter said. "And I don't think there's a legal problem here, I just wouldn't want to get scooped if the story got out, you know?"

"I can assure you Cindy won't talk to any competing reporters," Hannibal said. "Now how do you come to know Edwards' background?"

"Well after the interest you showed, I just had a feeling there might be a story there. So I took a look for Dean Edwards in the station's story database. What I found was his mother, who was convicted of murdering his father a little more than ten years ago." Irma's eyes became intense as her story evolved, and Hannibal could see her excitement at digging into the facts and finding a story. She was one of those people who got real joy from her job. "I searched out the video archives so I could hear the entire story, and got a look at his mother. The same woman who came looking for his picture before you."

Hannibal sat back from the table. "His mother. Maybe she just now found him."

"Sure," Cindy put in. "And he didn't want to have to tell Bea about his mom killing his own dad, so he ran. Poor boy. I hope he comes clean to her. She can certainly handle it."

Irma looked lost so Hannibal filled her in. "There's no crime involved with my job as far as I know, Irma. The person who hired me to find Dean Edwards is his fiancé e. But seems to me she deserves to know what you found out. Maybe I can even bring mother and prospective daughter-in-law together."

"Unlikely," Irma said. "She's gone." Now it was Hannibal's turn to look lost. Irma chewed a bit longer than she needed to, as if she was reluctant to continue. Hannibal's eyes prodded her, and they caught her attention.

"They're hazel, aren't they?" she asked. "Not green as I first thought, or even blue, but hazel." He nodded. "Black people don't have hazel eyes. Beautiful, though."

"So glad you approve," Hannibal said through a flat expression. "What do you mean she's gone?"

"Look I had the address, it looked like a story, you know, long lost son reunited with jailbird mother. So I went to that motel. Geez, what a dive. But the new husband, this Irons guy, tells me she ran off last night some time."

"Damn." Hannibal stood and paced into the next room, the living room. "I scared the woman off. I didn't know who she was. Never considered why she might be keeping such a low profile. I assume you questioned the poor Irons guy."

"Well I asked him a couple questions," Irma said, following Hannibal into the living room. Irma's face reflected a degree of excitement that brought a bad taste into Hannibal's mouth. "He confirmed her conviction, but of course he says she was framed. And he did say she saw a boy a few days ago who might be her son."

Cindy set a cup of coffee on an end table. With her hands she directed Hannibal to sit beside it, but her eyes were on Irma.

"Clearly she didn't want a lot of attention. Maybe she and Dean have run off together. Coffee?"

All eyes turned to the telephone when it rang. To Hannibal, it was one more unwelcome intruder barging in at a bad time. He picked it up, but the tone of his hello was not very inviting.

"You need to come right away," the panicked voice said. "I don't know what to do. It's, it's horrible."

"Bea?" Hannibal asked.

"I'm in that horrible little place over the garage," Bea said through her sobs. "Please. It's horrible. Dean he, he's in more trouble than I ever...please, please come right away."

*   *   *

Hannibal was not a happy man mounting the dark narrow staircase to the apartment above the Kitteridge three-car garage. First because he didn't know what he was heading into. But mostly because of the company.

As he pushed the door open he could hear Cindy and Irma behind him jostling for position. He was always pleased to have Cindy along on a case, but his skin jumped at the thought of being shadowed by a reporter. He wished now he had told her no, but he really didn't know how. And now she'd have her story.

The lights were on beyond the door Hannibal opened. The room was modestly furnished with mobile home type furniture and smelled as if the air had not been disturbed in a century. His attention was first drawn to the soft sobbing coming from the room beyond the nearly square living room. From that door, he traced the trail across the thin carpet back to his own feet. With his arms Hannibal directed the women around him on either side to prevent them from stepping on the series of red footprints pointing into the bedroom beyond. It was a man's spoor, in the pattern of an unusual shoe sole, a running shoe in fact, the unique Brooks Radius SC running shoes Dean wore at work that day.

Hannibal had to pull back on the tails of Irma's jacket to enter the bedroom first. The twin size bed projected from the wall to the right. Dean lay on his side curled into a fetal position. His shoes lay at the foot of the bed. Bea knelt beside the bed clutching his hands. Her face had been pressed against his but when Hannibal stepped into the room she looked up. A small smile broke through the dampness covering her face.

"Praise the Lord you're here," she said, her voice just above a whisper. "I didn't know what in the world to do."

Irma only got as far as, "Who is" before Hannibal's finger in her face froze the question in her throat.

"Don't you say a single word," Hannibal said. "In fact, I think you'd better be out of here right now."

Irma took a deep breath and leaned her determination right up against Hannibal's. "If I leave now I go straight to the station with the story, as much as I know."

Cindy pulled Irma aside. "Let's negotiate."

Hannibal ignored Cindy and Irma. "Okay Dean, this does not look good. Please tell me that isn't blood all over your shoes."

When Dean raised his head Hannibal hardly recognized him. The nervous kid Hannibal met at Kitteridge Computer Systems had been replaced by a dull-eyed man who fixed him with an empty stare. He had run from a manic state to what looked like clinical depression. He nodded slowly and managed to say, "It is."

"Whose?"

Dean's face collapsed on itself. "Oscar's. It's Oscar's. Oscar Peters is dead. Mama's done it again."

Hannibal turned from Dean to follow the red trail out the door. Not the end of the journey after all, but the first step.

-9-

The blood on Dean's shoes was fresh enough to retain its copper smell. The single bedside lamp shed just enough light for Hannibal to see there was no sign of struggle on Dean's face or hands. And the boy was hardly coherent enough to fill in much more. But Hannibal was overwhelmed by the implications of this new development, and his ordered mind wanted to close out one job before starting another. He stepped close to the bed, looking down at the fragile creature curled up on top of it.

"Dean, is Mary Irons your mother?"

"Irons?" Words came slowly, as if Dean was talking through a fog. "Oh, yes, she said she was using Mary Irons. Mary is her middle name. She's really Francis. Did she really marry again?"

Hannibal settled a hand on Bea's shoulder. He only had one comforting fact and he figured she needed it. "The woman who went to your apartment Saturday to see Dean wasn't a rival. It was his mother, Francis."

At the other end of the room, Cindy stood inches from Irma's face, speaking in low but intense tones. "What will it take for you to hold everything you know about this situation in strictest confidence?"

"Ah, someone I can deal with," Irma said, smiling in the subtle conspiracy all successful businesswomen have to be part of. "Look, all I want is the story. If I can stay I won't reveal anything to anyone until and unless the principals give me permission. Unless of course a crime has been committed."

Cindy returned Irma's smile. "If a crime has been committed in connection with this case, you will still maintain that confidence. You will not reveal any facts until the police already have them." Cindy held out her hand. Irma took it. Cindy whispered, "If you go back on this deal, I swear to God I'll terminate your career."

"As I will yours if you contradict anything I know to be the truth with a lie in court." The women nodded their agreement and shook again as a sign of professional respect. Then Cindy turned back to her man.

"I'm sorry to interrupt, Hannibal, but has anyone called the police yet?"

"Police?" Bea's eyes were wide with fear. "No. They'll put my poor Dean in jail. He's in no condition. Look at him. Mister Jones, now that you've found him won't you protect him? Please?"

Hannibal rubbed the back of his neck with one hand. "I'm on board as long as you want me," he said, but his eyes were on Cindy. He was always grateful for her ability to maintain the practical and legal views. "How much trouble are we in if we don't call the cops?"

"Probably none, until we confirm that a crime's been committed," Cindy said. "Mister Edwards, it looks as if you'll need legal representation very soon. Do you have a lawyer?"

Dean shook his head slowly.

"Can you represent him?" Bea asked. "Can I retain you on his behalf."

"Yes, unless he objects," Cindy replied. "Right now I want time to hear his story without pressure. And to keep him out of jail. Is he hurt in any way? Is any of this blood his?"

"He's not hurt," Bea said, unconsciously rubbing Dean's head as she spoke. "When he called me he could barely speak, I think. When I got here I found the... the mess. I took off his shoes and checked him over pretty well. He's okay."

Cindy dropped to her knees to be on eye level with Bea. "He doesn't look well, Bea. He looks like he's in shock, or maybe it's more than that. Do you know if Mister Edwards has been in therapy?"

"Therapy?" Bea said, her voice ripe with irony. "I didn't even know his mother was alive. How would I know? I know so little about him. I mean, he told me all his family were dead."

"Back home," Dean said, staring right through Cindy. "After Mama killed Daddy."

Hannibal leaned over Cindy. "Back home? Where's home, son?"

Dean seemed to find that a hard question. His brow knit in concentration. "Oh it's right there. The other side. Silver Spring."

"Mister Edwards," Cindy said, "Can you tell us the name of your doctor back home?"

"Oh, that was years ago," Dean said absently. "Years and years. Auntie, she took me to see Doctor Roberts after I saw it. That scared me."

"What did you see, sweetheart?" Bea asked, too late for Hannibal to stop her.

"You know. Daddy. What Mama did to Daddy with that knife."

Behind them, Irma whispered, "Oh my God."

"And... and Oscar," Dean went on. "He looked just like Daddy did. The same. The same. Blood everywhere."

Bea hugged Dean and he lapsed into silence. Cindy stood and turned toward the living room.

"I'm going to see if I can find this Doctor Roberts in Silver Spring. If I can, he's our best hope for protecting Edwards. He might be willing to help us keep his former patient out of the hands of the police. He'd have no trouble convincing a judge his condition is shaky."

Cindy moved quickly across the room but stopped when she came face to face with another woman on her way in. Joan Kitteridge stared past her until Cindy finally stepped aside. Joan didn't stop again until she was in the middle of the room. Her glittering brown eyes settled on Irma, then Bea, then Dean, and finally Hannibal.

"All right Jones, I can see this is your show. What the hell's going on here?"

At that moment Hannibal had the oddest thought: That there were just too many women involved with this case. "What makes you think something's going on?" he asked. "And do you make it a habit to walk in here unannounced?"

"Don't be flip with me," Joan said, her auburn locks flipping as her head snapped around so she could glare from the corner of her eye. "I went to get in my 'Vette and there's a trail of what looks like bloody footprints coming out of it, leading up here. Well Dean's been driving my car, and I want to know where he's been."

"I'm sorry," Dean said in a small voice. "I didn't mean to make a mess. I just went over to Oscar's. To talk."

"Oscar Peters?" Joan continued to speak only to Hannibal.

"Dean says Oscar's dead," Hannibal said. "I was just getting ready to call the police."

"Wait a minute," Joan said, hands raised. "Police. Shouldn't we know for sure what happened first? I mean, we don't even know if anyone's dead. Why don't we go around there and see what Dean saw? Oscar could be lying there in need of first aid or something."

"You're right," Bea said, clearly considering for the first time that Dean's report might not be accurate. "He could just look dead. Maybe we should send an ambulance."

"I need some sanity here, Jones," Joan said sarcastically. "He was driving my car and it's covered with blood. Don't you think we ought to check out the situation?"

-10-

The man running out of Oscar Peters' house was much too tall to be its owner. But half a block away from the nearest street lamp, that was all Hannibal could tell about him.

Joan had ridden with him because Cindy cautioned that no one should touch Joan's car. In a worst-case scenario, the police might accuse them all of an attempt to obstruct justice by tampering with evidence. They had barely left Hannibal's car when the house's front door opened. Joan called out Oscar's name and rushed ahead. Hannibal purposely hung back a bit, to see what interaction there might be between them. But then Joan stopped dead in her tracks, the man on the porch stared at her for a split second, looked at Hannibal beyond her, and sprinted down the street. Only then could Hannibal judge his height. He was much too tall to be Oscar, with long, black, stringy hair. He wore a black silk shirt and black jeans.

Hannibal charged down the street behind the running man. His breath came in short puffs while his body adjusted to the chase, but in seconds he was in his distance runner groove, arms pumping, lungs expanding to accept all the oxygen they could drag out of the air.

The stranger was a suspect, possibly a murderer. With him in hand, no mystery would face Hannibal. Dean Edwards would be in no danger, his mother would be in the clear, and Bea could perhaps convince him to return to a normal life. All that was motivation driving Hannibal down the street behind the rapid-fire clop clop of his quarry's footfalls.

But the other man was apparently driven by fear. That perhaps gave him an adrenal edge. In thirty seconds of running he had opened his lead to almost a block and then he turned the corner to the left. Hannibal cursed his suit coat and dress shoes as he watched the man disappear around the house on the corner. Hannibal still followed, nearly falling as he rounded the corner himself. Then he coasted to a stop.

Hannibal found himself on a narrow deserted lane. He moved to the middle of the street and pulled off his shades. Then he rested his hands on his knees and drew deep breaths as he scanned the street. His man could have run into any of the houses, or possibly reached the corner and turned either way. Of course, he could be hiding anywhere in the darkness. He dropped his head, mentally berating himself for being unprepared and missing a rare chance.

His head snapped up at the roar of a big engine coming to life. On the right side of the street a big car pulled away from the curb from behind another parked vehicle. Its headlights stabbed into his eyes as he tried in vain to see the person behind the windshield. Too slowly his mind registered that it was coming right at him. Too tired to run or reach for his pistol, Hannibal leaped to the side and rolled onto the sidewalk. As the big sedan pulled away he caught a fleeting glimpse of the license plate. Then his murder suspect disappeared down the darkened street.

On the long slow walk back to Oscar's house, Hannibal realized he could smell his own sweat from running in his black suit, which had picked up quite a bit of dirt while he rolled along the street. There was a nasty scuff on the toe of his left shoe. He opened the top button of his white shirt and pulled his tie away from his throat an inch or two. He had almost reached his destination before he could clearly see Joan sitting on the steps leading up to the porch. As she came within sight he slid his glasses back into place.

"Did you catch him?" Joan asked, getting to her feet. She smoothed her skirt as if she were just rising from a board meeting.

"Afraid not," Hannibal said. "He managed to reach his car and take off. So did you go in?"

"Are you kidding? There might be a dead body in there." Joan jerked her thumb toward the door and moved out of Hannibal's path.

Clearly, bodies were his business. He pushed the door open slowly with a gloved hand and took one step inside. The dining room light played over the stark ghastly scene displayed like a waxwork in the living room. Hannibal stepped carefully around the edge of the room to reach the corner living room torchere.

"You might want to stay on the porch, Miss."

More light didn't make it any more pleasant. Oscar Peters lay on his back, his head turned to his left. He still wore his glasses but behind them, his eyes were empty. His cheek was stuck to the floor by the large pool of blood. A couple of quarts had leaked out across the hardwood floor there, actually pumped out through his jugular vein. Oscar might have been staring over at Dean's footprint in the red pool. His face was frozen in shock. Well, yes, getting murdered is often a surprise.

Hannibal crouched beside the body, trying to hold a mental photograph of this last view of Oscar Peters. His facial expression was the result of the stab wound, one deep thrust to the solar plexus with the flat of the blade held horizontally. Too thick for a kitchen knife. Hannibal could picture the killer putting a hand behind Oscar's neck, or perhaps an arm around his shoulders, holding him still while he pushed his camp knife or hunting blade up into Oscar's middle.

"Oh dear God." That meant Joan had decided to come in after all. Well, now she knew why he wanted her to stay on the porch. Hannibal looked toward Oscar's pale face. The slash wound across his throat was deeper and from the pool of blood, must have been deeper still on Oscar's left side. Hannibal again saw the killer in his mind, stepping behind Oscar, sinking his blade into the left side of Oscar's throat through the big vein, then yanking it to the right and dropping him. No, not dropping him. He would have landed face down then. No, the killer stepped back and lowered Oscar to the floor.

Finally Hannibal lifted Oscar's cold arm and tried to bend it up a little. Judging by the stiffness, Oscar was at least two hours dead. Then Hannibal stood, recalling his brief tenure as a homicide detective in New York City. He remembered seeing lots more damage done to men. This was, in fact, the kind of neat work so often done by professionals and the mentally unstable.

"Now, Miss Kitteridge," Hannibal said without looking at her. "Now I think it's time to call the police."

Hannibal was pleased to see he had judged Joan correctly. Most people are frozen into shock by the sight of a dead body but she gritted her teeth, nodded her head, and reached into her purse for her phone. She did turn her back to the death, and step back out to sit on the porch while dialing. That was fine by Hannibal. He intended to stay in the house for a few more minutes.

Guilt was creeping in around the edges of his heart. While he quickly toured the house's first floor he was driven by more than a need to avoid Dean being charged with murder. For now he wouldn't think of that. He would look for some clue to who would want this little man dead.

Hannibal found nothing of a personal nature on the ground floor, if you discounted the knickknacks and kitchen utensils, so carefully matched and coordinated as to betray an obsessive attention to detail. Even Cindy didn't have salt and pepper shakers that matched the napkin holder, the toothpick holder, the canister set, even the breadbox, for God's sake. In Hannibal's mind, this guy was turning out to be a combined cliché. Everything he saw was what he would expect to find in the home of a young gay computer geek.

Upstairs was almost as infuriating. It was Hannibal's experience that you learned about a person from the nature of the mess they left. Nothing is as individual as the type of disorder we each leave behind. But Oscar Peters left none. Empty garbage cans. A totally orderly bathroom which did, at least, reveal enough in the products he kept to confirm his lifestyle. Quite a variety, in fact, of scents, oils and lubricants. Hannibal could only imagine how they came into play during contact between two male bodies. Closing the medicine cabinet he found himself staring into his own shaded eyes.

"But that's no reason to let a man die," he told himself aloud.

The other source of information Hannibal usually counted on was the clutter of paper most of us accumulate. A careful search yielded little there. Photo albums, address books, store receipts all told a person's story. But Oscar lived a nearly paperless existence. Hannibal assumed all such records were in his personal computer in digital form, and he would not have nearly enough time to find them.

The only papers in Oscar's bedroom lay neatly in a folder in his side table. Most of its contents consisted of a series of airline ticket stubs. Canada, Australia, Japan, and Russia all in the last year. The man got around.

The rest were personal letters, each folded and stored in the envelope it arrived in. The envelopes bore a return address in Heidelberg, Germany. Hannibal recognized the street because he grew up not far from it. He opened and read the most recent letter, which turned out to be from Oscar's mother. Oscar's parents, Foster and Emma Peters, had decided to remain in Germany when Foster retired from the Army. In her letter, Emma was trying to convince her son to visit them and patch up his differences with his father. Their disagreement apparently stemmed from Oscar's disapproval of his father's job as a Military Policeman.

The guilt twisted Hannibal's stomach harder. His own father had been an MP. When he was killed in Vietnam, Hannibal's mother raised him there in her native Berlin. Sergeant Jones may even have served with Foster Peters.

Then Hannibal's brow knit and he returned quickly to the airline ticket stubs. Not one to Germany. London was the closest he got. All over the world, but not one visit to his parents. Kept away by a feud that, according to his mother, started when he was in high school, almost fifteen years ago. And now, she would have to be told her Oscar died without reconciling with his father. Just as Hannibal's father died, a continent away, with no warning, no final hug, no good-bye.

The stairs seemed so much longer on the way down. Cool fresh air washed his face when he opened the door, and Joan turned to him expectantly. He had nothing to offer her except an address he had written on his note pad.

"Oscar's parents. You'll want to notify them."

"Yes, of course," Joan said, accepting the slip of paper as if it was much heavier than it appeared. Then they both turned to face the street and stood side by side in the gathering silence. After a few moments the silence became as heavy as that slip of paper. Joan wrapped her arms around her designer jacket.

"It's getting cold."

"Yes, probably two hours old," Hannibal said before he realized his mind was not on the same track as Joan's. "Sorry, I guess that sounded pretty callous."

"No," Joan said with half a laugh. "I can't think of anything else either."

Actually Hannibal couldn't get the cupric smell of Oscar's blood out of his mind, but he didn't feel the need to share that with this woman who knew the deceased in business and, as Oscar told it, socially as well. "I suppose you've been thinking about who would want him dead."

"I know it's a cliché, but as far as I know Oscar didn't have an enemy in the world." She turned to face Hannibal, staring as if she could see deep into his eyes through his sunglasses. "Can you tell me how a person can do that? Push a knife into another person's body?"

Hannibal could, but chose not to. He leaned against the pillar holding the porch roof up, and felt paint crumble behind his shoulder. "He traveled a lot, didn't he?"

"For business," Joan replied. "The computer industry holds conventions all over the world. It's an easy way to reward good workers."

"But none in Europe," Hannibal said. "None he could take advantage of to visit his parents."

"He never accepted the trips to Germany," Joan said. "And I never asked why."

A siren trailed off as a car with a flashing light on its roof rounded the corner. Two more followed and all parked in front of them. Hannibal knew what to expect and took Joan's arm to pull her to the side on the porch. A dozen or more men flowed out of the three cars like flies from burst melons. Or perhaps bees, Hannibal thought, because they gathered and buzzed around one central figure for a moment, as if getting instructions from the queen in a hive. Then, as if on some silent signal, they surged forward, not looking left or right, straight up the steps and into the house. The one man left outside walked behind them with the slow pace that is the privilege of the man in charge. He stopped in front of Joan, opened a wallet to display his badge and pulled out a notebook.

"Stan Thompson, ma'am. I'm the detective in charge of this investigation. I'll be back in a moment to ask you a few questions if that's all right." Joan nodded dully at his calm, almost smiling face. Thompson reminded Hannibal of a wall: tall wide and flat. His broad shoulders were part of that image. The pug nose and thin lips highlighted it. Even his straw-like hair seemed two-dimensional. He even wore a stone gray suit. When he turned to enter the house, Hannibal was almost surprised he didn't fall over. But since he was being ignored, he figured he'd follow and learn whatever else he could.

Which, as it turned out, wasn't much. Thompson stood just inside the doorway for maybe a minute staring down at the corpse. Finally, he nodded his head and muttered, "I've seen this before." Then he turned so suddenly he nearly stepped into Hannibal.

"And you are?" Thompson asked.

Hannibal gave his name as he stepped back onto the porch. Thompson switched on the porch light and turned back to Joan. Hannibal leaned against the low front wall of the porch, to Thompson's left and Joan's right. Thompson stood with pen and pad in hand, focused entirely on the woman before him.

"First I want to thank you for calling us, ma'am. Can you tell me how you came to find the deceased here?"

Whether it was his bluntness or his calmness, or the fact that he made no attempts to establish any kind of rapport with her, Joan was frozen. Her mouth moved a few times but no sound came out. For his part, Thompson stood patiently waiting for her to eventually answer. Hannibal noticed how harsh the lighting was on her face, casting hard black shadows that made her look much older than she was.

"She didn't," Hannibal said. "A man who is my client discovered him here less than an hour ago and told me and Ms. Kitteridge about it."

When Thompson turned to him, Hannibal produced his credentials and a card. Thompson stared hard at both, as if they answered his next few questions. When he had worked his way through them he moved on to the questions he still needed answers for.

"Your client's name?"

"Dean Edwards," Hannibal said. "He's up in Arlington right now."

Thompson began rocking back and forward from heels to toes. A sign of agitation Hannibal guessed. Now he ignored Joan. Hannibal had the impression this man could only encompass one person at a time.

"He didn't call the police when he found... this?"

"Mister Edwards was upset," Hannibal said. "This man was his friend. And we weren't sure if he was in fact dead. Mister Edwards has had some problems of an emotional nature."

Thompson's eyes came up from his pad without his head moving. "I see. Did you know the deceased?"

"Ms. Kitteridge is his employer," Hannibal said. Then in a lower voice he added "I met him today."

"All right. Now what about this man Ms. Kitteridge said was here when you arrived?" Thompson had turned a corner in his questions, but Hannibal knew he'd come back to the earlier line. A good cop who knew how to question a witness.

"Tall Caucasian male dressed in dark clothes, and a hell of a fast runner," Hannibal said. "Escaped in a large dark four door sedan with out of state plates that start with the numbers 902."

"You couldn't even see the make of the car?"

"It was dark," Hannibal said, looking down. He knew his guilt must be showing by now.

"How did you come to know the deceased?"

There it was. The lead to the pivotal question. The guilt that was clawing at Hannibal's mind suddenly burst in, and just as suddenly burst out through his mouth. "I was here earlier today. Mister Peters told me he thought his life was in danger. He told me he had received death threats."

"Really? And what did you do?"

"Nothing," Hannibal said through clenched teeth. "I didn't believe him. I didn't do a damned thing, all right? I blew it off and just a few hours later I'm standing here and he's....." It took just that long for Hannibal to regain his grasp on the guilt and shove it back down deep into his gut where it would roil around like a bad piece of meat, but he determined not to let it come spewing out again.

Detective Thompson looked at Hannibal as if he recognized what was happening to him. "When you've had a little time to think this through, then we'll both know this wasn't your fault. I know something of this Edwards and I think he'll be able to tell us more than you might think. In fact he's the obvious suspect, isn't he? We'll know more of course, after we speak to him."

Joan's voice was an unexpected intrusion. "I don't think you will." When Thompson turned to her, she said, "Mister Edwards is also in my employ. And right now he's under a doctor's care so I don't think you should be harassing him. Besides, your most obvious suspect is the man we saw running from the scene, don't you think?"

*   *   *

Hannibal had barely set the brake when Joan was out of his car again, headed for the steps up to the garage apartment. Hannibal had to run to keep up with her.

"That was something, you speaking up to that detective like that."

Joan stopped and turned to him. It had been a long day, and by now her hair was straying from its carefully planned design. Her makeup was wearing away. Her clothes showed the wrinkles of too many hours sitting. Still, he could again see how this woman could run a successful multimillion-dollar high tech company. That was in her eyes, which had not dulled or softened. "Mister Jones, these computer people, they're like children. I lost one of my charges today. I'm not anxious to lose another. Now let's get upstairs before the police arrive and make sure I haven't lied to them. My business influence won't stall them for very long."

But before they moved further, a short parade emerged from the door. Cindy led the way, followed by Bea who seemed to be supporting Dean by one arm. Even in the darkness his face appeared glazed over. They were followed by an older man wearing a thick gray beard and thicker glasses. Cindy pointed Bea and Dean into the back of a gray BMW in the driveway, then waved the older man forward.

"Hi honey," Cindy said, barely mustering a smile. "You were gone so long I got worried, so I did what I thought made sense. This is Doctor Quincy Roberts. He was Dean's therapist years ago. He was kind enough to rush down here and once he got a look at his former patient he agreed to have Dean hospitalized."

"I believe he's a suicide risk," Doctor Roberts said in a smooth voice. "I've given him a mild sedative, and now I'll drive him and his fiancé e up to Charter Behavioral in Rockville, where I've arranged to have him admitted. If nothing else it will keep the police from grilling him for a while. Maybe they can find their killer in the meantime. Believe me, Dean is in no way capable of killing anyone after what he's been through."

"What he's been through," Hannibal repeated. "Yes, I've heard. Can we get together tomorrow, Doctor? I'd like to learn more about what he's been through, and what he saw ten years ago."

-11-
TUESDAY

Hannibal started his day with a phone call to Anna Ingersoll. By the time he placed that call he was in his office, in his black suit and white shirt, on the clock as he would put it. He figured she would be in her office a few minutes before nine o'clock and he hoped to catch her before the day overwhelmed her. She sounded only a little harried when she answered.

"Anna this is Hannibal. How are you doing?"

"I'm okay," she said. "I called him last night. We talked for a while. I think he really listened to me, at least at first. Then the anger took over and I..." Hannibal let the silence hang, refused to let her off the hook. Eventually she added, "I hung up on him."

"Good for you," he said. It was a powerful indication that she was breaking from his dominance. They would heal their relationship or they would not, but now she was empowered to choose without being bullied in either direction.

"Thank you," Anna said. "I don't know how I could repay you." For his help or the encouragement, he could not be sure.

"Actually, I'm calling to ask for your help. I could use your expertise on a case I'm on, trying to find someone. Can you track a man down with a partial license plate?"

Hannibal could feel her smile across the phone lines. She loved the idea that she could be needed by someone. "I can sure as heck narrow your search, depending on how much of the plate you got."

"All I have is the first three characters," he said.

"That's not a bad start. Local registration?"

"I guess," Hannibal said. "It starts with 902."

"Hmmm....not Virginia. All ours start with three letters, except vanity plates of course. You don't know what state?"

Hannibal cursed away from the phone. "Guess I don't. So we're nowhere, huh?"

"I didn't say that," Anna said. He could hear she was already being distracted by something at work. "I can help you better when I've got more time at a PC. Can this wait until I can come over tonight?"

"Sure, no big rush," Hannibal lied. "If you can figure something out this evening, that will be great! I've got plenty to do today anyway, starting with taxi duty for a lady lucky enough to be able to take off from work whenever she feels like it."

*   *   *

Hannibal regretted his condescending thought about Bea Collins as soon as he pulled up in front of her home. She was dressed as if for work in a tasteful business skirt suit and black heels. Her makeup was carefully applied. Her raven tresses caressed her shoulders in gentle waves. Yet her petite form seemed shrunken in on itself. Her shoulders threatened to buckle under some invisible weight. She was perfectly framed by the backdrop of the day's low, dark clouds. "Thank you so much for coming," Bea said as she settled into the car. "I have to be there for him, but I couldn't have gone alone."

"I'm here to do whatever I can to help," Hannibal said, pulling out of the protected confines of the townhouse community. "I need to talk to Dean anyway. Find out what I can about his background. I'm afraid the police will try to make something of his history. A 'like mother like son' thing."

"Dean was in and out of full awareness last night, but he talked some," Bea said. "I found out he was raised by his Aunt Ursula after his mother, well, after they took her away. He asked me to call her, to tell her where he is. So I'll get to meet one member of his family at least."

*   *   *

Hannibal chased the last of the rush hour traffic around the Capitol Beltway, then branched north into Maryland and soon pulled into the visitors' parking area of the Charter Behavioral Health System Facility at Potomac Ridge, a suburb of Rockville, Maryland, which was itself a suburb of Washington DC. Bea stared hard at the front of the open, glass fronted building before she would approach it with him. To her, it must have seemed more a prison than a place of comfort.

"It's so big," Bea said as they entered the sterile environment of the reception area. "My baby will just get lost in here."

Hannibal could empathize. Too much white, too many smiles. And he knew most people still retained the snake pit image of mental hospitals. He took her hand as they approached the counter. "Relax, Bea. There are no amateurs here. Charter is the McDonald's of mental health. There must be a hundred of these places scattered around the country. This one has eighty-eight beds for adult inpatients, and almost as many more for adolescent patients. They have the benefit of a ton of experience."

Before they reached the receptionist, Doctor Roberts intercepted them. "You're quite an expert, Mister Jones. Have you been here before?" Roberts walked as smoothly as he spoke. In full light Hannibal could see that he was a round man, soft looking like a stuffed animal. There was a twinkle in his eye which, combined with his beard, reminded Hannibal of the line about the "jolly old elf" in "The Night Before Christmas." All that was missing was the smile.

"I visited someone else here not long ago," Hannibal said. "At that time I spoke to her doctor in a little waiting area right over here."

For Hannibal, it was a heavy dose of deja vu. Just like the last time he visited Charter, the room was empty and painfully quiet, with a smell of vanilla he figured someone sprayed on some regular schedule. Bea perched on the edge of one of the green plastic covered sofas. Hannibal sat beside her and Doctor Roberts pulled a chair close to them.

"How is Dean?" Bea asked as soon as they were settled. "Is he all right? Can I see him?"

"Of course," Roberts said. "He is feeling better, although he's a bit confused about things, the sort of confusion that so often goes with depression and anxiety. But I don't think he's in great danger."

Hannibal tried to match Roberts' carefully measured smile, but he could not imitate the doctor's melodic, hypnotic voice. "Doctor, I need to talk to Dean for a couple of minutes about what he saw last night. The details could be very important."

"I'm sorry. You can speak to him if you like, but you must not discuss the events of last night. At least for a couple of days, all right?"

The air conditioner sighed and Hannibal felt its cold breath on the back of his neck. "I don't know if you understand, Doctor. Ms. Collins has asked me to protect Mister Edwards. To do that, I need to know exactly what he saw. I think I can prove he had nothing to do with this murder."

"On the contrary, I believe I do understand," Roberts said. His smile never changed. "But for the next couple of days, it could do real damage for him to discuss those matters. And I am charged with protecting him also, Mister Jones. Protecting his mental health. I wasn't kidding about his being at risk of suicide. I won't risk stirring up those dangerous self-destructive feelings until I'm sure it's safe."

The door hinges were silent but Hannibal must have detected the movement of the air when it opened. He looked up to find Detective Thompson moving toward them with a long stride that ate up distance with a minimum of effort. A pair of uniforms stood outside the waiting room. Thompson nodded toward Bea and Hannibal, but his face betrayed no surprise.

"Doctor Roberts. Guess I should have expected it to be you," Thompson said. He stood over Roberts looking down on him in every sense. "As you might expect, I need to question him in regard to last night's homicide."

"As you might expect, you may not." Roberts shifted in his seat, but did not crane his head up quite far enough to see Thompson's face. "As I was just telling his fiancée and his friend here, Dean's emotional balance is too delicate right now to..."

"A man is dead," Thompson said as if this would surprise someone. "The boy is at least a material witness, more likely he's the killer."

Roberts' smile never changed, even when Thompson threw his rage at it. "I'm sorry detective. Dean's under sedation anyway. He could not very well answer your questions. And he's no murderer."

"Lucky for us all you're not a cop," Thompson said. "He was there last night and he left the scene covered in the dead man's blood."

"Actually," Hannibal put in quietly, "Only his shoes were covered with blood."

"So you say. If he'd reported his so-called discovery, I'd have seen him last night and I'd know if that was the case."

Hannibal rose slowly to his feet, staring through his lenses into Thompson's eyes, which hung three inches above his own. They stood like two boxers just before the bell for round one.

"I don't think you want to call me a liar, big man."

A woman's voice called, "Stan? What brings you here?" All eyes turned to a frail looking figure entering the room. Her face was worn by life's erosion, her makeup a little too heavy as if trying to conceal that fact. Her gray hair pulled back into a bun. Her belted flowered dress hung to her ankles. When Thompson saw her his posture softened.

"Ursula. I didn't know if you'd heard."

"Well, my good friend Stan Thompson didn't call me, did he?" Ursula made it a soft accusation. "As a matter of fact, Dean's fiancée called me to let me know the trouble he's in. Awful to meet such a person under these ugly circumstances, and over the phone at that. But at least she was considerate enough to call."

Hannibal turned to face Ursula. "Detective Thompson doesn't seem to be much on introductions. I'm Hannibal Jones and this lovely lady is Dean's fiancée, Bea Collins. Bea is a very successful interior designer in Georgetown."

Ursula's smile faltered when she realized who Bea was, but she still offered a hand and said. "Pleased to meet you. I didn't know, I mean over the phone you didn't sound..."

Thompson cut across their uneasy handshake. "I still need to question that boy, Doctor."

Roberts stood up to Thompson, literally and figuratively. The police detective towered over the psychiatrist, but it didn't seem to matter. "And I have already told you that you will not discuss this grisly business with him now. He is under sedation."

"Please," Bea said, speaking for the first time. "He didn't do it. Why persecute him?"

"Stan, be reasonable." Ursula said. "You know how weak he is. You don't want to make it worse for him. I'll take full responsibility."

Thompson's gaze went from face to face as if he did not know who to respond to. Watching this disparate group rally around Dean Edwards defensively, Hannibal thought there must be something good in him to inspire such loyalty.

Roberts turned to Ursula as if Thompson had already left. "He has asked for you, and he has asked for Miss Collins. I will take you to visit him, just you two, and just for a few minutes. I think it will do him some good."

Turning his back on Thompson, Roberts took Ursula's arm with one hand and Bea's with the other. Hannibal followed them out of the waiting room, leaving Thompson standing helpless behind them. A short walk down a soundless antiseptic hall brought them to an elevator door. While they waited, Roberts turned to Hannibal.

"I meant what I said in there, Mister Jones," Roberts said. "Only these two ladies."

"I understand, Doctor," Hannibal said, matching Roberts' smile this time. "I'll be happy to wait right here if you'll return while they're visiting. If I can't talk to Dean I'd sure like a chance to talk to you for a couple minutes."

*   *   *

From the front, Charter looked every bit the efficient contemporary edifice dedicated to healing. But to the side of that building, by facing the right way, Hannibal could almost forget it existed. The grounds constituted a well-maintained park, reminding him of a golf course, except with young trees scattered about the fairway. Maples dominated the landscape but it was the pine that scented the area with their sharp sweetness. The occasional squirrel stopped to watch him. They knew, as did the residents in that building behind him, that this was a safe haven. The first cardinals of autumn chattered at one another, perhaps making romantic plans for tonight. Walking here, Hannibal thought, would be therapy for anyone, even the most dedicatedly sane.

"I'll bet people go nuts just to get to come here," Hannibal said.

Roberts smiled his soft, professional smile. "Sometimes what a person needs most is a chance to relax and lose the cares of the day. For some of my patients, this is the only socially acceptable way to do that."

"But not Dean Edwards?" Hannibal asked, not looking at Roberts as he walked.

"Dean was one of those people who hated his weakness," Roberts said. "He worked very hard for six years to avoid ever being in a place like this. I honestly hoped I'd never see him again, but of course a precipitating event like this, well."

The sun burst through its cloud cover and Hannibal stopped in a small clearing, where he could be bathed in light and Roberts had the option of shade. "So how did Dean become your patient anyway?"

"Well originally I was Ursula's client," Roberts said. "She was my insurance broker. Soon after the tragedy happened, she started bringing Dean to me. He had a lot of guilt issues and confused loyalties to deal with."

"Doctor, everyone seems to know exactly what this tragedy was but me."

Roberts looked at Hannibal as if deciding what degree of truth was called for. "Sorry. A little over ten years ago Dean's mother stabbed his father to death. They were already separated you see. Dean's father, Grant, had moved in with his sister because he thought his nine year old son needed a woman's influence."

"Any idea what broke them up?"

"Not really," Roberts said. "Apparently they argued a lot. Or rather she argued with him. Grant was not a strong man, and from all accounts his wife dominated him. She was a strong woman. As was Ursula. Now that Francis is back I wouldn't be surprised if she went after Ursula."

Hannibal was looking at Roberts now, watching the beard move up and down. "Back?"

"Miss Collins told me Dean had seen his mother. Isn't it so?"

"Was Dean your patient during the trial?" Hannibal asked.

"Yes. I'd like to think I held him together during that difficult time."

"Losing his father must have been tough, but seeing his mother convicted of murder would be worse," Hannibal said, starting to walk again. "Was there any doubt? I mean, any chance she wasn't guilty?"

"Mister Jones, you've met Stan Thompson. Does he strike you as the type of man who leaves anything to chance? He was the investigating detective."

"What?" Hannibal's feet stopped dead, and the sound of the birds faded from his mind.

"Oh yes. He was up here back then. That case made him, Mister Jones. Moved to Virginia not long after at a much more impressive salary."

"And you don't think there's any chance a mistake was made?" Hannibal asked. "Sometimes evidence can be misleading."

"Their case didn't depend on evidence, Mister Jones," Roberts said. "And it could hardly fail with Dean as an eyewitness.

*　　　　　　*　　　　　　*

Hannibal's office was dim with only the corner lamp lit. Anna was perched in Hannibal's desk chair, her toes dangling just above the floor. To her right and a little behind her Hannibal sat with his legs stretched out in front of him, looking over Anna's shoulder at his computer screen. He had surrendered his jacket, gloves and shades and even rolled up the sleeves of his white shirt, but in his mind he was still at work.

"Is it a rule you can't relax while we do this?" Cindy asked, handing him a glass of wine. She had already placed one in front of Anna and held one for herself. When Hannibal shook his head, she turned to drop onto his lap.

Anna turned just enough to smile a thank you toward Cindy as she sipped her wine. "Here's the site I was looking for," she said. Hannibal saw the words "License Plates of the World" and checked the URL: http://danshiki.oit.gatech.edu/~iadt3mk/index.html. Way too complex to try to remember.

"Bookmark that, will you Anna?"

"Will do," she said. "Now, we're assuming the car you're after is registered in the U.S. right?"

"Yeah," Hannibal said, sipping his wine. Cindy had chosen a fruity white wine that he knew would lighten his spirits. "So let's start looking. There's only fifty of them."

Anna tapped a few keys and a group of plates came into view. "I guess alphabetically is as good a way to approach it as any, eh?" she said. "Here's Alabama."

"Nope, way too light," Hannibal said. "The plate we're looking for is dark, maybe a real dark blue, with white letters."

"And the first three characters are numbers, right?" Anna added, tapping more keys. "Alabama always has a letter in the first three. Alaska's next."

Cindy squirmed down comfortably into Hannibal's lap. "So did Doc Roberts say what got Dean into the hospital?"

"Oh yeah," Hannibal said, kissing her forehead just because it was within reach. "Dean discovered his father's mutilated body."

"Oh God," Cindy moaned.

"He and his dad had been alone in the house. His mother came over but Dean didn't go to greet her I guess. From another room he heard them arguing, apparently about finalizing their divorce."

Anna skipped Alaska, which starts with three letters, and Arizona, which has a light blue plate. "Kids don't go near when that's going on," she said.

"Roberts says he heard her leave," Hannibal said, hugging Cindy to his chest. "Then the door opens again, in Dean's words, like she forgot something."

Anna skipped past Arkansas, California and Colorado for color or number combination mismatches. "Maybe she was just getting up her courage."

Hannibal wondered if she was projecting her own feelings. "For whatever reasons, the next thing Dean heard was a grunt, then something heavy falling to the floor. Then the door slams again."

Cindy emptied her wine glass, even while watching the monitor. "Hey what about Connecticut?"

Hannibal leaned forward. "Dark blue, light letters, three numbers a dot then three letters. That could be it!"

"I'll bookmark this page too, and move on," Anna said. "So then this kid walks out and finds his father dead, right?"

Hannibal nodded grimly. "I'm afraid so. Terrible thing for a boy that age."

"You lost your dad when you were even younger," Cindy commented. She refilled glasses while Anna flipped past Delaware and the District of Columbia, plates they were all familiar with, and glanced at Florida and Georgia plates which were the wrong colors.

"That was different," Hannibal said. "I lost my dad to a faceless enemy a thousand miles away. And I didn't have to see him dead."

Anna never turned from the monitor. Hawaii, Idaho, Illinois, Indiana and Iowa all failed to match Hannibal's description. "That's a terrible thing, but does it make him an eyewitness?"

"That's kind of where the story gets muddy," Hannibal said. "Bea told me he never actually saw his mother in the house. But he testified she was there to please his aunt. That probably explains some of his guilt."

Cindy resumed her seat. "Sure. He thinks he's the reason his mother's in jail."

Hannibal watched license plates flash across the computer screen over her hair: Kansas was a loser.

"What about Kentucky?" Anna asked. "The numbers. Fairly dark at the top."

Hannibal leaned in close. "No, I don't think so. I seem to remember a dot. A dot after the first three numbers. And Doctor

Roberts admitted Dean thinks he's responsible for a lot, including his father's death and Oscar Peters'.

Cindy kissed his neck. "You think the two murders are connected somehow, don't you?"

Louisiana, Maine, Maryland and Massachusetts were the wrong color. Michigan could have been it, but the plate started with three letters instead of numbers. "Connected? Well let's see. Stabbings both times. In the victim's living room at night both times. Knife gone both times. Men in Dean Edwards' life both times. Dean finds the body both times. Yeah, I'd say they might be connected."

Anna fanned past the next five states. Hannibal was momentarily distracted because Cindy pressed her mouth against his and he was enjoying the sweetness of the wine mingled with her kiss.

"Hey cut that out you two," Anna said with a grin. "How about this one, Hannibal?"

Hannibal pulled himself free of Cindy's embrace and stared hard at the monitor. The license plate was cobalt blue with three numbers and three letters separated by a dot. The raised characters were silver, with a reflective quality Hannibal recognized. That and a number of subtle visual cues he couldn't name made his heart quicken beyond what the wine and Cindy's kiss could do.

"That's it," he said softly. "Now we know what state the real killer drove in from."

-12-
WEDNESDAY

Silver Spring was a community in search of an identity. Like its sister communities
Bethesda and Chevy Chase, Hannibal thought of it as a growth on the northern skin of Washington, growing up into Maryland, technically independent but too close to call a suburb. Coming in off the capitol Beltway, a driver slid into these cities and could never know he had crossed over into The District if not for signs indicating a change.

Hannibal had a couple of errands to attend to in Silver Spring, which is tucked into that three or four mile space between the Beltway and the District. In that narrow space it graded rather quickly from affluent suburb to inner city business district as it merged with the narrow dirty streets of Washington. So almost as soon as he was off the highway Hannibal was turning right into an older neighborhood, older but still proud and, to the extent it could be, exclusive. In many ways the neighborhood reminded him of the woman he was here to see, Ursula Voss.

Anna Ingersoll had verified that this year's Nevada license plates held three numbers followed by three letters, not counting vanity plates and special plates of course. She promised to check the Nevada motor vehicle database today and give him a printout showing which of the seventeen thousand possible combinations starting with 902 were currently issued in Nevada. In the meantime, he had little to go on to help solve Oscar's murder. So he decided that he would try to find out more about the death of Dean's father. Ursula was the most likely source of information there.

On the telephone, Ursula told him her office was in her home and that she could give him a few minutes if he came fairly early. Less than an hour after that call, Hannibal pulled up in front of Ursula's house and set his parking brake. The large brick structure was probably forty years old. He'd bet Ursula bought it new at a time when the idea that it would one day be worth a quarter million dollars would have raised a laugh. And he was sure she had lived there ever since. Despite the bay window, the porch was reminiscent of the one on the front of Oscar's house.

Hannibal tightened his gloves before he rang the bell. When Ursula opened the door she was wearing a blue flowered dress that could have come off the same rack as the one she had on the day before. A pair of reading glasses hung from a chain around her neck.

"I'm quite busy Mister Jones," she said after they exchanged good mornings. "Believe it or not, the tax season's already underway for us accountants."

"I won't take up too much of your time," Hannibal said. He took one step over the threshold and stopped. A wave of deja vu struck him and it took him a moment to sort it out. The room was more broad than deep, with a fireplace in the far wall which looked as if it had not been used in decades. Vaulted ceilings kept the room cool and imparted the slightest echo. But it was the decor that struck him. Oscar Peters might just as likely have picked this flowered wallpaper, only different from his in color. The sparse furniture was placed in analogous positions. The standing lamp in the corner, even the drapes at the windows were similar in style to what Oscar had in his house. Hannibal's eyes dropped to a particular point on the floor. It was a hardwood floor, just like the floor in that other house where Oscar Peters stretched out in front of the door at that exact place and let the blood out of his body.

"That's the spot," Ursula said with ancient hatred. "That's where Dean found Grant. Is that what you came to see?"

"No ma'am," Hannibal said, backing toward the living room sofa. "But it does help me understand what happened to Dean."

"And just what does that mean?" Ursula asked in a sharp tone, settling into the love seat, positioned kitty corner to the sofa.

He meant he saw Dean as a man standing just one step over the knife-edge line separating sanity from madness. He imagined Dean opening the door to that house decorated so much like the house he grew up in and looking down and seeing a dead man lying, for all practical purposes, where his father was that night, his body positioned as his father had been, with all the blood spilled in the same pattern on the hardwood floor.

"Nothing, Miss Voss," Hannibal said, forcing the image out of his mind. "I just let my imagination run away with me there for a minute."

"Well let's get down to business," Ursula said, pulling a silver cigarette case from her purse. "What did you need to see me about?"

"Actually I came to ask you for a favor, something I didn't want to broach on the telephone." Hannibal had expected the offer of coffee or tea but clearly this woman did not intend to make his visit any longer than necessary.

"I see," Ursula said, touching the flame from a silver lighter to her cigarette and inhaling deeply. "Unless it will help my nephew somehow, I hardly see why I would be doing you a favor."

Hannibal had little motivation to play softball with this hardened woman. "I've been hired to try to help him, and I wouldn't ask anything of you outside that context. But after you told Thompson where he was, I couldn't be sure how much you cared about Dean yourself."

Ursula leaned back as if he had hit her. "What? What makes you think I told him?"

"Please Miss Voss. Only a handful of people knew Dean was hospitalized, and none of us had any motivation to inform the police of his whereabouts. But then, Thompson didn't tell you it was his case, did he?"

"Stan Thompson and I go back a long way, Mister Jones," Ursula said. "Since he's working in Virginia now, I figured he could tell me just what kind of trouble my nephew was in. I needed to know what that murdering whore had gotten my poor Dean into. And no, he didn't tell me he was involved with the case." She forced the last sentence through clenched teeth.

"Ahh, Bea must have told you his mother had visited him. I take it you didn't like her very much, even before Dean's father died."

"That woman was white trash from the beginning. The kind of white trash you find in the hills in West Virginia." Ursula spoke through a cloud of smoke and Hannibal could almost see the venom dripping off this black widow's fangs. "Poor Grant was seduced by her wanton body, but we could all see through her. He married her against our will."

"Our will?"

"The whole family was against it," Ursula said, filling her lungs with smoke again. When she pulled the cigarette away from her mouth, lipstick clung to the filter like a bloodstain. "Wasn't long before they were arguing violently. Grant, he was too gentle a soul for that and she just ran over him. When he finally came to his senses he and little Dean moved in here. He was the spitting image of the little brother I helped raise, not a drop of his mother's violent blood in him. That cold-blooded murderess."

She had no way of knowing Hannibal had looked into Francis Edwards' china blue eyes himself, and failed to find a murderess there. "Odd for a cold-blooded murderess to be on the street in ten years, eh?"

"That trial was a travesty," Ursula said. "Manslaughter they gave her, not a murder conviction. Her lying trickster lawyer Walt Young convinced those idiots it was a crime committed in the 'heat of passion,' I believe is the exact legal term he used."

"And just how did he manage that?"

Here Ursula leaned forward and lowered her voice. "He convinced those sheep on the jury that Grant had another woman. As if my brother would have strayed, even from that lowlife, before his divorce was settled. She admitted she came to the house that night because she got the final papers and was trying to talk him out of it. If only I'd been home. Dean heard them arguing about the divorce. Poor Grant finally stuck to his guns about something and she...she...and poor Dean had to see it."

Hannibal wondered why he was not inclined to comfort this woman. "Yes, and Dean told a court that he saw his mother with the knife."

"Yes, that's right. If he hadn't that whore might have gone free."

"So I gather," Hannibal said. "But Dean now says he didn't see his mother at all. He lied, Miss Voss, to please the grownups, he says."

The drapes were parted, and the blinds threw prison stripes across Ursula's form. Her mouth held firm but her eyes moved down and for a moment Hannibal let her stew in the silence. When she finally spoke she had left the past behind. "I'm a busy woman, Mister Jones. What did you come here for?"

"I gather you and Thompson are old friends," Hannibal said with an edge in his voice. "You wouldn't have called him otherwise. He thinks he's got his killer, Miss Voss, but I think he's wrong. I saw a man running from the deceased's house just before we found the body. But I need time to find him. All I want is for you to ask your good friend the police detective to back off Dean for a few days. Give me time to find the real killer."

When she looked up at him he saw indecision on her face so he pressed harder. "You know he'll accept anything as evidence to prove a shaky case. Give me a chance to find the truth."

"I'll call him."

-13-

The Silver Spring Boys and Girls Club wasn't far from Ursula Voss' home, just off Forest Glen Road. The practice field behind it was a vast space of sparse grass bordered by closely planted oaks whose denuded branches swayed gently, sweeping the underside of the clouds above. Hannibal sometimes wondered why trees planted in a linc often seemed to stop at an agreed upon height, forming a clean line at the top.

The man waiting for Hannibal near the goal post stood with his hands deep in the pockets of a black windbreaker. Hannibal didn't recognize the logo on the jacket, sort of an orange claw striking from under the word "Predators." The man inside the jacket flashed a bright smile from the middle of a very dark, round face. Even at a distance, he seemed too pleasant to be a football coach.

"Thank you for meeting me here, Mr. Lee," Hannibal said, offering a hand.

"No problem, I've got to be here tonight to run the practice anyway. And please call me George." The man had a strong handshake that challenged Hannibal to match it. "Now you said you wanted to talk about one of my boys, Ingersoll. Is he in some kind of trouble?"

"I'm involved in a dispute with his wife," Hannibal said carefully. "She has asked me to advise her. But if I'm going to be fair I need to know a little more about Isaac." Lee would probably think Hannibal was a lawyer, which was fine for now.

Lee nodded, then started walking toward the sidelines. "He hit her didn't he?"

Hannibal followed, enjoying the quiet of the unused field. "I understand he has a problem with his temper. Is that your experience?"

Lee laughed, turning along the sideline and strolling slowly down field. "Yeah, he's a hothead. But he's a hell of a guy to have on the line. The Predators wouldn't do nearly as well without him. I just wish he wasn't such a sore loser."

"I'm surprised he's even on a semi-pro team like the Predators," Hannibal said. "I mean, if a guy's too violent for the Redskins, he must be downright dangerous."

Lee stopped at the thirty-yard line, turning an eye toward Hannibal's face. "Is that what he told you?"

"That's what she told me."

Lee shook his face at the ground. "Well that's probably what he told her. Too violent? Not sure if that's even possible. Mister, Ingersoll was cut from the Redskins for the same reason guys usually get cut. He just wasn't good enough. The fact that he didn't get along with most of the guys, well, that was just an added incentive to show him the door."

"So is this the usual next step? Drop down to a semi-pro team?"

Lee turned again, stepping farther away from the street, into the private peace of the football practice field. "Sometimes. If you can play at all, you can usually get a spot somewhere, like the Diamond League where we play."

Hannibal looked to the side and imagined Isaac Ingersoll crashing through a line of defenders, racing down the field to crush a quarterback. It would certainly be where he felt most alive, most at home. "I guess a guy like him just needs to play."

"Lot of the big guys do," Lee agreed. "I just hope he comes up with his dues, or else I can't even allow him to practice with us tonight."

The grass must have been mown just that day, the sweet smell of freshly cut grass bringing a gentle smile to Hannibal's face. "Dues? Is he getting fined for something?"

Lee spun at the fifty-yard line, one foot erasing the chalk line as he did so. "You don't know a damn thing about football, do you?" Hannibal snapped back, startled by Lee's sudden burst of energy. "You're looking to get money out of him for the wife, is that it? You come down here thinking Ingersoll's getting paid for playing."

"Isn't he? I guess I just assumed..."

"What, you think this is like baseball? You fail in the majors so you go down to triple A ball?" Lee stepped in close to stare into Hannibal's lenses and suddenly, he looked exactly like what Hannibal expected a coach to look like, a mama grizzly bear protecting her cubs. "Those guys swinging a bat, they play for money. These guys are different."

"They really don't get paid? How do you recruit them?"

"Don't have to, brother," Lee said. "They find us. They play for the love of the game, something you couldn't possibly understand. There's more than four hundred of these little teams around the country you know. Minor league teams in forty different leagues like the Diamond league. And not only don't these guys get paid to play, they have to pay their dues to get on a team. Plus they buy the gear. Most of the time, they have to pay for their own transportation to and from games."

"I feel like an idiot," Hannibal said. "That's why you have to practice at night."

"Yeah. You got to have a job to be able to get the chance to come out here and grunt, and sweat, and get run into by another bunch of guys who love this game."

$$*\qquad *\qquad *$$

When his car was moving again, Hannibal pushed a CD into the player. After his football lesson, Hannibal needed noise. Only when he was alone did the serious rock and roll come out. He grew up on this music thanks to the American Forces Radio and Television Service but, for reasons too hard to think about, he stuck with R&B or jazz in public. But the truth was, he could think more clearly surrounded by Sammy Hagar's power chords. He didn't want to believe yesterday's murder was in any way related to the one that cost Dean his parents, but if the acts were as similar as Dean thought, it seemed likely they were. It would help to know more about the older killing from a more objective source.

Once on the Beltway heading south and east, Hannibal set his cruise control at seventy and pressed a preset on his car's hands-free phone. Within a minute he had Cindy's voice filling the car with him.

"So do you get a consultant's fee?" he asked her.

"I'll take it out in trade, lover. What do you need?"

"How hard will it be to get the records of Francis Edwards' trial?" he asked.

"Depends on what kind of detail you're looking for."

The long ribbon of asphalt stretched out before him, and it would have been easy for Hannibal to think he had all the time in the world. "Well, what I really need is a transcript of the court proceedings. I want to hear the other side of this case."

On the other end of the phone he heard a familiar huff. He could see Cindy in his mind, jaw forward, top lip curled in, blowing a puff of air upward. "Right," she said. "You don't have the date of this event, do you? Or happen to know for sure where it took place? How about the prosecuting attorney's name?"

Hannibal dodged a tractor-trailer and eased down into the right lane. His exit wasn't that far off. "What I know, baby, is that Francis Edwards was convicted of manslaughter. That her lawyer raised the specter of another woman and must have convinced the jury it was a crime of passion. That little Dean Edwards at nine years old was forced to testify against his mother in open court after he'd just lost his father. And that the murder victim Dean just saw yesterday looked very much the way his father did when Dean found him."

For a while Hannibal heard nothing but Steve Perry's crystalline tenor as Journey eased through *Open Arms*, but he knew she was just putting it all together. He knew his woman well enough that he almost heard her answer, "I'll see what I can do," before she said it.

"Knew I could count on you, darling. Think you can get away for dinner? I don't expect much movement on this case in any great hurry."

Driving through his neighborhood, Hannibal was still struck by the study in contrast. The boarded up buildings of Southeast Washington DC were painted a rainbow of pastel colors, as if someone wanted to make sure they would be able to find their way back to the right abandoned tenement. Men and women, almost all black, walked the streets in the most expensive designer clothing or in rags, neither noticing the other's mode of dress. Just a few blocks away in one direction, the Navy Yard did mostly administrative business for the sea service. A few blocks the other way the grand buildings of the Smithsonian Institute hosted millions of tourists every year.

Hannibal pulled into his parking space, the one right across the street that no one ever seemed to park in. In the late summer sun his block looked a bit cleaner than the surrounding area. He knew his neighbors were working class people, struggling to make a living, but it always seemed to him that a bubble existed around his building that separated him and his neighbors from the surrounding depressed area.

As he climbed the front steps to the stoop, his mind wandered backward down his life's trail to the days when he and a handful of new friends first walked into this three-story brick monstrosity that had become a crack house. With Sarge and the others, he had driven every sort of human garbage out of there: drug dealers, winos, the lot. And for reasons still beyond his own understanding, he had stayed here to make a place for himself.

The outer door stayed unlocked during the day. As he pushed inside, the glaring sun was replaced by a shadowed darkness some might find gloomy, but which he always found somehow comforting. For a moment he was undecided if he would go left to his apartment or right to his office.

The decision was taken from him by a huge fist that closed on his right shoulder and shoved him into his office door. The frames of Hannibal's Oakleys dug into his cheek and the blackness deepened for a second.

"Where is she?" It was Isaac's beer-laden breath in his ear, Isaac's hand on his right shoulder, Isaac's elbow pinning his body to the door. The pressure kept him from catching a good deep breath and his feet could barely gain purchase on the floor. But the brief flash of fear he felt quickly transformed into anger.

"I called all the shelters." Isaac said. "They wouldn't tell me nothing. I been to the police. Where the hell is she?"

Hannibal's right hand formed a claw. With stiffened fingers he snapped back toward the voice behind him. The strike wasn't very hard, but it didn't have to be. Isaac released him and backed off. Hannibal turned to face his huge attacker, who stood with one hand pressed to his eyes.

"I guess she just got tired of taking your shit," Hannibal said, drawing himself up into a fighting stance. "And frankly, asshole, so have I."

Isaac Ingersoll was very big, very strong, and quite fast for a man his size. But Hannibal had been kickboxing since high school and right then was filled with the kind of rage that comes when frustration gets overlaid with a layer of indignation. It was quick, and it was ugly.

A series of jabs flashed between Isaac's upraised hands until blood from his nose was running freely down onto his lip and chin. Then Hannibal got serious and started mixing it up with side kicks to his opponent's right thigh. Isaac swung. Hannibal dodged and attacked - left, right, kick - until Isaac finally just stopped trying and stepped back absorbing the punishment.

Finally a sharp wheel kick caused Isaac's knee to buckle and he fell against the wall and sank into a crouch. Hannibal raised his fist to drive a right cross down into Isaac's face and finish it. The big man's eyes never closed or turned away and that was what made Hannibal pause.

Isaac's injured blue eyes looked up into Hannibal's face and he moaned, "where is she?" in the voice of a child on the verge of tears. Try as he might, Hannibal could not see a vicious wife-beater. He was looking at a lost boy who needed his mother. He saw a brief flash of Dean huddled on a bed and recognized his facial expression mirrored here. With a sigh he dropped his fists, suddenly ashamed of the blood on his gloves.

"Come into my office. And I swear to God if you give me any more trouble I'll kick your big ass."

Isaac meekly followed and dropped into the seat he was directed to. Hannibal turned on the cold water in the kitchen, soaked a towel, wrung it out, and gave it to Isaac to clean himself up with. Then he sat behind his desk.

"Why did you come here?"

Isaac looked up into his own head before answering, and Hannibal got the feeling this was a man who just did not express himself well in words. "To get your help. To find my Anna. You could make her come back to me."

"She's not your Anna, Isaac," Hannibal said. "She's a grown woman, her own woman. I can't make her do anything and neither can you. And she's just decided she doesn't have to accept being beaten up, understand?"

Isaac nodded, and at that minute he did appear to understand that much. His eyes cast around as if he was searching for the solution to that problem. It occurred to Hannibal that the man could only express himself one way.

"Do you love her?" he asked before he knew he would.

"I love her," Isaac answered, "as much as I know how. I need her. I can't live without her. What can I do? What do I have to do?"

The telephone's bell jangled Hannibal's nerves from the base of his skull downward. Without thinking he snatched it up to stop the noise. His eyes widened in surprise, mostly because he did not believe in coincidences.

"Some news for you Hannibal," Anna said. "And not all good. There are more than nine hundred current license plates in Nevada that start with 902. But I was able to narrow it down some."

Hannibal considered how badly he wanted to hear what Anna had to say, but only for a second. "Anna, would you hold on a second? There's someone here who wants to talk to you."

*   *   *

Anna hesitated for just a beat before climbing into Hannibal's car. He pulled away from the DMV building and headed toward nearby Springfield Mall. Before he passed the first traffic light he asked the question he'd been sitting on since he handed the phone to her husband.

"Do you love him?"

"What the hell kind of a question is that?" Anna asked. In just a few days she had come completely out of her thin shell and was showing the self-confidence of a successful professional woman.

"The kind of question I need answered before we get there," Hannibal said. "The kind of question that will tell me what it is I should be trying to do."

He kept his eyes on the road, but he felt or sensed Anna's face going through a range of expressions. The question took in a wide variety of concepts, emotions and ideas. It always does. People don't usually notice that, but Anna appeared very aware of it right then. Ultimately the answer came. "Yes."

"He answered faster," Hannibal said. "He needs you, Anna, and I think maybe you need that too."

"I'm afraid for my son."

"Your husband needs help," Hannibal said. "He says he's willing to get it, if you'll stick by him. I just want you to talk face to face."

"I've already said okay to that," Anna said. "Now, do you want to hear about the license plate?"

"We're here. Hold it for when we're inside."

Hannibal had not chosen Mozzarella's because of its cuisine, although he was partial to its version of commercialized Italian food. Nor was its reasonable price range a factor. What mattered was its proximity to Anna's job, and the fact that it would be pretty full at lunchtime. Some people were a lot less likely to misbehave in a crowded place and Hannibal had judged Isaac to be one of them.

Lighting was dim for a lunch place, perhaps to mitigate the bright reds and yellows accenting the cuisine. Garlic butter and oregano were the dominant aromas. Conversation was low but constant, creating a pleasing background hum of white noise. Anna hesitated once more when they came within sight of the booth. Isaac stood as she approached. While Hannibal wore his black work suit and Anna a neat charcoal skirt suit, Isaac was dressed in jeans and a knit shirt. Still, Hannibal noticed that at one time or another, every woman in the room stole a glance at the big, well-muscled blonde.

Hannibal eased Anna into one side of the booth, then subtly shoved Isaac into the other side and sat beside him. They ordered quickly and tried to settle into being comfortable in what was by definition an uncomfortable situation.

"So," Hannibal said before any other conversation could start, "more than nine hundred plates that could belong to our murderer. But you said you were able to narrow it down? How?"

"Well, I actually went down the entire list checking make and model." Anna's smile returned as she spoke. She so wanted to be useful. Maybe she needed to be needed as much as Isaac needed her. "First I eliminated all the cars I know to be compacts. You said it was a bigger vehicle. Well that got us to six hundred twenty-five cars."

"Pretty smart," Hannibal said. He had wanted Isaac to see her in a professional capacity before they talked. Maybe he'd gain a little more respect for her.

"Then I had another thought and went through again, striking all the trucks and vans," Anna said. "That brought the number down to three hundred twelve. Still a lot of people to check but then I got daring."

Now Hannibal was grinning. "You are quite the detective. Now what do you mean by daring?"

"Well, you said it was a man driving, right?" Anna didn't stop when the waiter arrived and placed their food in front of them. "So I figured the car probably wasn't registered to a woman. Scratching those cut it down to two hundred nine. Nevada has a lot of unmarried women you know."

"That will make a big difference if this comes down to a real search," Hannibal said. "I sure appreciate your effort." He gestured for Anna and Isaac to eat, then dug into his own food. The smoked sausage stuffing his ravioli was bursting with that flavor that can only come from charcoal, and it blended perfectly with the sweet marinara sauce. He watched his two booth mates eyeing each other cautiously while he ate. Isaac was first to speak.

"So how have you been Anna? And how is my Nicky?"

"We are both fine, thank you," Anna said, not looking up. "I can take care of myself. And my son."

Little more was said until Hannibal finished his lunch. Isaac looked toward him several times, as if waiting for him to make something happen. Anna's eyes wandered that way a few times as well. When Hannibal did put his fork down he turned so he could see them both easily.

"All right, you two, I've got to get going," he said, which drew startled looks from both Isaac and Anna. "Before I go, Anna, Isaac and I discussed some ground rules and I wanted to get your agreement to them. First, he accepts the separation and will never try to make you go home with him. Right Isaac?" Isaac nodded, and Hannibal continued. "In exchange you agree not to refuse to see him any day he wants to spend some time with you, like today. You pick the place, you say how long, but you agree to see him and talk to him. Okay?"

Anna took a deep breath and bit her lower lip, but nodded her head as well. "Fine. Now I discussed with Isaac the idea that he needs some counseling for his problem of hitting people he loves. He can do that and I think maybe get his problem fixed if you give him some support. What do you say? I mean, is there anything else that makes it unacceptable to live with him as man and wife?"

Anna's eyes widened like a doe startled by a flashlight at night. "Well, yes, that's basically it."

"Well good. You two sit here and work out a plan to do what has to be done. I got the check. Here's cab fare back to work. Like I said, I have to run. But I'm sure you'll call me tonight to tell me how it went."

"Yes, you can bet on that," Anna said, her face sending overlapping messages of hate and thanks. "But wouldn't it be better if you stuck around to hear for yourself?"

Hannibal had an answer prepared, but his phone saved him the trouble. Smiling, he pulled it out of his pocket and flipped it open. The smile dropped from his face instantly and his mind shut out everything but the voice in his ear.

"Calm down Bea. Where are you?"

"The garage apartment," Bea said through tears Hannibal could almost see through the telephone. "I came to pick up some of Dean's things and, and, Hannibal they've found the murder weapon."

-14-

Hannibal's tires squealed when he reached the driveway. Only pure luck had allowed him to avoid a ticket on his way to the Kitteridge house. He ran through the door and took the steps three at a time until he stood face to face with Stan Thompson in the modest living room. Bea sat on the sofa, alone, still crying.

"Would you mind showing me what you got?" Hannibal said, fists on hips.

Thompson looked down at him and grimaced. "You know, for someone who has no official standing in this case, you sure do turn up with a lot of questions."

"Just trying to keep you from embarrassing yourself, chief," Hannibal said. "Just thought it would be nice to see the supposed murder weapon. I know I have no rights here, just asking."

"What the hell, over there," Thompson said with the arrogance of the man who thinks he has all the answers. The weapon lay on the coffee table where anyone in the room could examine it, in a simple ziplock bag. Hannibal squatted beside the table for a closer look.

It was the right tool for the job. A genuine Marine Corps issue Ka-bar fighting knife. Marines started getting them in nineteen forty-two and their popularity never flagged because they were tough knives made for combat. This one was the regulation size, a little less than a foot long, with about six and a half inches of that being the parkerized blade. It retained most of its black coating, except of course for its glittering razor edge. The dark brown stains up under the hand guard were certainly dried blood, and he could guess whose. The handle's compacted leather discs were stained unevenly dark, assumably from absorbing the sweat from the hand of its owner.

"That thing couldn't be his," Bea whined, and Hannibal suddenly remembered she was there. He moved to the couch and put a comforting arm around her shoulders. "I swear I've never seen that knife before," Bea went on.

"Just try to relax," Hannibal told her. "This is all circumstantial."

"Give it up, lady. Your boyfriend's cooked." Thompson had moved unnoticed to stand over them, staring down like a judge. Hannibal released Bea and stood slowly, so that he was nose to nose with Thompson. The bigger man took a small step back. Hannibal advanced, keeping his voice low.

"That woman's suffering right now. Part of the collateral damage that surrounds every murder. There's no good reason for you to be rough with her. Unless you think she had something to do with Oscar's death?"

Thompson took Hannibal's arm and guided him into the bedroom. Hannibal thought for a moment he would get the chance to get physical with the detective but once out of Bea's sight Thompson dropped his arm and spread his hands wide.

"You're right," Thompson said softly. "You're right and for what it's worth, I apologize. I know what you're talking about. I saw what Grant Edwards' death did to my good friend Ursula Voss." Something in Thompson's eyes said they were more than friends.

"She seems, on the surface, to be a pretty tough woman," Hannibal said. "Wouldn't think her grief would show."

"You don't know," Thompson said, dropping on to the bedsprings. The mattress stood on edge against the wall, one result of the search, Hannibal assumed. "Cancer took her husband, not three years after the wedding, and she never married again. She had a big hand in raising her little brother and always felt protective toward him."

Hannibal sat beside Thompson. "Look chief, it'll kill her if her nephew gets dragged into a murder trial."

"Don't you think I know that?" Thompson asked. "But what can I do? This is certainly enough to warrant my demanding Dean be taken into custody. I mean, this isn't just some forensic indication here, it's almost certainly the murder weapon, hidden in his home."

"Okay," Hannibal said, standing. "Where'd you find it?" Thompson pointed at the mattress. A slit had been cut into the middle of it, just about a foot long.

"One of my men turned the mattress over and found that. And when he stuck his hand inside, he pulled out that knife. You can see dried blood on it, up by the hilt."

"Yeah, and I can name a dozen people who could have put it there since the murder, including me."

Thompson stood, smiling. "You know I've got enough to question him."

The room smelled even more stale than it had before. "If you were at his mother's trial, then you've known Dean Edwards for a long time. You think he's a killer, chief?"

"Frankly I don't think he's got it in him," Thompson said, staring out the window. "But I think if I sweat him a bit I can get him to give up the real killer."

Hannibal wandered over next to Thompson, staring down at the same wide, well-kept lawn. "And that would be?"

"His mother. A known killer. I checked. She's out of prison already."

"Motive?" Hannibal could see the main house from there and wondered idly where the Kitteridges were during all this investigating.

"Well there's plenty of evidence Oscar Peters was gay. And witnesses tell us he and Dean were close. Maybe mama didn't approve."

Hannibal watched Langford Kitteridge step out of his house, wearing a jogging suit, and begin a series of slow stretching exercises on the lawn. Then his attention returned to Thompson. "Because the murders look the same, you think maybe they were done by the same person, eh?"

"Let's just say I'm getting the blood on the knife tested against two different samples," Thompson admitted.

Hannibal didn't want to obstruct the investigation, but he sure wanted to protect Dean from being hauled in as a suspect. And maybe, he realized, he could forestall it. He moved off to the living room, followed closely by Thompson. He sat beside Bea, pulled his telephone from his jacket pocket and looked up at Thompson as he dialed.

"You don't want the press to pull Dean in yet, chief. It'll look like a helpless, emotionally wrecked man being persecuted."

Hannibal ignored the puzzled looks on Bea's and Thompson's faces while he listened to the ringing sound, grateful when the right person answered.

"Hi, this is Hannibal."

"Hannibal? Hannibal Jones?" Irma Andrews asked.

"How many Hannibals do you know?"

The pleasant voice at the other end changed, and Hannibal could imagine her eyes narrowing. "What's up? You got something for me? Something bankable before the 6 o'clock cast?"

"I keep my promises, Irma," Hannibal said. "This case is about to become news, and you've got it exclusively if you move. Remember where we went together last night?"

Hannibal could hear Irma shuffling papers, perhaps taking hasty notes. "Sure, Dean

Edwards' place. Is there a serious development?"

"I'm there now. I'm looking at Dean's fiancée, the investigating detective on the case and what is almost certainly the murder weapon. But your story is that Dean is under a psychiatrist's care, hospitalized, and the police want to drag him downtown. Bea can give you all the details and if you hurry, the police are still searching the place. Lots of nice B-roll of cops dusting and searching and...."

"Jones, I owe you a big kiss! Be there in twenty minutes!" In this case, Hannibal understood being hung up on without so much as a good-bye. A glance at Bea told him she understood what was happening. One look at Thompson's face told Hannibal that he did not.

"Were you just talking to the press?"

"That's right," Hannibal said. "Have a good rundown of the case ready when they get here. Bea's going to tell them all about Dean's condition and how unfair it would be to haul him out of the hospital."

"Under these circumstances," Thompson said slowly, "Taking him into custody will be out of the question until we've definitely confirmed that this is the murder weapon."

"Buys me a little time," Hannibal said, moving for the door, "so I better make the most of it."

Hannibal was down the stairs before anyone had a chance to ask more questions, jogging lightly to the main house. He pulled up in front of Langford Kitteridge who stood touching his forehead to his knees. When he straightened his tall slim form he smiled a greeting at Hannibal, then became more serious as his eyes strayed to the garage.

"Nasty business over there," Langford said. "They tried to keep me out of it but it's my property, you know. Joanie told me all about it. Nasty business."

"Yes," Hannibal agreed, noting the impatience in Langford's hopping from one foot to another. "I'm surprised she's letting them tear around in that place without her here."

"Oh, Joanie's out of town," Langford said, beginning to swing his arms and twist from side to side. "Big trade show. Had to leave last night."

"Really? Rather sudden decision, eh?"

"Oh, no," Langford said. "This thing was planned months ago. She's a featured speaker I think. But I am surprised she didn't cancel. I mean, I thought she really liked that Oscar. Dated a couple of times I believe. But sometimes, she's a little too much business first, if you know what I mean. And for the computer industry, the shows in Las Vegas are critical."

"Las Vegas?" Hannibal repeated. "Yes I think I do know what you mean. And I think I'll stop by her office and see just what was so important about this trip that a murdered friend didn't make her change her plans."

-15-

The same thoughts cycled and recycled through Hannibal's mind during the drive to Kitteridge Computer Systems and all the way up in the elevator. Considering the degree of responsibility Joan showed toward her employees, how could she fly across the country the day after one of them was murdered and another was about to be accused of that murder? And what of the Nevada license plate on the fugitive's car? Hannibal didn't believe in coincidences.

Mark tried to make Hannibal feel welcome in his office, but he was clearly distracted. While Hannibal watched, he labored to put stacks of paper in some sort of order.

"Yes, Mister Jones, the software expo this week is one of most important events of the year in our industry. It would have been very bad for our business if Joan wasn't there. In fact, I believe she's giving a talk."

Hannibal wondered briefly how this guy found his way into the computer business instead of standing on runways in Tommy Hilfiger's latest gear. "I see. You say this thing goes on all week. Any way I can get in touch with her?"

"I can give you a phone number," Mark said, not looking up. "I should have been able to give her a message tomorrow when I went, but...." Mark shuffled papers harder, and turned to his computer to tap information into a form. Hannibal felt forgotten.

"Change of plans?"

Eventually Mark said, "Well, yes. I would have followed Joan... Miss Kitteridge... this evening. But I'll be at Reagan National tonight instead. Oscar's mother is flying in from Germany. I've been tasked to pick her up. Not that I mind doing it, it's just..." Mark looked up at Hannibal for sympathy.

"His mother? Not his parents?" Maybe his father was ill. Or perhaps the feud he had read about in her letter to him was more serious than he assumed. "When does Mrs. Peters arrive?"

Mark looked chastened, and his next words stumbled over each other coming out while his hands wandered through drawers, finally producing a flight itinerary. "I didn't mean it like that. Of course it's our duty to host the lady while she's in town. Joan would have done it herself but for, you know, the importance of this expo. And she's getting here this evening. Nine oh-seven to be precise."

Hannibal stood, pushing his hands into his pockets, curling them into fists there. He imagined a woman in her forties or fifties, alone, stepping into a strange city in the middle of the night after eight hours in an airplane. She deserved to meet a sympathetic face. And he owed her something, somehow. Maybe just because he shared the guilt in Oscar's death.

"Look, why don't I meet her at the airport," Hannibal said.

"Really? I mean, would you?" Mark flashed his fashion model smile and quickly gathered papers to hand him. "I can give you her hotel reservations and everything. You're a lifesaver."

No, Hannibal thought. That's why she's coming here.

*   *   *

It was a bone weary Hannibal Jones who returned to the Charter facility to meet with Bea and Doctor Roberts that night. He had watched the touching news piece on Channel 8 at six o'clock that portrayed Dean Edwards as another victim of Oscar Peters' murderer. Stan Thompson had done his best, but still came across as the hard-bitten detective determined to bring in his man. The camera treated Bea well, her courage and love projecting right into the screen. To any viewer, she would be the heroine of this drama as it played out. Hannibal wanted to hear first hand about her television interview.

The nurse at the reception desk was pleasant and so soft spoken, Hannibal wondered as he had on earlier visits if she thought he was a patient. Or maybe she could not tell patients from visitors, so she treated everyone the same. She looked up from her computer screen with the same frozen solicitous smile worn by every woman he had ever seen in that chair, as if it were issued to them when they came on duty. She apparently had his name on a list of acceptable visitors because she directed him to Dean's room as soon as he identified himself.

Bea greeted him with a hug so intense he was glad he decided not to bring Cindy along. Dean even mumbled hello, but he seemed to be looking through them. Hannibal reassured Bea that Dean would be safely hospitalized for a few days while he, Hannibal, searched for Oscar's real killer. They talked briefly about her experience in front of the camera. Apparently Irma had led her gently with the right interview questions, soliciting the answers she wanted without actually putting words into her mouth. Then Dean moaned, Bea turned to hold his hand, and Hannibal eased Quincy Roberts out of the room. Hannibal said he had three questions for him, which he asked while they slowly strolled the antiseptic hallways, amid the murmurs and moans of the discontented residents.

"If the police could get through the proper channels they might get a writ of habeus corpus in three or four days. Will Dean be fit to be questioned by then?"

"Perhaps," Roberts said. "At his present rate of progress it's possible. Can't be sure, you know. It's not an exact science. He has a lot of issues to deal with."

"One of those is his mother's guilt," Hannibal said. "Dean told me Oscar's murder looked just like his father's. Do you believe there's any chance Dean's mother did kill again?"

Roberts dragged his fingers through his beard and his voice wandered from its usual even timber. "Mister Jones I'm still not convinced Mrs. Edwards killed anyone. And if she did, to imagine she would repeat her crime within a year of release from prison is the merest fantasy."

Hannibal nodded. "Doctor, do you have any reason to believe that Grant Edwards had another woman when he lived in his sister's house?"

"Oh, I for one am quite sure he did." Roberts stopped walking and looked around as if he might be overheard. Hannibal guessed he was wondering how far into client confidentiality he would allow himself to be pushed. "That is another issue Dean has to resolve, Mister Jones. A part of him feels his father deserved to be punished. You see, he was aware of his father's affair with his baby-sitter."

-16-

It wasn't that often that Hannibal wondered just what he was doing or why. Most often his professional work involved some variation of protecting a sensible person from a bully. A person is threatened, something very dear to them is stolen, a child is involved with a gang and parents don't know what to do. Other people's troubles became his own. That was how he made his living since he resigned from the Treasury Department.

The sequence of events that lead him to an uncomfortable seat in the customs area of Reagan National Airport at ten in the evening was not so clear. It really had nothing to do with Dean Edwards, the man he was being paid to help out of a terrible situation. Nor did it have anything to do with the murder of Dean's father. That wasn't his job, but the news about Dean's baby-sitter did provide another suspect for that killing. Another jealous woman may be lurking out there. And if Grant Edwards' death and Oscar's were related, clearing Dean's mother of the earlier murder would help clear her of the second.

The twin doors popped open and Hannibal stood with the rest of those lining the velvet ropes that formed a chute for the international travelers to flow through. First out were the families pushing mounds of luggage stacked on carts. Military from the men's haircuts, arriving at the end of a permanent change of station. Then a few European tourists, just as easily identified by their clothing and an air of unfamiliarity. And a few vacationers, looking exhausted, as if they had tried to see all of Europe in their few days off.

Among the last to enter the cool but brightly lit cavern was a lone woman carrying a single suitcase. Florescent lights gave her hair a bluish tint. Her slightly bent posture and slow shuffling gait made her appear older than Hannibal thought she must be. But something in her soft, warm features told him this had to be Oscar's mother.

"Mrs. Peters?" he asked to be sure. When she nodded with a numb smile he took her suitcase.

"Thank you, young man," Mrs. Peters said. Her makeup had almost worn away during the long flight. "And thank you so much for meeting me like this. I haven't been in my own country for almost twenty years. I've been moving for more than thirteen hours and I'm just about all in. You work with, I mean, you work for the company my Oscar..."

"No ma'am," Hannibal said, not wanting to make her finish the sentence. "I'm Hannibal Jones and I'm involved in the investigation. The people your son worked for asked me to meet you and get you to your hotel. I had no idea your trip was so long."

Mrs. Peters shuffled along sticking close to Hannibal as they headed out into the parking lot. "Oh my, yes. Crossing the Atlantic was more than a ten-hour flight because from Frankfurt they don't fly into New York, but rather go straight to Atlanta. Then you sit there for a couple of hours before the final hour and a half flight here, and then there's the customs nonsense, like I was some kind of foreigner. Although after twenty years, maybe I am."

"I flew out of Templehof when I left Germany for the last time," Hannibal said as he pushed her suitcase into his trunk. "We lived up in Berlin." The night sky was unusually clear and a mass of stars crowded together to comfort one another over the river. It appeared that there was no one to comfort Mrs. Peters. She seemed very alone, but then she looked as if she was used to it. Hannibal thought his charge should be in her mid-sixties at most, but everything about her seemed from the previous generation. Hannibal waited until he had his passenger settled in his car and belted in place before he broached a new subject.

"Tired, ma'am?"

Emma Peters looked at her watch, a diamond studded lady's Waltham that might have been there for the whole twenty years abroad. "A bit. I guess my body thinks it's about three a.m."

"I was surprised to learn you were traveling alone." Hannibal said while she reset her watch. "Your husband is ill?"

"Yes, but that's not why he didn't come. My husband hasn't spoken to Oscar since our son ran away from home. He couldn't face this."

Hannibal guided his car down the darkened tunnel that was the tree-lined George Washington Parkway into Alexandria. "Must have been some disagreement to last these years. I'm sorry." He decided not to pry further.

"Oscar's father was an MP, Mister Jones. You know what that is?"

Hannibal smiled. "Yes ma'am. My dad was military police as well."

"Really?" Emma seemed to look at him with new eyes. "Well, Foster is a conservative man as you can imagine. Very proud of his position, his duties. When Oscar accused him of covering up a murder, well, that was the end of it for the two of them. I tried, but I could never bring them together again."

There was that word again, and Hannibal's resolve quickly evaporated. Another murder? He did not believe in coincidences. "Oscar had information about a murder?"

"Oh, no," Emma said with a wave of a withered hand. "But he certainly thought he did. The truth is, poor Carla's death was accidental. But my Oscar was only sixteen, and he had such a crush on her, he could never accept that, well, that God could be so cruel I guess."

"Carla?" Hannibal asked as he turned onto Route 1 toward the towering hotels of the Crystal City district. "Someone you knew, then?"

Emma nodded, and leaned back, as if reviewing slides being shown on the Volvo's ceiling. "Oh, yes, the whole family did. Her husband, Gil Donner, was the Provost Marshall at the time. Sort of Foster's boss, really, but we socialized from time to time. I think it was hard for poor Oscar sometimes, since Carla was one of his teachers. Freshman social studies, I believe. I remember that one organization day. A big picnic and we and the Donners..."

Hannibal parked in front of the Hyatt Regency hotel and popped his trunk. In the light from the lobby he could see the recollection had brought a tear to her eye. Perhaps this one happy memory of her son was lonely in there. He grabbed her suitcase from the bellhop, handing him a tip anyway, and got Emma checked in. Then he followed her to her room door. Exhaustion hung across her shoulders like a shawl, and he figured she would be asleep as soon as she found her bed. But as he opened the door she stopped and more of the story bubbled up out of her.

"They fought after poor Carla died. He was at that age, raging hormones and rebellion, you know. I remember he called Foster a commie, said it was all a plot. Oh, flew into such a rage that day. How he hated communists. It was the worst thing Oscar could have said, if he wanted to hurt his father."

Hannibal carried her suitcase into the room, watching her face. Emma did not look sad, but rather warmed as if she clung to these memories for company. He considered that maybe any memory of her husband and son together was valuable after all these years. She settled onto the bed but seemed unaware that Hannibal was about to leave.

"Funny, a freshman in high school and he thought he knew everything," she said. "He was a, well today they'd call Oscar a conspiracy theorist I think."

"Ma'am I have to get going now."

"He even said he knew a witness, an eyewitness to Carla's death. Actually, assassination was the word he used."

Hannibal's hand rested on the doorknob, but he could not quite bring himself to turn it. "Really? Did he say who?"

"Oh of course not," she said, shaking her head. "He withdrew into his fantasy world of conspiracies. Pulled away. And then, that summer, he left. Ran away to America."

"You mean he disappeared?"

"Oh no, not to me, just to his father." Emma was drifting, sleep pulling on her. "He wrote to me. When he lived in New York with some people he met. Then he was in Chicago. Wandering. He found out he had a flair for computers, even back then. I sent money. He took courses in California. Even when he was staying in that sinful place Las Vegas two years ago, he wrote to me. I think he fell in with a bad crowd there. But he wrote. He was never a bad boy."

Her motor seemed to have run down. She sat staring at the floor. Hannibal took her shoulders and helped her lie back on the bed. Her eyes closed, her breathing slowed, and her speech slurred a bit. "And now," she murmured, "and now I have to bury my son alone, because his father hasn't the strength."

Hannibal waited until her breathing deepened fully before he turned off the light and quietly slipped out the door.

-17-
THURSDAY

Hannibal's eyes opened when the key slid into the lock. The gray outside his window was a lighter shade, and the street lamps were out, but the sun was not quite up. By the time his feet touched the carpet he could smell fresh coffee brewing. He pulled on a pair of sweatpants he had left on the floor and headed toward the other end of the apartment. She was starting his day with a smile, as she so often did.

"Morning, lover," Hannibal said stepping into the kitchen. Cindy looked up, caught in the act, putting cream cheese and marmalade on the tray with the bagels. Her smile, warm and radiant as the summer sun, held his attention before he noticed the other surprises. Instead of business attire Cindy stood before him in her own sweat suit. Her face, usually so carefully made up, was scrubbed clean. He spotted a small overnight case on a kitchen chair, which, he assumed, contained her day's clothing.

"I missed you last night," she said. "Got to thinking about breakfast in bed. And then I decided, why not?"

*　　　　　*　　　　　*

Snuggled under Hannibal's comforter they chewed raisin cinnamon bagels and Hannibal watched the sun make its debut over Cindy's shoulder. The coffee was hot and strong, the way he liked it, with just enough cinnamon added. Hannibal loved the time he spent with his arm around his woman, just relaxing. Once again he considered asking Cindy if she'd like to wake up together every day. And again he wondered what this independent professional woman's answer would be.

"How would you feel about going away together for a day or two?" he asked.

"Away?" Cindy asked, pushing a last bit of a bagel into her mouth. "Away where?"

"Out of town. Actually, Oscar Peters' hometown. Frankfurt."

She turned to face him, her nipples brushing his chest. "Frankfurt? You mean as in Germany? Wait a minute. Aren't you on a case, lover? How will Bea feel if we just take off?"

"Oscar's mother tells me he may have known something about a murder, back when he was in high school," Hannibal said, his eyes dropping from Cindy's face. "If what he told her is true, the culprit was never caught. It's another motive for his murder if it's true. I think I should follow it up."

"Follow up?" Cindy asked, her brow crinkling. "Oscar's probably fifteen years out of high school. You think you can solve a murder that's been sitting so long? And what about the guy running from the scene of the crime?" she asked, her brow crinkling.

"If I'm right he's driving back to Vegas, which is a good four day ride. He'll keep. Come on."

Cindy considered his words, her mouth bunched to one side. Hannibal leaned back against a pillow and sipped his coffee. When Cindy was pondering this way, it was best to leave her alone. Besides, the warmth of her thigh against his was pleasant enough without any further activity.

"Let me see if I have this straight," she finally said, sitting up straight. The comforter fell away from her ample bosom, further distracting Hannibal. "You want to interview people and check out the scene of the crime, right? So we fly to Europe for you to do that, spend a day there, and jet back? That's crazy. You really think there can be any kind of connection between this possible murder Oscar was talking about and his death?"

"I've got to follow my instincts," Hannibal said tangling his fingers in the soft curls flowing in waves about her shoulders. "A man is murdered. The accused killer saw his father murdered. Now I find out the dead man claimed to have knowledge of yet another murder. Can I just accept all that as coincidence?"

Cindy shook her head slowly. "And why drag me along?"

Hannibal slowly ran his fingertips softly down her spine to finally cup her bottom against the mattress. "I guess I just figured we needed some time away together. And there's something over there I'd like to show you."

-18-
FRIDAY

A voice filtered through Hannibal's sleep-fogged brain telling him to bring his seat to the upright position and fasten his seat belt. His watch told him it was five minutes after five in the morning. A flight attendant announced that the local time was eleven-oh-five. Cindy's head lifted from his shoulders.

"Why don't you reset your watch, Cin? I'll stay on Eastern time."

Cindy smiled into his face as their Boeing 737's tires skidded, then rolled onto the runway. "I liked the way yesterday started a lot better."

Hannibal agreed, although after their leisurely lovemaking it had turned out to be a busy day. They had gone together to explain their plan to Bea. She was surprisingly agreeable to any straw clutching Hannibal might have in mind as long as she knew Dean would be hospitalized. Cindy had gone alone to explain the situation to Dan Balor, senior partner in her law firm. He had agreed to let her arrange for tickets and hotel accommodations through the firm. Hannibal had visited Mrs. Peters again to get her home address and phone number. She thought he might convince her husband to attend his son's funeral. He made no effort to persuade her either way. And at seven p.m. their plane lifted off from Dulles Airport and they settled down for the first airline dinner of the trip.

Hannibal tucked into his seat and went to sleep almost immediately after the meal. They were diving into the early morning sun over London before he learned that Cindy had sat awake almost two hours longer then he did. Seven in the morning was two o'clock to their bodies. Cindy had no interest in breakfast so they spent the hour and a half in Heathrow Airport watching other planes come in. Cindy dozed a bit while Hannibal drank British coffee, which is a transitional step between American blends and the stronger European grinds and a good explanation of why British citizens still drink a lot more tea then coffee.

The hop to Germany was barely as long as the London layover, but they passed into another time zone to further confuse their systems. Hannibal's first stop was a vending machine that turned his American cash into German Marks. Then they stopped at one of the numerous stands in the Frankfurt Main for breakfast. It was close to noon, so breakfast consisted of a fat sausage Hannibal recommended. They ate on their way to the Avis booth to pick up their car, each carrying an overnight bag. Cindy babbled, something Hannibal only knew her to do when she was over tired.

"What a rude people," she said under her breath. "They stare at you, or ignore you, and they don't know how to smile, do they?"

"Really?" Hannibal said through his bratwurst. "I don't find them rude at all. Maybe they're staring because they don't see too many Latin beauties like you come through here."

In fact, Hannibal found Frankfurt Main very much like New York's Kennedy Airport. The decor, the hustling crowds, even the general layout of the sprawling terminal seemed very American to him. And the people looked and dressed like New Yorkers. He actually missed being surrounded by people who clearly had someplace to go and wanted to get there.

"Well, maybe it's easy for you because you speak their ugly language," Cindy said. In fact, Hannibal had hardly noticed that he ordered their food in fluent German. Once on the ground, with his mother's language pouring into his ears, it came as second nature.

Cindy began to relax when they had found their way out of the parking lot and were on their way down the A5 Autobahn toward Heidelberg in a rented Volkswagen Jetta. An hour's worth of countryside flew past, looking more like New England than

Virginia, and when they turned off the highway she actually smiled.

"Well, is this more like it?" Hannibal asked as he slowed to a stoplight. "If I wanted to sell Germany to anyone, I'd always start them off in Heidelberg."

The Hotel Neu Heidelberg looked like an overgrown cottage, its peaked roof and wraparound porch reminiscent of Smurf village homes. The woman at the desk greeted them in English, asking if they were new to her city. Hannibal explained that while it was Cindy's first visit to Heidelberg, he grew up in Germany as an American military dependent and knew the town pretty well. The remark seemed to increase his popularity.

Their hostess was older, heavyset and very Aryan in appearance, but she welcomed them with the kind of smile and grace one gets in America only when one has a platinum card or serves in public office. Minutes later they were installed in a room Cindy admitted was comfortable and downright cozy. She was particularly pleased that the furnishings were clearly individual, not part of a stock of hotel furniture. She would have been happy to sit for a while and catch her breath, but Hannibal was anxious to get on with the mission, as he put it.

*   *   *

The Peters home was a modest brick structure perched on a slight rise, far enough north of the hotel that they had a clear view of the sparkling waters of the Neckar River. Hannibal expected Cindy's attention to be arrested by the river that dominates the city, but instead it was on the door they were approaching.

"Don't you think we should have called first?" Cindy asked as they walked up the path between carefully tended flowerbeds.

"He's expecting us," Hannibal said. "Mrs. Peters called and he said he'd be home this afternoon to talk to us. Calling would have given him the opportunity to cancel."

Hannibal lifted the heavy doorknocker and let it drop against the wood panel twice, then waited. Any soldier would have identified the man who opened the door seconds later as a sergeant major, regardless of his lack of uniform. Foster Peters wore a well-pressed white shirt and charcoal slacks that matched the hair at the sides of his head. The gray at his temples graded up to hair as black and shiny as his shoes. The man stood ramrod straight, his dark eyes boring right through Hannibal's dark glasses. Hannibal subtly straightened his posture.

"You're the people who knew Oscar," Foster said. A statement, not a question.

"Yes sir," Hannibal said. "Your charming wife told me we could have a few minutes with you this afternoon. I'm Hannibal Jones and this is Cindy Santiago."

"Come in," Foster said. He shook Hannibal's hand, nodded to Cindy and executed a smooth about face. "I can offer you some refreshment. But please don't call me sir. I work for a living."

He led them through a front room that clearly was his wife's area. All the collectibles were there: the cuckoo clock, the hand-carved miniatures, the Hummel figurines. But when they entered the den, Hannibal knew this was the man's space. The displays on the walls were military awards, or commemorative firearms, or paintings with a military or hunting theme. Foster stepped behind the bar and busied himself without looking at them.

"I know we're less than an hour from the Weinstrasse, the heart of the German wine country. But the term 'German wine country' never made much sense to me, anyway, so how about a beer? I've got some Rauch bier on tap."

"Rauch?" Hannibal asked. "As in German for smoke?" Foster cocked an eyebrow, so Hannibal added, "I'm an army brat, sergeant major. Grew up in Berlin."

Foster nodded, then drew three schooners from a home tap and placed them evenly in a rank across the bar. "Berlin used to be a good town. Like Frankfurt was. Twice the military city Heidelberg will ever be. This place loves its tourists too much. But USAREUR moved here back in ninety-four and after twenty-five years the Army had become my life I guess. Got a good civilian job with V Corps after I retired." He and Hannibal lifted their glasses and drank together. The brew was almost black, with a yeasty aroma and smoky flavor that combined to make it one of the best beers Hannibal had ever tasted.

Cindy tapped his elbow. "Who moved here?" she asked quietly. "You-sar-your?"

"It's an acronym, honey," Hannibal replied. "It stands for United States Army, Europe. See? USAREUR."

"Oh." She sipped from her glass, smiled politely, and put it down. Foster looked at her as if his suspicions had been confirmed. Then he pointedly ignored her, turning his attention to Hannibal.

"But you didn't come all this way to hear about local military history. What'd you want to ask an old soldier like me?"

Hannibal really wanted to ask how a man could miss his own son's funeral. Instead he leaned an elbow on the bar and said, "I understand that you led the investigation into the death of a woman named Carla Donner some years ago. It seems Oscar disagreed with the official reports. Would you be willing to tell me what really happened?"

At the mention of the name Donner, Hannibal could see Foster stiffen and draw himself even straighter, if that was possible. His weathered face grew harder, like cement setting into granite. His eyes focused on Hannibal's face and he hardly blinked as he spoke.

"The case was a simple one, albeit tragic. Carla was alone in the house. She slipped in the tub, banged her head against the edge and drowned. End of story. Oscar, well Oscar was confused about some things."

"I see," Hannibal said, raising his glass again. It was good beer, but he hardly tasted it now.

As if she had received a secret signal, Cindy spoke up. "You knew the Donners, didn't you?"

"Gil Donner was a good friend," Foster said. "And still is. While I had to investigate his wife's death, I had to get him through the ordeal."

"Friends of the family," Hannibal said. "So Oscar knew them as well?"

At that Foster smiled. "Yes, Oscar actually had quite a crush on Mrs. Donner. She was one of his teachers. It was his freshman year of high school. He took her death hard, as did we all, but he took offense at the fact that the investigation was kept low key."

Cindy finally poured dark beer onto her soft voice before speaking again. "Gil Donner was Major Donner then, isn't that right? He was Provost Marshall at the time. Now I don't know much about the military, but I think that made him your boss, isn't that right? Is that why you kept the circumstances of her death so, what did you call it? Low key?"

Foster walked around the bar and pulled a large but thin hardcover book out of a shelf. He began to leaf absently through it while he talked. "People may have thought that, but they were wrong. No matter who he was, there was no point in hurting him further by letting the details out."

Hannibal stood beside Foster, looking over his shoulder at what he thought at first was a photo album. "Well, Mister Peters, I doubt those details would matter to anyone now."

"It might still matter to Gil. You see, Carla was cheating on him. Too close an investigation would have surely brought that out."

The ruffle of pages being turned was the only sound in the room for a while. Hannibal returned to the bar for another big swallow of beer. He realized now that Foster Peters had never really given up on his son.

"Oscar sensed some secret was being kept. And you never told him?"

"I'm a professional, Mister Jones," Foster said, not raising his head. "You don't make exceptions for family, especially frantic teenagers."

Hannibal looked to Cindy to ask the hard question.

"Mister Peters, I understand why Oscar might think Carla was murdered. But why would he tell anyone he knew a witness to that crime?"

Foster looked up calmly. "Miss, he lied. He lied to make it look as if I would falsify an investigation. He knew that impugning my police work was the most effective way to hurt me. He was good at that."

Hannibal drained his glass. Watching Foster stare down at the glossy pages he realized he had gotten all he could from this man. Foster Peters was more alone than Hannibal ever wanted to be.

"We'll be going now," Hannibal said. "Thank you for your time."

"Oh here," Foster said, flipping the book to Hannibal as they walked toward the door. "Take that with you."

Hannibal caught the book but immediately held it out toward Foster again. It was a yearbook from Frankfurt American High School. "You don't want to give this away."

"Why not?" Foster held the door open for them. "Maybe his friends in the States will want to see it. It was all I had of him until he got back, but now he's not.... you think I should be there, don't you? With his mother. Well, it's too late now, don't you see? Too late to have him back again."

Cindy averted her eyes and moved off toward the car. Hannibal hesitated, then realized it was too late for this man. "I'll give this to your wife," he finally said. "I don't think she'll let him go so easily."

*   *   *

"I'll never call my neighborhood in Alexandria, Old Town again," Cindy said, clutching a painting she had just purchased from a street vendor.

"Yes, this is the real thing," Hannibal said. He was glad to see Cindy smiling again. Their conversation with Foster Peters had left her depressed, but he didn't think that man's self serving bitterness should be allowed to ruin her day. Besides, that was not what he brought her to Germany for. So he took her to Heidelberg's old town, thinking a stroll there would lighten her mood.

In the crisp clarity of the afternoon sun, he walked her to Hauptstrasse walkplatz, the half-mile long pedestrian mall in the middle of the old town district. He felt a brief moment of deja vu because Alexandria, Virginia's old town area clings to the banks of a narrow river as well. But the Neckar River flows more swiftly than the Potomac, and so is much cleaner. This day the sun skipped golden discs across its crystal blue surface when he caught sight of it.

Cindy wandered aimlessly through the warren of cobblestone streets with Hannibal in tow. An endless flow of shops and cafes caught her attention, offering all the usual tourist paraphernalia and a few less usual choices like artwork and antique books.

They shared an outdoor table at a small but delicious smelling restaurant before reality again intruded, and it was Cindy who broached the subject at hand.

"So, do you think Oscar might have been right about a murder?"

Hannibal bit into his schnitzel like a long lost friend. The pork was crisp and golden beneath the thick brown sauce. He made an "mmmmm" sound and smiled contentedly behind a faraway look.

"Hannibal, please." Cindy said, grinning herself. "It's a pork chop in mushroom gravy for crying out loud. Now what do you think?"

"Schnitzel is not a pork chop," Hannibal said with a nearly straight face. "And jaegersoße is not simply mushroom gravy. And I'm not sure what to think about Oscar's suspicions. There's certainly good reason to wonder. I mean, his father pretty much admitted he was covering something up."

"True," Cindy said, and then, as if it was part of the same conversation she added, "It certainly is charming here. And the people are so, I don't know, hospitable. Not like Frankfurt at all. Rather surprising."

"Why?" Hannibal asked, sipping his wine. "Is Washington like Pittsburgh? Heidelberg is kind of the romantic heart of Germany."

"Poetic," Cindy said, digging into her own potato salad. "So are we finished with business here?"

Hannibal sat back and took a big swallow from his glass. He had chosen an alt bier from farther north, thick and dark with a nice malty flavor. "I'm thinking I might like to chat with Donner a bit about his wife's death."

"Sometimes you're like a terrier with a bone," Cindy said. "How do you figure to find this Donner character, anyway?"

"Just like back in the States, babe. I'll look in the phone book."

*   *   *

Hannibal wandered through the bar in his working clothes and glasses, feeling out of place for the first time since he returned to Germany. Gil Donner had insisted Hannibal come alone, and picked a place they could be anonymous.

The place was The Schiwmmbad, and it was more American than Hannibal wanted to believe. First the place was huge. There were two dance floors, a theater, two bars and a stage in the building. And the place was loud. The music was live, and the sort people call alternative these days. To Hannibal it was rock music that just missed the target. But the young crowd, about half American military, seemed into it.

Hannibal hated pushing through crowds. He hated the drunken laughter that surrounded him, mixing with the music. And he hated the stale beer smell that seemed to rise out of the hardwood floors. All in all, he wanted this to be over.

A fellow who looked as if he just stepped out of an Army recruiting poster appeared at Hannibal's side, tapped his shoulder and pointed. The man at the booth ahead stared at Hannibal with a disappointed half smile. His gray sport coat and open collared white shirt seemed out of place in that bar. His eyes were hard deep blue marbles, which had retained the sharpness of youth while everything around them had fallen to the will of time. Donner's cheeks sagged into a double chin. What hair he retained, around the sides and back of his head, was peppered with gray. His body in general had softened, but Hannibal could see the hard core at the center of him that his eyes betrayed.

When Hannibal reached the booth, his Ranger type escort signaled that he should sit opposite Donner. Hannibal imagined being pinned into his seat by this hard looking kid and shook his head. On second appraisal, the young fellow had to be six foot two, maybe one eighty, and the leather jacket and pants did little to hide his trim muscular frame. His hair was so light a blond that the severely Ranger haircut left him looking almost bald. His brown eyes were as hard as Donner's.

"After you," Hannibal said, waving a hand toward the booth. The Ranger type grabbed Hannibal's right arm and pushed, looking surprised at the resistance. Hannibal's left fist curled, his arm pulling back.

"It's okay, Cook," Donner said. The Ranger type stopped pushing, and slowly released Hannibal. Hannibal stepped aside and again pointed to the vinyl-covered seat.

"Sit," Hannibal said, as if addressing a trained hound. Cook's eyes went from Hannibal to Donner and back, then he slowly slid into the booth. Hannibal settled beside him and turned his attention pointedly to Donner.

"I'm not here looking for trouble," Hannibal said, lacing his gloved fingers on the table. "I'm just looking for the facts."

Donner sipped from the only beer on the table. When he spoke he did not raise his voice above the room noise, forcing Hannibal to lean in to hear. "Mister Jones, this is all a mystery to me and I don't like surprises. Carla, rest her soul, is fifteen years in the grave. Why on earth are you asking about her now?"

"I don't think the truth can hurt you at this point, Mister Donner, but it could save a young man a jail sentence."

Donner nodded, and sampled his beer again. He stared into the glass like a crystal ball. "You mean the man accused of killing Foster's son, Oscar. You are concerned with the motive, yes? But you spoke with Foster. I believe he told you all there is to know."

"He didn't tell me who found the body," Hannibal said, raising his voice as the band blasted louder. "Or where the crime took place."

Donner stared deeper into the glass, as if reading a script there. "I found the body, Mister Jones. Me. I found her lying in that tub."

Cook's presence, Donner's attitude, a dozen subtle subconscious clues prodded Hannibal's thinking into a new direction. What was not said suddenly seemed important. "She wasn't home, was she?"

"Why do you ask?"

"Because you didn't say," Hannibal said. "And because of Foster. He lied about the investigation back then. Maybe he's still lying. Lying for you. And maybe Oscar did know something that got him killed."

Cook's hand rested lightly on Hannibal's shoulder. "You don't want to be calling Gil here a liar."

Hannibal heard a barely detectable click and glanced over at Cook, then down toward his lap where his other hand held a narrow knife blade poised to jab toward Hannibal's ribs. Hannibal returned his attention to Donner, who wore that expression men get when they think they're in control. That, more than the knife, got on his nerves. His own face betrayed none of his feelings.

"We're not going to play it this way," he said in a matter-of-fact tone. Then his left fist snapped up from the table, pivoting on his elbow, smashing into Cook's nose. His right hand darted across his body under the table to grab Cook's right hand and yank it straight out to the right. He didn't think the shoulder was dislocated, but right then he didn't care much. What mattered was that Cook's elbow was locked out. Hannibal's left forearm pressed forward against Cook's shoulder. Donner jumped when Cook's bloodied nose thumped down into the table.

"He doesn't need that shoulder in his work, does he?" Hannibal asked through clenched teeth. "Now, I don't think I've asked you who killed your wife. What I need to know is how she was killed. That's enough to provide a motive for the murder my client's been accused of."

Donner saw the fear in Cook's eyes, a young soldier getting his first real-life experience with violence and the kind of real pain one never experiences in a training exercise. His eyes jumped to the side when the knife clattered to the floor.

"Let him go. You'll ruin him."

"The longer his shoulder stretches like this, the longer it will take him to recover normal range of motion," Hannibal said. "What are you covering up, Major?"

The mention of his rank seemed to stir something inside Donner. "I retired a full colonel," he said. "And my wife. Carla. Carla killed herself, you bastard."

Hannibal released Cook, who sat up quickly, his hand leaping to his injured elbow. Hannibal turned to him and raised the right side of his suit coat, showing the space under his right shoulder. "If we were in the States, there'd be a Sig Sauer automatic sitting there, and I might have decided to use it to put your shoulder out of action for good," he said. "But then, you might not have learned your lesson so well that way. Now you behave and let the grownups talk." Then he turned to Donner and said "Details."

"Details?" Donner repeated. "Details. I pulled the radio out of the tub."

"Back up. Where was she? Not at home, right? Peters told me she was seeing another man."

Donner looked at Cook who pointedly looked away. This was information he was not meant to hear. Hannibal nodded and stood, keeping a foot on the dropped knife. Cook slid out of the booth and walked to the bar, not out of sight but out of earshot. Hannibal sat and stayed quiet, waiting. Donner swallowed the last of his beer. When he began again, it was the opening of floodgates, releasing a torrent too long locked away.

"Carla and I married during the seventies, remember. Times were different. We trusted each other enough to, well, a broader variety of experiences kept the relationship fresh, and..." Donner was fading.

"You're saying you maintained an, er, an open relationship?"

Donner met Hannibal's gaze at last. "Exactly. An open relationship. Of course, the Army frowns on that kind of a lifestyle. It can stop an officer's career cold. So we maintained this little apartment across town in Frankfurt. We had our... other meetings there."

"And that's where you found her?"

"She was lying in a tub full of water. She had carried a radio into the bathroom. She plugged it in up by the sink where you could plug in a shaver, but she had set it on the edge of the tub. And then she must have just... just...." Donner's eyes clamped shut so tight they squeezed a few drops of liquid out of his eyes.

Hannibal tried to picture the scene. "She pulls the radio into the water. Teeth clench, body convulses. Head snaps back. Skull trauma. She sinks below the water, lungs keep pumping. Without the radio, you could sell most medical examiners on the accident story. But why? Despondent over her lifestyle, maybe?"

"Who can say?" Donner said. "She never said anything. No note was found. I can only say she seemed depressed and irritable the last few days. If only she'd told me."

"Look," Hannibal spoke slowly. "I'm sorry I dredged all this up. I needed to know what happened. I hope you understand."

Surprisingly, Donner nodded and returned a small smile. "Believe it or not, I do. I was a Provost Marshall remember? I've done my share of investigations. And, hey, I'm sorry about Cook."

"Not a problem. He maybe learned an important lessons about the difference between threats and combat. About readiness. Could make him a better soldier in the long run."

As Hannibal prepared to stand, Donner said, "Can I ask you something?" Hannibal nodded. "What was your father's first name?"

"Charles. Why?"

Donner seemed fully back to present-day reality. "The reason I agreed to meet you at all. Charlie Jones. Common enough name, of course. But I worked with an MP NCO named Charlie Jones back during Nam. He was a whole lot blacker than you, but he married a local national so it could be. He was a hell of a good soldier. Just in case it matters."

-19-
SATURDAY

"You know what I think?" Cindy asked as Hannibal pushed their car up the Autobahn "I think you came over here hoping you'd meet someone who knew your dad."

"Do we have to talk about that now?" Hannibal asked, enjoying the sun in his face, coming in sharply from his right as he drove north. They had enjoyed a wonderfully pleasant night at the hotel, and had gotten out early to start their day. He was working hard to maintain good spirits for his errand today. They had already passed Frankfurt before Cindy mentioned business again.

"Sorry. I just wondered. So, you think this Donner character was telling the truth?"

"Impossible to guess," Hannibal said, sliding in behind a Mercedes making excellent time. "He sure looked sincere about his loss. I believe he loved his wife. But the rest of the story only hangs together if you don't look too closely. Anyway I know all I need to. There was a cover-up. That means several people had a good reason to go after Oscar."

"I follow that, but if someone saw Oscar as a threat, why would they wait so long to do anything about it?"

The world became familiar as Hannibal wheeled into the outskirts of Berlin. He saw that a great deal of construction was going on, and that Berliners in general still dressed a couple of years behind Americans, but mostly, it was his childhood home. Except of course he didn't see soldiers and American children everywhere.

"Playing devil's advocate, counselor? Well, from what his mother told me, it could be our theoretical assassin just couldn't find him. He's been on the move since he came to the States."

It occurred to Hannibal that Cindy might have been trying to distract herself from the purpose of their trip with her questions. As they rolled slowly through the ivy-covered gate of the small cemetery she hushed entirely. The gate itself had a thin peaked roof, below which hung a white sign with black letters. Hannibal translated Gottesacker der Brüdergemeine as the Bohemian Parish Cemetery. They parked among a haphazard collection of vehicles and Hannibal reached into the back seat for the flowers before he got out.

Lilies. White lilies, he remembered, were her favorites. He stood waiting for Cindy to take his arm before moving off, his shoes crunching on the gravel path between carefully tended monuments. The Germans did care for their dead, he had to give them that. The grounds were meticulously kept, the trees deep green with that flush of health trees in such places always have. Hannibal stopped in front of a row of low white marble stones. The space behind the monuments was covered with ivy, while a carpet of grass lay in front of them.

"Her whole family's out here someplace," Hannibal said. "Or at least was here. My dad is one of the few Americans here, even though that's the America Memorial Library up there on Blücher Square. Actually, I understand when they built Blücher Street on the northern parts of the cemetery in the seventies, that's when they tore down the north wall and some of the memorials and graves were destroyed."

Cindy remained silent. Hannibal wondered if she thought his ramblings were some sort of avoidance technique. Well, it didn't matter what she thought. He saw no purpose in grief. It was merely respect for those you loved to visit them once in a while and honor their names. He lowered himself onto his haunches and looked closely at the stone. Funny. Both their names were there, but he always thought of this as visiting his mother. Maybe that was because he had twenty years of memories of her, and so very few clear memories of his father. That void, that emptiness, still ached from time to time like a node of poison in his body. As if someday that poison sack could rupture and kill him if he disturbed it too much.

So when he gently laid the flowers down on the grave, he imagined handing them to his mother, and could again see her face light up as it always did when he offered any small gesture of his love. When he stood he was aware of passersby, here to acknowledge their own loved ones. Germans never looked at others in these places. They respected the privacy of other people's feelings. He stood before the stone, alone in his silence, except for the small hand squeezing his.

"I think I finally understand," Cindy whispered. "War took your father, but your mother's life, and yours, were no less destroyed. You were ... what did you call it?"

"Collateral damage," Hannibal said. "Father was a casualty, and our lives were part of the collateral damage."

Cindy nodded and returned to silence. After a time he turned to her and said, "We've got a plane to catch at twelve-fifteen." They returned to the car but Hannibal sat a moment before starting it. He opened his mouth to speak a couple of times. A nearby tree moved with the soft breeze, its leaves casting shadows across his face. He licked his lips and gripped the steering wheel.

"Thank you," he finally said. "Thank you for coming here with me. I don't know if I was alone..."

Cindy wrapped her hand around his. "Oh no, baby. Thank you. Thank you for bringing me, for letting me see it. And letting me see you, this way."

He looked up at her, wanting to tell her he loved her, wondering why that was so hard sometimes. Cindy nodded and smiled and just said, "I know."

*   *   *

The flight home was direct from Frankfurt to National Airport. Flying westward they had watched the sun and almost kept up with it for nine hours, holding hands much of the time. Between long naps they sat wrapped in their own private thoughts. Thanks to the time zones it was only three o'clock in the afternoon when they touched down. Between the arrival gate and the car Hannibal related his plans for the day to Cindy. It was time for action to prove Dean's innocence, and he was asking Cindy to get the ball rolling while he took care of one social obligation first.

At Cindy's townhouse, Hannibal took a quick shower and changed clothes. Of course he pulled on another black suit, indicating he was still at work. Then he left her to make phone calls while he drove to the Hyatt Regency. After a short elevator ride, he tapped on the door softly, almost hoping he had made the trip for nothing. But it was only seconds before he heard Emma Peters' soft steps approach the door. When she opened the door he saw the expectant look lift from her face like a mist when the sun hits the land. She nodded twice and smiled wistfully.

"Well Mister Jones," she said. "Good afternoon. What brings you here this afternoon?"

He had simply wanted to end her suspense. Now he wanted to ease her loneliness. "Well I rather suspected you were sitting up here in your room. I thought you might want to go downstairs and have a cup of tea or something."

In the elevator, Hannibal learned that Emma had not bothered to eat lunch that day, so once they were seated in the hotel restaurant he ordered a small salad and a cup of soup for each of them. Only three other people sat in the room with them, two older couples dressed as tourists and a woman who may have been working the hotel but doing it quietly. Emma looked at each of them closely. She seemed to look at everyone closely.

"I wanted to thank you, young man," she said after their food arrived. "Thank you for coming in person to tell me what I already knew would happen. What did Foster actually tell you?"

"Ma'am?"

"His reason," she pressed, pouring vinaigrette on her salad. "What reason did he give you for not coming to his own son's funeral?"

Hannibal looked down into his clam chowder. "He kind of said it was too late. I think maybe he doesn't want to deal with the loss."

"Oh no," she said, chewing each bit of lettuce slowly but completely. "He can't face it. He's been waiting for an apology for fifteen years and now he knows Oscar was as proud and stubborn as he is, and he'll never be back to say he's sorry."

It could have been a hard statement, but Emma's grief was so heavy it would not even let her anger push out from under it.

"Whatever his other feeling, he misses his son," Hannibal said. "While I was there he was leafing through Oscar's high school yearbook." He almost mentioned that he had it now, but thought it might be hurtful to her to know he parted with it so easily. "Mrs. Peters, could Oscar's attacks on your husband have been part of a cry for attention?"

"Oh, I don't think so," Emma said. "Oscar was a real conspiracy theorist, even at his young age. He started to hate the American government, to think everything it did was wrong. And his father symbolized all that to him."

Hannibal sipped his coffee thoughtfully. "Not so unusual. But most kids don't believe strongly enough to run away from home."

"I think maybe he fell in with a bad crowd," Emma said. Then she started rummaging around in her purse. "He ended up in Las Vegas for a while, and oddly enough, that seemed to straighten him up some. Maybe coming face to face with all that sin did something. Anyway, he met a girl out there. Here, take a look."

Emma produced a photograph that looked as if it had been riding in her purse for longer than a mere year. Hannibal indulged her by looking at it, but in seconds his face dropped. It featured Oscar standing in a park with a woman beside him, half her face cut off by the sloppy photographer. On Oscar's left, a young man was reaching around Oscar to slap playfully at the woman. Pulling out of range of that slap would be the reason she was mostly out of the picture.

The young man beside Oscar was tall and thin with long, dark, stringy hair, and dressed in dark clothes. Something about him, the shape of his head, the angle of his shoulders, was too familiar for comfort. Hannibal guessed this man was a hell of a fast runner and drove a dark, four-door sedan.

140

*　　　　　*　　　　　*

Sliding wooden doors whose top halves contained a dozen small windows separated Hannibal's office from the next room. By pushing the doors back into the walls he had effectively doubled his office space.

Hannibal stood leaning back against the wall behind his desk. His seven guests sat around the room, mostly in folding chairs brought in for them. All held cups of coffee or tea, except Monty whose coffee Cindy had taken rather briskly, replacing it with cocoa before sitting beside Hannibal. It was a lot of people for the room to hold, including one who had only been there once before.

"I guess before we start, some introductions are in order," Hannibal said. "If you watch the news on Channel 8 you might recognize the redhead on my far right as Irma Andrews. She's involved in the case I've asked you all to help me with. I've promised her an exclusive on the story. In exchange, she's agreed not to mention any of you without your express permission."

He turned to the four men seated in a group on his left. "These guys are my neighbors in the building here, and they sometimes help me on cases. That's Virgil," Hannibal said, indicating the tall black man with yellowed eyes. "The white guy is Quaker, Sarge is the big guy with the Marine Corps tattoo on his arm, and the little baldheaded troublemaker is Cindy's father, Ray."

"Hey," Ray snapped, "Watch your mouth. I ain't quite bald."

Everyone chuckled and Hannibal continued. "The twelve year old who thinks he's grown is Gabriel Washington, but he'll only answer to Monty, as in three card. He's a little hustler, so watch yourself."

"So this is the part," Monty said, "where you're supposed to say 'I suppose you're wondering why I called you all here,' right?"

"I guess it is," Hannibal said, hands in pockets. "By now I think everybody knows about this Dean Edwards case I'm working on. He's the likely suspect in the murder of a guy called Oscar Peters. I was at the scene of that murder soon after it, and spotted a real suspect. He got away from me, but he was driving his own car, and I've traced it to Las Vegas. The fact that he drove all the way from there implies he didn't want to make it easy for anyone to trace his visit here through airline records. I've got a partial license plate to go on, and I want to find this guy in a bad way."

Watching the faces aimed at him, Hannibal figured he was the only one who noticed Irma pushing the record button on a palm-sized tape recorder. He cleared his throat, hoping he could construct decent sentences in case he was to be quoted later in the press.

"When I spoke with Oscar's mother Irma today she showed me a photograph of her son with a friend who could well be the man I chased. So I just might recognize him when we see him."

"When we see him?" Sarge repeated.

"That's right, Sarge," Hannibal said. "I'm going to ask you, Virgil and Quaker to fly to Vegas with me. We can split up a list of possible license plates and the addresses they're registered to, and hunt this guy down."

"Do the police have the partial plate?" Irma asked.

"They have no interest in leads when they've already got their suspect," Hannibal said.

"Las Vegas!" Monty said, the way most people his age might be expected to refer to Disney World or the Superbowl. "I really think you'll need more help out there, Hannibal. I can scout cars real good."

"Appreciate the offer, Monty," Hannibal said, holding a palm toward his young friend, "but I need you here for another important job. See, I think there might be a conspiracy going on here involving something Oscar knew about a previous crime, maybe about a couple of previous crimes. Something somebody didn't want him to know. And whatever he knew, his mother might also know. So I'm going to ask you and Ray to keep an eye on Emma Peters while I'm gone. Between you, you can be inconspicuous. Even alert people often don't notice kids, or taxis."

"You'll call me if you find this guy?" Irma asked.

"Of course, but I hope you won't be just sitting and waiting to hear from me," Hannibal said. "I figure you can help figure this whole thing out."

"And just how do you expect me to do that?"

"Well, I'm not sure I've got a handle on this entire mystery," Hannibal said, "but I've got a feeling Joan Kitteridge is very much in the middle of it. The day after we discovered Oscar's body she left town. Headed for Las Vegas, coincidentally enough. If you believe in coincidences."

"Really?" Irma looked up, her piercing blue eyes widening as her mind raced. "She strikes me as a cold one, capable of anything. I understand she had been to Oscar's house before. And she did turn up rather suddenly, right after we got to Dean Edwards' place. Where was she right before that, while Oscar was being murdered?"

"You're the reporter pursuing this story," Hannibal said with a smile. "I figure you can find that out more easily than anyone else."

"Sounds like tomorrow's going to be a busy day," Cindy said. "Sure wish I could join you on the scavenger hunt in Nevada. But I better hang here to protect Dean from the police."

"Yes," Hannibal said, turning his smile to Cindy. "And there's one other important thing you could do, sweetheart. I sure wish you'd go to Oscar's funeral. It's likely to be a pretty thin turnout."

-20-
SUNDAY

It was more of a light mist than actual rain, but it would still ruin Cindy's hair. She stepped out of her taxi and straightened the skirt of her black suit, the one she only wore on occasions like this one. She stepped up the path toward Oscar Peters' final resting place, balancing carefully on her heels which sank hazardously into the immaculately cared for turf. She had to admit there was no more beautiful or more solemn place for a burial than Arlington National Cemetery.

Oscar, of course, had no military experience. But she knew that being the son of a retired soldier he was entitled to a space in a national military cemetery. Someday his parents would certainly join him in that hallowed space. Still, she knew the schedule here was cramped, and remaining spaces few. Retired Sergeant Major Peters must have made at least one influential friend to get his son buried here, and to make it happen so quickly.

Traffic on the George Washington Parkway had been heavy for a Sunday morning and Cindy was barely on time. She would not reach the chairs beside the grave much before the pallbearers who were stepping slowly from the other direction, carrying their load with easy and palpable dignity. The Old Guard was the ultimate burial honor, ramrod straight soldiers of the same height in their dress blues and white gloves, glittering shoes and grim expressions. Their precision always took Cindy's breath away.

Two women stood at the graveside as she approached and for a moment she was unsure which was in mourning. Hannibal had described Mrs. Emma Peters well: bluish tinted hair, slightly bent posture, soft, warm features. The other woman was taller with a cloud of white hair and thick glasses. She would be one of the Arlington Ladies, a little known group of veterans' widows with a most charitable mission. One of these women attends every funeral at Arlington, to make sure no service member is ever buried here without someone on hand to mourn him. When a widow is present, they are there to comfort her.

Cindy stopped at the edge of the rows of chairs, observing the ceremony from behind the two women. She had not expected the man. He and Mrs. Peters were of the same generation and at first Cindy thought her husband must have come to his senses at the last minute. But this was not the man she met in Germany. They stood closely enough to make it clear that he was familiar. An old family friend perhaps, who hurried to her side when he learned she would attend her son's funeral unescorted.

Well, she could not simply stand back and observe. Cindy shook herself into action and moved forward to introduce herself to Mrs. Peters before the chaplain began his service.

*　　　　　*　　　　　*

On the outskirts of Las Vegas, Hannibal stared at his twenty-fourth license plate of the day, then checked the number off on his list. All of the numbers on the list were similar, and one of them could well match the license plate on the car he saw only in the dark in Virginia. The plate he was looking at was number twenty-four on his long list of possibilities, but he was sure the gleaming new Lincoln Town Car attached to it was not the vehicle that nearly ran over him back home. There was no need to knock on the door looking for the tall, dark-haired driver

Pale yellow sunbeams reached over the edge of the earth and poked in around the frames of his sunglasses as he returned to his rented Ford Taurus and consulted the map laid open on the passenger seat. He had hoped his quest would not continue beyond dinnertime, but here he was, still crisscrossing Las Vegas' dusty streets. This kind of legwork was boring, even in a nice town.

After living in Berlin, New York and Washington, Hannibal found Las Vegas unexpectedly stale. Berlin was an ancient city,

145

dating back to the thirteenth century. New York had three hundred years of history. Even Washington, the planned community that was young compared to most national capitols, went back a couple of hundred years. They all had their run down areas, their aging quarters. But they all had grown and aged through a normal life span, if cities can be said to have such things.

By contrast, Las Vegas was an infant, incorporated as a city almost a dozen years into this century. And while the other cities grew to adulthood in the normal, legitimate way, Las Vegas was corrupted when it was adopted by the criminal mastermind Benjamin Siegal, called Bugsy by the press of the time. So, while the city rose anew out of the desert in nineteen forty-six, it was corrupted by organized crime. And so decay had set in early. The city had grown up and grown old in a very short time. It showed all the signs of decay generally found in cities several times older. Like prematurely aging women, Las Vegas wore way too much gaudy makeup. And like many aging women, it was not hard to look past the makeup, to see the damage time was wreaking underneath.

Hannibal and his small team had stepped off the plane into intense morning sunshine. His first act after renting cars for them all was to buy several maps. After seeing just how small the town really was, he had divided it between Quaker, Sarge, Virgil and himself. Each had a map rectangle to cover, about fifty miles long and maybe ten miles wide. Within that space, they each had a list of fifty some odd plates to check out. The job was even bigger than it seemed. Hannibal had prowled the city's back streets and pocket neighborhoods all day, whittling down his list of possible license plates. Now, the neon fronted gambling houses were just lighting up, like the flying insect traps he had seen hanging in suburban backyards. He saw the night flies hovering at the entrances, not even trying to avoid being drawn in and zapped.

The guidebook told Hannibal that Las Vegas was a city of barely a quarter of a million people, not counting tourists. The tiny District of Columbia held two and a half times as many people. To Hannibal, Las Vegas looked like a frontier town from a western movie. The Hollywood style main street was a series of gaudy flats. Behind them, you could see the sagebrush between houses. There were no condemned buildings standing in a row, their shoulders pressed together to remain upright the way they were back home. But he was surprised at the number of addresses that turned out to be trailers surrounded by sand. And when the houses really were houses, they seemed too far away for his taste.

He had to admit, driving down uncluttered blacktops with the desert receding flat and brown in every direction, that his body liked it out here. The air tasted different, sweeter than he was used to. It was warmer, but dry enough to keep his clothes from sticking to him. And every time he stopped his car, the silence fell in on him, as refreshing as a massage. And when people saw him staring at their cars, or at them, they smiled. Dropping back into his seat and pulling the door closed he considered it again. His body really liked it here.

His mind, however, was restless. It was like some form of sensory deprivation. He realized that some part of him craved clutter, needed the background noise a real functioning city provides. So he breathed easier as the nightlife stirred into wakefulness. And he found himself smiling when his telephone rang.

"Hey Hannibal!" Quaker's frantic voice jumped into Hannibal's ear. "I think we got a pretty good suspect here. Tall guy inside. Big black car outside. Come take a look."

*   *   *

Hannibal reached the address Quaker gave him in less than two minutes. The old, rambling house was styled like an old Mexican hacienda with stucco walls and a low-pillared porch. There were no other structures within easy walking distance, giving the impression that this one grew up out of the desert sand of its own accord. Frantic music pouring out of the building did not cover the laughter or the sound of dancing feet. Rolling slowly past, Hannibal saw two figures dancing spastically on the porch, shadowed by the light behind them. They were certainly dancing together, but by form both were clearly male.

A low wall wrapped its stone arms around the large parking lot just past the house. Quaker sat atop it not far from the entrance. As Hannibal approached, he stood, his gangly arms waving Hannibal in. As he brought the car to a stop, Hannibal powered his window down.

"This is somebody's house?"

Quaker thrust his face forward, wearing a weary grin. "Nope. I was stopped behind this guy at a light and I noticed the plate was like the ones we were looking for. The car kind of looked right, so I followed him. When he parked here I called you. Come on around inside and I'll lead you to the car. Sure hope it ain't another false alarm."

"Amen to that," Hannibal murmured. He had already done this eight times that day, on occasions when Quaker, or Sarge, had found a car that could be right, but could not find the owner to confirm they fit the description.

As Hannibal turned the wheel to follow Quaker across the hard ground of the parking lot, another Ford slid up behind him. Headlights bounced off his rear bumper, allowed him to see Sarge's silhouette in his rear view mirror. Seconds later he saw yet another similar vehicle fall into line behind Sarge. Their short convoy bounced along the path through close-parked cars, reminding Hannibal of a trip through a drive-in theater's grounds. The cars were mostly new and expensive at the beginning of his journey. As they neared the back of the lot they approached a small gathering of older models.

Finally Quaker stopped and pointed at a large, dark-colored vehicle. The space beside it on the driver's side was vacant, and Hannibal pulled into it, stopping too close to the target car. Sarge parked in the nearest space, seven cars away. The other car, Virgil's, passed him to park in the next row. Hannibal killed the engine, listening again to the way the open spaces seemed to suck the sound away. Voices carried clearly from the house nearly a hundred yards away. And as he opened the door he stared up into a very clear, star-speckled night sky. A broad full moon hung directly overhead. Just what I need, Hannibal thought.

Sarge's footsteps crunched toward them, the beam from the flashlight in his beefy fist jiggling across the ground to finally rest on the bumper of the big car Hannibal now stood behind. Hannibal nodded slowly. Bright silver characters raised against a cobalt blue background: 902, a dot, then JZB. More importantly, he recognized the shape of the deep blue vehicle, a Lincoln Town Car at least a decade old. The differences between this car and the new vehicles he had seen earlier in the day were subtle but at the same time obvious. Very quietly he hissed, "Yes. This is the car that almost hit me."

"Neat ain't it?" Quaker said. "Now we know the guy you want's a fag."

"Excuse me?"

"This place is a gay club," Quaker said, his pale angular face a grinning death's head in the moonlight. "If he's in there, he's a fag."

Hannibal paced a few feet away. "A customer you think?"

Virgil's gravely voice rumbling in from behind him. "Not by this car. A hustler. Working the crowd."

"Sure," Hannibal muttered, looking around himself. "This is where the hired help park."

"So, you'll know him when you see him?" Sarge asked. When Hannibal nodded, he added, "So I guess we go in and get him."

Hannibal leaned against his car's trunk. "That might not be the best plan. He might have a lot of friends in there, he might recognize me... it could get messy."

"Well, I sure ain't up to waiting out here all night until he decides his night is over," Sarge said.

"Besides," Quaker added, "when he does come out, he'll probably have company, if you know what I mean."

Virgil listened to the others, then took a deep breath and let out a long breath through his nose. "I'll go get him," he said in a low monotone.

"But you don't even know what this guy looks like," Hannibal said.

"Doesn't matter."

*   *   *

Virgil was dressed casually, in slacks and a knit shirt, but he drew several stares when he entered. First, he was taller than almost anyone in the room. He was a big, solid man and his skin had a sheen like black leather. He strode through the crowded room and something about his manner made the sea of writhing bodies part before him. He looked neither left nor right on his path toward the DJ's station. The flashing lights in the darkened room did not seem to affect him, nor did he react in any way to the booming music battering his ears. It seemed to be some bizarre hybrid of country and disco, and the men on the floor were twisting themselves into pretzels trying to dance to it.

Inside him, Virgil's entire being was clenched like a fist. The all male group here made his flesh crawl. Memories clawed at his mind, memories of days and nights in prison when he had to fight both the drug addiction he could not feed and the predators who needed sexual release so badly they turned to members of their own sex and sometimes did not care if their partner was willing or not. Years of successfully defending himself did not make the thought any more pleasant.

At the far end of the dance floor he leaned forward but still had to shout to the bald, leather-clad DJ over the music. After a second iteration the DJ nodded, winked at him, and gave him a thumbs up sign. Virgil turned and made it most of the way across the floor before the DJ lowered the music and spoke into his microphone in a voice just a bit higher than Virgil thought it should be.

"That tall, dark, beefy man heading toward the door has a message for you all. He's had a little mistake in the parking area and he wants to make it good. So if your license plate number is 902 - JZB, catch him at the door to talk about what he's willing to do to make it up to you."

Virgil stopped at the bottom of the porch steps and lit a Lucky Strike. He had managed to avoid the use of illegal substances for five long years and he never drank alcohol because he knew where that could lead. But as he filled his lungs with smoke he knew he could never call himself drug free until he lost this habit too.

The man who burst through the doorway behind him raised a smile on Virgil's face. He was almost Virgil's height, six foot four, with straight, black, stringy hair. His slender frame was wrapped in a buckskin shirt and leather pants. He bounced up to Virgil, talking very rapidly, pointing into Virgil's face.

"Are you crazy man?" the newcomer snapped. "I know you didn't put a ding in my ride. That car's a classic, man. Do you have any idea what parts for that thing cost?"

Virgil rolled his yellowed eyes and held his hand forward. "Virgil," he said.

The other man, startled by this simple action, calmed a bit and took Virgil's hand. "Fancy," he said.

Virgil puffed air out of his cheeks in a stifled laugh and pointed with is head toward the parking lot. The two moved on, Virgil walking in his usual slow steady manner. Fancy moved more frantically, taking two steps when one would do, swaying left to right on the path. As they neared his car, Fancy's high-heeled cowboy boots began dancing a flamingo around Virgil and his arms waved wildly.

"Holy shit, man. Look at that. I can't believe you parked that close to my ride. What the fuck's the matter with you? I can't even open my damn door."

Fancy started around his car to the passenger side, but stopped as Quaker rose up from between the vehicles, a short length of pipe in his right hand. "Sucks, don't it?" Quaker said.

Beside Quaker, Hannibal rose to his feet and stared hard at the face framed in the moonlight before him. He watched as anger and indignation slowly gave way to recognition in those eyes. The man's lower lip began to tremble as Hannibal's focus shifted to a space over his shoulder.

"This is him," Hannibal said. "The man in Emma's picture."

Fancy spun to see a human bulldog with receding hair slapping a baseball bat into his left hand. "Then I guess he's coming with us."

*   *   *

On closer inspection, Hannibal decided this Fancy was too dark to be a white man. His hair, hanging about his shoulders, betrayed a native American heritage. His nose was broad as a black man's, his eyes dark and piercing as he stared up from the chair in Hannibal's motel room. He wondered how many tourists went straight to the major hotels on the strip and missed the many small single level motels like this one that surrounded the city.

"So," Hannibal said, pacing in front of Fancy while he tightened his black gloves, "Shoshone? Hopi? Ute? Paiute?"

"Hopi," Fancy snapped, "Like you give a shit. What the hell is this? Why'd you grab me?"

"You know why," Hannibal said, placing a foot on the bed and resting his elbow on the upraised knee. "I chased you away from Oscar Peters' house... let's see, it will be a week ago tomorrow I think. You sure can run, I'll give you that. I want to know why you were running, Mister...."

"You don't need to know my name," Fancy said, sitting up straighter.

"I need to know if you murdered Oscar Peters."

"Yeah, right," Fancy said, propping his hands on the arms of the chair. Sarge, Quaker and Virgil held his eyes. "So now you interrogate me, is that it? You and your little gang of leg breakers?"

Hannibal considered for a moment. This man may well be a cold-blooded murderer, but his words were those of an experienced victim. He could, after all have been set up by someone who never thought anyone could trace him back here.

"No," Hannibal said softly. "Just me." He hooked a thumb toward the door while maintaining eye contact with Fancy. He felt, rather than saw, his partners leaving. Quaker first, then Virgil, and finally Sarge. Hannibal heard the door click shut behind him and saw Fancy's shoulders drop an inch in relative relaxation. Hannibal opened his top button and pulled his tie down a bit. Half his face smiled at the absurdity of the situation.

"So the question is whether you put a knife into Oscar Peters' throat. And I really would like to know your name."

"Many Bad Horses." When Hannibal looked up in surprise, Fancy repeated. "My real name. Victor Many Bad Horses. Most people just call me Fancy. And no, I didn't cut Oscar. He was like that when I got there. You a cop?"

Hannibal pulled a two-liter bottle of root beer from the little refrigerator and filled two glasses. "Not a cop, but I have an interest in this murder." As he handed Fancy a glass he said, "I used to be a cop though. A cop would ask you, if you're innocent, why'd you run?"

Fancy took a long drink that nearly emptied his glass. Hannibal thought Virgil had been right. This man was a hustler by trade. He was looking for the angle. Staring into the ice cubes in his glass, he must have thought he saw it. "Sure, I see now. Joan sent you, didn't she? Well she ought to know she can trust me. I might have stayed around awhile, or even called the cops myself if she wasn't there. But she recognized me, and I didn't want to get twisted up with whatever the hell she was planning."

Hannibal nodded and raised his glass in salute before taking a drink himself. Then he nodded, his lower lip protruding, as if considering Fancy's story and deciding it sounded about right. "And what would you tell the cop who asked why you were there in the first place?"

"The truth," Fancy said, leaning back and crossing his legs. "Oscar invited me over to help him out. We got to be pretty good friends when he was living out here last year."

"Really?" Hannibal stood and drank the last of his soda. It tasted good, but left a bitter after taste, like Fancy's story. "I didn't think the boy was that type. And anyway he moved to the other side of the country. Why would he be calling you? And why now?"

Fancy's long fingers wrapped around the arms of his chair and Hannibal could see muscles bulge under his shirt. "What do you know? Oscar had a big heart, big enough to find affection on both sides of the fence. He had lots of people wanting time with him out there in Virginia, but when he was in trouble he called me!"

"Trouble?"

"Somebody threatened him, he said, somebody he took real serious." Fancy drained his glass, and reached to refill it himself. "I didn't want to fly out, because plane tickets are too easy to trace. So I hopped in the old Lincoln and drove on out there. I called him when I got there...."

"Which was when?" Hannibal asked, pacing slowly across the room, staying between Fancy and the door. Fancy was becoming a bit too agitated for his taste. Hannibal felt the tension bleeding off him, bouncing about in the deep shadows at the corners of the room.

"I got out there Monday, early," Fancy said. "Couldn't get Oscar on the phone so I rang Joan. She said she had a date with him that night, but I should come by early in the evening. So I found a motel, took a long nap. When I woke up I went out for some dinner then went on to Oscar's place." Fancy's eyes dropped to the floor and his voiced dropped into a raspy lower register. "I waited a bit too long. Got there a bit too late."

For a brief moment Hannibal wasn't sure where to take his interrogation. It would be easy to believe Fancy's story, and just as easy to believe he was practicing a script handed him by a cunning killer. Right that minute, Joan looked like the most likely actress for that role. And that suggested a line of inquiry that made Hannibal smile.

"Tell me, Fancy, how well do you know Joan Kitteridge? I mean, you only met her last year, right?"

Fancy's eyes were hooded. A thick silence surrounded the room, holding his words inside. "Well, yeah, we met when she spent last summer in town here. And I never laid eyes on her again until she turned up here today, asking me all those questions. Except for that night in front of Oscar's house, of course. Why? What are you getting at?"

"Oh nothing. She stay at the same hotel back then?"

"Uh-huh," Fancy nodded. "She says she likes The Orleans because it's off the strip and...."

The single lamp cast much of Fancy's face in shadow as he stood straight, but Hannibal could see his face twisting into an angry mask. His voice, low again, had an ugly hiss behind it. "Joan didn't send you, did she?"

Hannibal stood easy, hands at his sides but very alert. "I don't believe I ever said she did."

Fancy pulled his right foot up on the chair he had been sitting in. From it he pulled a long narrow dagger and turned to wave it in circles, its point poised to open Hannibal's navel. "All right, just who the hell are you, mister?"

"I can't believe you don't recognize me, Fancy man," Hannibal said, his knees slightly bent. He could almost smell the adrenaline flooding Fancy's body. "You almost ran me over with the old Lincoln less than a week ago, a couple blocks from Oscar's house."

In the glare from the lamp Fancy's eyes seemed to glow with a fire of their own. He swiped with the knife from left to right a couple of times, but Hannibal knew he need not worry about the first couple of feints. His own hands curled into gloved fists and he assumed a comfortable fighting stance. Fancy's boots danced on the floor, his teeth bared in hatred. Hannibal bounced slightly on his toes, but did not back up.

"So, am I supposed to be frightened?" Hannibal asked.

Fancy made a sound someplace between a shout and a growl as he drove his knife forward. Hannibal pivoted to his right. The blade slid past his body, slashing into the inside of his suit coat. His left fist shot forward, clipping Fancy's jaw. Surprisingly, Fancy kept his feet and slashed backward. Hannibal barely avoided the knife, its tip making a whooshing sound as it sliced the air an inch in front of Hannibal's throat. Then Hannibal's right foot snapped upward with crushing power between Fancy's legs. The taller man was paralyzed just long enough for Hannibal to land a right cross that twisted Fancy's head around, then a left hook to his midsection, and finally a right uppercut that landed him, unconscious, across the bed.

The sound of Fancy bouncing on the bed was drowned out by rushing feet as Quaker and Sarge burst into the room. Hannibal was panting but waved his friends to relax.

"He get frisky?" Sarge asked.

"Not so you'd notice," Hannibal responded. "But grab that blade. Then I think we should have no problem getting him to the police. They can hold him on suspicion of murder based on what

I know now. Then we'll swing across town. Somebody I know is in town and I think I ought to drop in and say hi."

-21-

Standing in front of the wall of dancing lights holding a bunch of cheap flowers, Hannibal thought he might choose to stay at The Orleans Hotel and Casino if he ever decided to stay in Las Vegas for pleasure rather than business. The Orleans was no less garish than all the other adult penny arcades in town, but it did stand at the southern end of the city on Tropicana Avenue. One face of the flashing Christmas tree of a building did offer a breathtaking view of the lively and festive Las Vegas strip. But he could see that by choosing the right room, a visitor could instead have a window full of the sweeping mountain panorama that surrounded the valley Las Vegas was snuggled down into.

At his elbow, Virgil murmured, "Just like the French Quarter," in his trembling base. Hannibal wasn't sure about the architecture, but he did recognize the magnolia trees, looking so out of place, standing in front of the urban desert inn.

"I think I better do this one alone." Hannibal said. "Cover the exits best you can while I go inside and try to find out which of these eight hundred rooms our girl is vacationing in."

Actually, there were eight hundred and forty rooms, as Hannibal learned from a brochure while he waited for a desk clerk to notice him. He would need help to locate his quarry. The flowers were just camouflage.

"I just got to town, and I want to surprise a certain little lady," Hannibal said. "I know she's staying here, but I'm not sure of the room." He leaned forward and smiled like a drunk, hoping that the twenty-dollar bill under his hand on the desk was the appropriate tip for such a favor. The desk clerk's nod reassured him that it was.

Dixieland jazz pulsed in the lobby, lifting his spirits momentarily before a rocket-powered elevator thrust him onto the seventh floor. Then he was tapping on a gilt-edged door before he realized how late it was. If Joan was a typical Vegas visitor, she would not be behind that door, but rather downstairs enjoying the casino, or perhaps at a table in the showroom where he had read that Al Martino was performing tonight.

Hannibal heard the rustle of what might have been a silk robe, but could just as easily be silk sheets, he supposed. Cat-like footsteps followed, and whoever had padded to the door hesitated a moment before pulling it open a crack. Joan's face peeked through the space and Hannibal saw it was indeed a silk robe. He found her face lovelier as it was, fresh scrubbed and makeup free, than any of his past views of her. Joan's hair was tossed a bit, as if she had just been roused from a nap.

"Are you decent?" Hannibal smiled like a schoolyard conspirator. "I'd like to chat for a minute if you don't mind."

Joan's eyes flashed at the flowers, then roamed the hallway, looking for an acceptable way out of this situation. Finally they settled on his lens-shielded eyes, her face showing new respect for him. "Is there any point in my asking how you found me here?"

"You may want to know," Hannibal said. "And I would gladly tell you. But not out here in the hall."

Joan drew in a deep breath, released a heavy sigh and pushed a handful of perfectly manicured fingers through her wavy auburn tresses. Then her face regained its customary degree of intimidating confidence and she pulled the door open, almost sucking Hannibal into the room.

Actually, it was a suite Hannibal stepped into, beautifully appointed and fully fitting his notion of luxury. Light coming through the windows he faced cast a sensual yellow highlight on everything in the room. Joan had chosen the view of the strip. He moved quickly to follow her into the sitting area. His eyes lingered long enough to note that he had heard both silk robe and silk sheets, and that Mark Norton was sitting beneath those sheets looking like a kid caught during a game of hide and seek.

"Do you like rum?" Joan asked as Hannibal entered the sitting room. "It's Bacardi light."

Hannibal nodded and Joan filled two glasses on the little table. Then she carried her own drink across the room and took command of the love seat. She drew a gold lighter from a pocket of her robe, and a cigarette from the other. She lit the cigarette with all of Lauren Bacall's body language. Hannibal stood beside the table and poured a few drops of the liquid fire down his throat. Less than two hours ago Fancy had threatened him with a knife, but this was the first time he had felt in danger since he landed in Las Vegas. While he considered how this conversation should go his eyes cut briefly toward the other room.

"Something on your mind Mister Jones?" Joan asked, her long legs crossed under the white silk.

"Actually, I was just thinking what they told me on my first job, you know, about what you don't do where you eat."

Joan smiled, and he had to admit to himself that she was alluring. What man could say no to this woman? She was not just a lovely package, she was a force of nature. She filled her lungs with smoke, then sipped from her glass and almost shivered as the liquor slid down into her.

"Why Mister Jones, I believe you are a prude." Smoke carried her words out into the room. "How sweet. But you needn't worry. Mark is my husband."

One reason Hannibal wore his sunglasses almost all the time was that no one could see his eyes widen in surprise. "I see. And the reason you haven't made this public knowledge is..."

"Is really none of your business," she said, leaning to one side and stretching her legs out farther. "But in fact I do have a good reason, and I would really appreciate it if you would keep my confidence."

Hannibal thought he had some small advantage in this game and with such an opponent he needed to push that edge as far as he could. He swallowed half his drink before speaking. "Speaking of secrets, how long have you known Fancy?"

Joan slowly sat up straight, and Hannibal could almost see her conniving mind working. He watched her consider lying about knowing Fancy, then reject the idea. She must know he would not make such a statement unless he was sure. She ordered her thoughts without losing eye contact with him, something most men could not do in a poker game. But this businesswoman was a master game player.

"I see," she said, then licked her lips. "Fancy is a close friend of Oscar's, Mister Jones. Or was, I guess. I met him when I was out here in August. You can check that I was here easily enough."

"And when you saw him leaving Oscar's house?"

Joan leaned forward earnestly. "Well I wasn't going to give him away to the police if that's what you're thinking. I knew they were friends. I didn't think he was the killer for God's sake."

"So you hurried out here to ask him about it," Hannibal said. Her eyes never wavered.

"Actually this trip has been on my calendar for months," Joan said. "But yes, I did want to know what he was doing there that night. He satisfied me that he was innocent and hadn't seen anything important."

Hannibal saw no point in quizzing Joan extensively. If she and Fancy were involved in a conspiracy together they would have their stories lined up very carefully. Besides he had a lever, the marital secret, to apply whenever he needed more from her.

"Is that it?" Joan asked. "You just wanted to know my connection to this Fancy?"

"Just like to have all the details straight," Hannibal said. "Thank you for your time."

As he turned to leave, Joan called, "And just how did you find me here?"

He turned to watch her breathe out a gray stream, adding to the translucent cloud now hanging above her head. "I'm a detective."

*   *   *

Outside, a hot dusty wind was blowing in out of the desert from the south. Hannibal's three friends met him across the street from The Orleans. They stood between a juggler entertaining for fun and a folk singer working the street for handouts.

"I take it you confirmed when her last visit to this burg was?" Sarge asked. "We ready to head for the airport?"

"I think I found out what I went up there for," Hannibal said. "But I think I want to change the plan. Just me and Virgil fly out tonight, if it's okay with you and Quaker."

"I'm game," Quaker said. "But for what?"

"Well now that I know when she was here, I'd like you two to stick around long enough to find out exactly why."

-22-
MONDAY

Hannibal breathed easily, taking in the scent left behind on Cindy's pillow, his eyes closed against the morning sunlight bursting in through his bedroom window. The silence was broken only by the sound of her flesh moving against his own. She was naked, straddling his body, their skin tones almost a perfect match. Her knees felt hard pressed into Hannibal's waist, and her fingers pressed hard into his back as she kneaded the muscles on either side of his neck. He had to admit, the girl gave great back rub, but he was most aware of the heat coming down from her body on his behind as she straddled him. Or was he just imagining that?

Hannibal had dragged himself home just before dawn, bringing with him the deep confusion he often felt in the middle of a case he saw no end to. But after a short nap he had awakened with an unfamiliar intuition. An odd excitement he could hardly describe to himself, let alone explain. The sense that it would all come down today, one way or another. A peculiar thrill that had nothing to do with the wonders of joy Cindy had shown him earlier in the morning.

"I got a funny feeling baby," he mumbled into his pillow. "Like everything is going to come to a head today."

"God I hope not," Cindy said, kneeling up straight. "You haven't had enough sleep to face any real trouble."

"Slept on the plane." Hannibal turned over and pulled his woman down into a hug. "Did I seem under rested when I woke you up when I got home?"

Cindy moaned softly through a smile. "No, you seemed to have had enough energy at the time. Made me wish I was with you in Vegas instead of stuck here. And all for no good reason."

Hannibal ran a hand through Cindy's hair and kissed her face at random, enjoying her weight on him. "You mean Mrs. Peters didn't appreciate your being there?"

"Well, not like she was alone or anything. She had a gentleman there to comfort her." Cindy squeezed Hannibal tight, then slowly forced herself to stand up. "We really need to get out to the hospital, lover. Bea's going to be waiting for us."

Hannibal sat up and filled his lungs with life. "A man? Not her husband I assume. Well, maybe she had a lover here in the states, a man from her past?"

"Sure didn't look like it," Cindy said over her shoulder on her way to the shower. "I mean I didn't see any signs of intimacy. And this far from home, why would she hide it?"

*   *   *

Dean Edwards' quarters at Charter looked more like a motel room than a hospital room. There was none of the usual antiseptic smell Hannibal always expected. If it was ever there the vase full of fresh flowers on the round table drowned it out. Bea sat in a chair on Dean's left, holding his hand. Doctor Roberts, standing beside her, occasionally jotted a cryptic note on a clipboard. Cindy stood with her hands braced on the foot of the bed. Hannibal chose a chair on Dean's right so he could watch Bea's face and Roberts. The windows at Hannibal's back flooded the room with brightness, but his Oakleys cast a slightly blue light on the scene.

"He has largely withdrawn into himself," Roberts said, scratching at his thick gray beard. He turned to face Hannibal, his thick glasses magnifying his eyes into huge brown marbles. "I think perhaps his mind is working overtime trying to process all these sordid events."

"Yeah?" Hannibal's face twisted into a bitter scowl. "Well I think it's from people talking about him like he's not in the room." Hannibal leaned forward to tug on Dean's cotton pajama sleeve. "Hey Dean! I talked to your mom a few days ago. I could probably find her again if you wanted to talk to her."

Dean answered Hannibal with a stony silence, but did not speak.

"Look, my friend," Hannibal continued, "if you won't tell us what happened when you went to Oscar Peters' house, some very bad people are likely to come in here and take you to prison."

"This is unacceptable!" Roberts said. "I want you out of here immediately."

Those words, coming from Roberts' round teddy bear form brought a smile to Hannibal's lips, but he stayed focused on Dean. "The doctor can't protect you forever. The police are just not going to believe all the strange connections in this case are coincidences." Then the weight of those coincidences pushed one of the puzzle pieces into an unfamiliar slot in Hannibal's mind and he spoke almost before he realized it.

"When you were in Las Vegas last year, I'll bet you hung out with Oscar's friend Fancy."

"Joan's friend," Dean corrected reflexively. The room lapsed into silence and even Dean's face showed surprise. Bea squeezed his hand staring at Dean as if his just speaking was a miracle.

"Old friends?" Hannibal asked after a moment.

Dean turned to him, squinting into the sun behind him. "Actually, Fancy worked for Joan, at the very beginning of the company."

"Did Joan tell you that?"

"Well, I guess they both did," Dean said. "It just kind of came up in conversation one night."

Hannibal leaned back in his chair. "What an odd thing to lie about."

The soft purr of Hannibal's telephone was like an electric current arcing around the room, jolting everyone there. Hannibal recovered first and pulled the device out of his suit coat's inside pocket. When he heard Ray's voice, he stepped back toward the windows. Cindy followed, as if to give Bea some privacy. Bea had leaned forward to wrap her arms around Dean, and he was more responsive than he had been since Oscar's death. Hannibal watched his clients while he asked Ray what prompted his call.

"Just earning my pay, Hannibal," Ray said. "Got the kid with me, and we watching Emma Peters."

"Wait a minute. Monty's not in school?"

"He said you cleared it with his grandmother," Ray said. "Didn't you?"

Hannibal snorted. "We can talk about it later."

"Well, anyway, Emma just had a nice long breakfast in the hotel restaurant and now she's leaving. There was a man with her, but they're splitting up now."

"A man?" Hannibal could hear traffic sounds from Ray's end of the telephone connection. He would be in his cab, ready to move. Which meant Hannibal needed to think quickly. He pulled his mind away from the puzzle of Joan's past and centered it on the grieving widow.

"Describe the man, Ray. Maybe her husband came over after all."

"I rather doubt that," Cindy whispered. "Bet it's her new friend."

Hannibal held up a hand to quiet Cindy, then began to repeat Ray's words. "Okay. Around her age. Yeah? Medium height. Blue eyes, droopy jowls, double chin. Bald on top, gray around the sides.... " Hannibal flipped through available photos in his mind, and his jaw literally dropped open. "That's Gil Donner. It's got to be!"

"That's him," Cindy called, "That's the guy from the funeral."

Hannibal again waved to shush Cindy, and spoke into the phone. "Yes, I understand. No. Yeah, stay with him. And since he's there, put Monty on Emma. I don't think she'll be real mobile. But I got to know where Donner goes."

When Hannibal hung up, Cindy asked, "You think there's something going on between those two?"

"I don't think he'd have traveled this distance for romance, and now I've got two people who've told me they didn't act like lovers a thousand miles away from prying eyes."

"Who cares?" It was Bea, still caressing Dean but with her tear-stained face pointed at Hannibal. "My heart goes out to Oscar's mother, but what has either of these people from Germany to do with freeing Dean from these awful accusations?"

Hannibal approached the bed, but spoke to Dean who, for the moment, seemed the most rational person in the room. "The fact that Gil Donner came to the U.S. makes me think I'm not the only one who sees a connection between Oscar's murder and Donner's wife's death. I'm not convinced she was a suicide. In any case, if Donner does see a connection, he must not think you're the killer or he'd be here. I need to see what trail he's following, because one thing's for sure. He knows more than I do."

Roberts pulled his thick glasses from his face and began to clean them on his tie, directing eyes down and away from Hannibal. "You have an interesting theory, Mister Jones," he said, "but I fear a court of law would require a good deal more than that to see a connection between murders clearly separated by both time and distance. And the third murder, Dean's father, doesn't seem to figure into any of this at all."

That remark seemed particularly callous to Hannibal with Dean sitting there, but before he could respond his phone rang again. He flipped it open, but didn't get the chance to speak first.

"Dispatch? This is Santiago."

"Ray?" Hannibal said into the little phone.

"Listen, the radio's out so I'm calling in on my phone," Ray said. "Just picked up a fare in Crystal City, headed to a Doctor Walter Young's office up in Silver Spring. You copy?"

"Yes I do," Hannibal said, a smile growing on his face as he hung up. "So what do you think, Doctor Roberts? Donner hailed a cab and my partner picked him up. He's making a beeline for Walt Young's office."

"Walter Young?" Dean leaned forward so quickly he broke free of Bea's embrace. "That was my mother's lawyer's name. Never forget that name."

"You're right on target there Dean," Hannibal said. "And I can't think of any reason for Donner to know Young exists unless we assume there is a connection between the three apparently separate murders."

-23-

Even with his windows rolled down, the sunlight was turning Hannibal's car into a white leather oven. An occasional bead of sweat appeared on his forehead, but he wiped it away with a handkerchief before it could roll down into his eyes. His shirt chafed his neck just a bit, and the noise from cars and passersby on the busy street was helping a small headache to start up at the base of his skull.

Beside him, Cindy was not so relaxed. In fact, she fidgeted constantly, shifting in her seat as if she was afraid her nylons might permanently weld themselves to the car seat if she sat still for any length of time. She occasionally stared at Hannibal but said nothing. He guessed she had no idea how he could stand this waiting.

But Hannibal learned about surveillance in the New York City police department, years before he ever applied to the Treasury Department. He remembered hot days and cold nights when he waited for several hours for something to happen. So he settled into his car seat twenty yards from the entrance to the target office building.

This time he stared through his dark lenses for less than an hour before Gil Donner pushed through the door and stalked down the street, doubtless looking for a taxi. Hannibal watched him move off in the direction of the District until he vanished from sight beyond the fast flowing cross traffic. Then Hannibal left his Volvo and led Cindy quickly through the door Donner had come out of.

As Hannibal reached for the doorknob to enter the third floor office he realized he could not remember the last time he had seen a door quite like this one. Its stencil read simply, "Walter

Young, Attorney" in plain block letters. A single lawyer's name on the glass top half of the door, in this day of corporate thinking and legal teams. The mark of a man holding with very specific moral beliefs about how law should be practiced. Or, just as likely, the mark of a failure who refused to give up.

The door swung in as Hannibal reached for it, and he found himself face to face with a beefy man whose hair was cut long on top but short at the back, allowing a few strands to hang across his face in his haste. His tweed suit was cut loose on his stocky frame and his florid Irish face made Hannibal think of Spencer Tracy in those old movies his mother had loved so much.

"Walt Young, I assume?"

The man nodded as he shook Hannibal's offered hand. "Yes, sorry, but I was just on my way out for a late lunch. Why not arrange an appointment with my receptionist?"

"Sir, it is quite urgent that we speak with you right away," Cindy said from behind Hannibal. "A man's life is at stake."

"Well yes, isn't it always?" Young said, yielding no ground despite being no more than a hand's span from Hannibal's face. "Doubtless he will survive until after I've had lunch."

"When I talked to Francis Edwards she gave me the impression that you were more the concerned type," Hannibal said. "You couldn't save her, but we hoped you'd help us keep her son from the same fate.

"You spoke to Francis?" Young asked, taking a step back.

"Yes," Hannibal said. "A week ago yesterday. Actually she goes by Mary Irons now, but it was her all right. Miss Santiago here represents her son Dean. He's accused of a murder very similar to his father's death."

Cindy stepped forward, more fully blocking the door. "Mister Young, we've been able to keep Dean out of police hands because he's emotionally fragile right now, but time is running out. I don't believe Dean killed anyone, but because of the M.O. the next most likely suspect is his mother. We need your help to sort out the connections between the two murders."

Young stared at the two intruders for five silent seconds. Then his shoulders dropped and he turned, waving them into his office.

As he passed his receptionist's desk he muttered, "Alice would you please order in for us all?"

*   *   *

Young's inner office was tastefully appointed in dark wood. A traditional coat rack stood beside the door. Hannibal noticed the only full-size wooden filing cabinets he could remember seeing. Those, and the absence of a computer in the room, gave him the feeling of falling back to another time. He imagined this was the way Young's office looked the first time Francis Edwards walked into it.

"Have a seat," Young said. He dropped into his own chair and Hannibal and Cindy settled into a pair of ladder-back chairs facing Young's heavy wooden desk. Young smiled approvingly, but at what, Hannibal wasn't sure. Perhaps he simply approved of their posture.

"So which is it?" Young asked. "You want to talk with me about this murder Dean Edwards is accused of, or ask me about the murder his mother was convicted of?"

"Both actually," Hannibal said. The room smelled of smoke and Hannibal wondered how long it would be before Young needed to light up. "I'm convinced there's a connection between the two, and also between them and the death of Gil Donner's wife."

Young's eyes never reacted. He simply repeated the name, "Gil Donner?"

"The fellow who just left here?" Hannibal said.

"Yes. Tell me, were you tailing him, or am I under surveillance?" Young asked, just the hint of an edge in his voice. "And just who are you? I understand the young lady's interest here but..."

"My role is simple," Hannibal said, handing over his card. "Dean's in trouble. I'm trying to get him out."

Young stared long and hard at Hannibal's card, as if trying to draw some extra meaning from it. Hannibal and Cindy allowed him the time to think. When he looked up he was nodding his head, his lips curled. "Yes, I've heard a little something of you.

Some from another old lawyer type, Dan Balor. Told me you helped him out a bit too. And you, Miss Santiago is it? You are one of Dan's young lions, eh? Or lioness I suppose."

"I'll take that as a compliment," Cindy said. "I think my client is innocent of the murder he's accused of. I think. I think the guilty party may be responsible for the other two deaths, or perhaps Oscar Peters died because he knew something about the others. And, sir, unless he's a client, I would really like to know what Gil Donner wanted to talk to you about this morning."

Alice entered without knocking and dropped two big paper bags on Young's desk. She had clearly been with him for several years, a thin woman with a lead from one ear piece of her glasses to the other so they would hang around her neck when she wasn't wearing them. As she emptied the bags she spoke, not to anyone really but just to the room.

"Hot pastrami on rye. Roast beef on wheat. Turkey on white. Mustard, mayo, ketchup. And three sweetened iced teas."

Like that, she was gone. Young leaned back and said, "Call it, Miss Santiago."

Cindy appeared stunned, not sure what she should do, so Hannibal pulled his chair closer to the desk, unwrapped a straw and shoved it through a plastic lid. "Come on Cindy. Turkey, roast beef or pastrami?"

"Um... turkey I guess."

Hannibal shoved one of the wax paper bundles her way and pulled off his gloves. He opened the roast beef sandwich, shoving one of the small paper plates included under it. The sandwich was fat, but the roast beef was lean. His kind of lunch. He noticed Young was much more relaxed at this human level.

"Well, Donner came here to ask me about Mrs. Edwards' murder case," Young said. He opened the pastrami sandwich and crunched on half of the dill pickle before continuing. "He never mentioned his wife's death, but he did ask a lot about the circumstances of Mr. Edwards' murder. I think he was looking for similarities between it and the more recent murder of Oscar Peters."

"Well the two murders do have a lot in common, and my client was shown to be present soon after both." Cindy said. She finally spread a paper napkin on her lap and nibbled at her sandwich.

"Well your client was too short to run a knife over his father's throat at the time," Young said between bites. "And his mother didn't kill his father anyway."

"I don't think so either," Hannibal put it. The roast beef was juicy and tender and he made a mental note to get the name of the deli it came from before he left. "Of course, for me it's all conjecture. Why don't you tell us why you're so sure she's innocent."

Young stopped chewing for a moment, then looked at Hannibal more sternly. "Take them glasses off." Hannibal complied and Young returned to chewing his food while he stared some more. Hannibal kept his head up but continued with his lunch. He liked a man who judged by eye contact. Young finished the first half of his sandwich, wiped his mouth and took a long sip from his drink.

"What you really want to know is, why'd I plead her out for manslaughter on a heat of passion defense."

Hannibal glanced at Cindy, who still didn't look comfortable, so he turned back to Young. "Forgive me for saying so, but innocent does have a nicer ring to it. If she was."

"Oh she was, Mister Jones, count on it. But sometimes the truth only carries so far in court."

"You had a suspect?" Cindy asked.

"What I know for sure is that Grant Edwards was having an affair," Grant said, picking up the second half of his lunch. "And I know that girl he married was full of spit and fire but it wasn't in her to kill the man she loved. And make no mistake about it, she loved Grant. His family pulled him away from her."

"Couldn't kill him?" Hannibal asked. "Even if he was fooling around with another woman?"

"How did you know of the affair?" Cindy asked.

"One at a time," Young said. "I knew about the other woman because the boy told me. But Dean wouldn't put that on his dad on the witness stand, not so soon after his death. And I do understand that. And no, Francis could never have killed the man

171

no matter what. But I figure the other woman's man, or maybe her father, slipped in and did the deed."

This introduced a new source of guilt for Dean. By not vilifying his father, he pushed his mother closer to a conviction.

Cindy emptied her mouth completely before speaking again. "Why not simply subpoena the other woman and let the jury judge for themselves?"

At that Young slammed a hand down on his desk. "Don't you think I would have if I could find her? I had no clue to her identity. Who could have helped me? The boy wouldn't talk. The sister, Ursula, didn't want to see anything except for my client to go to jail. She hated Francis, even before the murder."

"You know," Cindy said, "Your ten year old suspicions might not seem so silly today, and they might help establish reasonable doubt for my client. One theory is that Dean told Oscar something about Grant Edwards' murder, something someone didn't want Oscar to share. Dean might trust you enough to open up a little bit. Would you consider coming in as co-counsel on this?"

"Perhaps. If you can explain to me how these three murders might be connected."

Hannibal finished his lunch and noisily emptied his drink. "Cindy can explain all the theories to you. I want to interview Joan Kitteridge again to try to verify a part of her story. And if you two don't mind, I'm thinking maybe I can get Emma Peters to tell me more about Gil Donner's involvement in all this. I'm going to stop by her hotel room and have a little chat with her."

The first errand was somewhat disappointing. Emma's room was empty. For a small gratuity he learned from a bellman that she had left with a man whose description matched that of Gil Donner. Of course Monty was nowhere in sight. He would have followed at a discreet distance. When he could get to a telephone he would let Hannibal know of any significant activity. Hannibal cursed himself for not getting a phone for Monty.

So he turned his car to the offices of Kitteridge Computer Systems, Incorporated. The Stepford Wives receptionist smiled with recognition when he entered and anticipated his first question.

"If you're looking for Miss Kitteridge, Mister Jones, she isn't in today."

With an effort Hannibal managed not to focus his frustration on her. "That's all right. Could you buzz Mark Norton for me please."

"Oh dear, I'm afraid Mister Norton isn't in today either."

Hannibal nodded, his eyes closed behind his dark glasses. That, he supposed, was predictable. He thought they would fly back in the wee hours to make their relationship less obvious, but he supposed they just decided to enjoy a long weekend together. That, or they had disappeared for good. Joan's absence only made her connection to Oscar's murder more suspicious. He was about to leave when he decided to try another wild shot, his second of the day.

"There's one other person who could help me. Do you know a native American named Many Bad Horses?"

The girl smiled her chilling mechanical smile. "Victor? Of course, one doesn't forget a name like that. But he's, um, no longer with us."

"Really?" Hannibal said, trying hard to sound conspiratorial. "A talent like him, I would have expected Miss Kitteridge to hang on to. Was he, you know, let go?"

The receptionist lowered her eyes and smiled. "Well, he was allowed to resign of course but..."

Hannibal lowered himself into the chair beside her desk. "But?"

"Well there were rumors," the woman said. "I heard Miss Kitteridge asked him to go because she caught him messing around in the employee files, you know, digging into people's personal information. You know those computer types. Can't stay out of files marked confidential."

"You're so right," Hannibal said. And what did this mean? Was it an indication that Fancy was in the blackmail business? That would certainly point to a motive for Oscar's death. Did he learn something from his good friend that got him killed? Or did he pass information to Fancy which was traced back to its source?

Hannibal was the lone rider in a down bound elevator when his phone rang again. He flipped it open, hoping to hear from Monty, but prepared for bad news from Cindy about Dean's hospitalization. When he heard Sarge's voice, he remembered that he should have expected a call from him as well.

"Hey, my man, what's the latest from out west?"

"Hey, we're having a good time, man," Sarge said. "Quaker's already gambled away his fee for this little jaunt. But I think we found what you were looking for, so maybe we can get back to DC before we go completely broke."

"So Joan was in Vegas last summer to do the chapel thing?" Hannibal asked as he got into his car.

"Close but no cigar," Sarge said. "It was a divorce she was after, and she got it finalized too,"

"Divorce? I thought they were relative newlyweds."

"Different husband," Sarge said. "They wouldn't give us any info about the man down at the courthouse, but they said Joan Kitteridge got divorced. Didn't want to tell us that much but, well, we kind of finagled it out of this broad."

"I probably don't want to know the details," Hannibal said. "Enough to know she was married before. And for some reason or other, she sure didn't want it to be public knowledge. Gives me a bit more to talk to her about. And since she didn't go to work today, I think I'll just head over to the house and roust her."

Hannibal roared up onto Route 395 headed north and east to Arlington. Afternoon traffic was light and in a handful of minutes he was again in the driveway of the substantial Kitteridge home. He was wondering if one of its occupants was as solid as that structure. It even crossed his mind that perhaps he should have brought Virgil along as backup. Could the woman really be dangerous?

When Langford Kitteridge opened the door, Hannibal thought he saw worry lines on his face, but as he registered who his visitor was, he broke into a smile and waved him inside.

"Mister Jones, here's a surprise. Won't you come in."

They went into the living room, furnished in very modern black chrome decor. Between that and the spring in Langford's step, Hannibal had to remind himself that this man was not his own age. Like a good host, Langford went straight to the wet bar and poured out a pair of cocktails. Hannibal didn't know they were martinis until the olives dropped in. He seemed to be meeting a lot of people lately who thought they knew what he wanted.

As Langford handed up the glass he said, "Well, have you talked to Joanie in the last couple of days?"

"Actually, I came by hoping to see her here." Hannibal removed his glasses to admire the military oil paintings hanging in well lighted places around the room, and his eyes were drawn to one framed certificate. It expressed the thanks of the President of the United States for thirty years of faithful service. The retirement certificate of a brigadier general in the United States Army. Well that went a long way to explain the man's level of fitness, no to mention his ramrod straight posture. But then his face drew Hannibal again, the worry lines returning.

"I haven't seen her," Langford said, as if speaking of a small child. "The girl hasn't been home in three days. Hasn't called. Not even an e-mail note."

No, Hannibal thought, she was busy spending time with her hidden husband and dealing with her old employee. For now, Hannibal suspected Oscar had been blackmailing her with information he got from Fancy. She would want to silence the source somehow, but it's dangerous to kill an old pro at the blackmail game. Maybe the secret had to do with the divorce she kept so quiet.

"Tell me, has she been behaving oddly lately? Like since her divorce?"

"Divorce?" Langford tipped his glass up and settled onto a bar stool. "I think perhaps you've gotten hold of some bad information, my young friend. A person has to be married before they can be divorced. And my Joanie's just never found the right fellow. Afraid to stray too far from home I suppose. Besides, as soon as she got out of school I started KCS and gave it to her to run. It's kept her out of trouble, but it's also become her life."

For Langford, this was a spate of running off at the mouth. Hannibal saw Joan as aggressive and independent. Her uncle's doting must suffocate her. He could almost see that as a motive for keeping a marriage secret, but not quite. Either way, he saw no reason to hurt the old man.

"Sorry, must have gotten something mixed up. When I got the report of her time in Las Vegas last summer..."

At this, Langford threw his head back and laughed, his white hair shaking behind him. "Oh my, you have been sold a bill of goods. Joan wasn't even in the country most of the summer. She went down under for a computer conference and made a long vacation out of it."

"Really?" Hannibal tried to suppress his reaction. But now he knew for sure that Joan was up to something she did not want her uncle to know. "Was she in touch with you during that time?"

Langford smiled even wider. "Come downstairs with me, young fellow, and let me show you something."

Langford ducked his head and led the way. A long flight of stairs led them to a broad family room complete with big screen television and yet another bar. Off to the right was a smaller, more intimate den lined with maple bookcases, all filled with hardcover volumes. On the left stood a small fireplace. A computer console dominated the right side. Langford dropped into the well-cushioned chair and began tapping at the keys faster than Hannibal could follow. He saw an e-mail account come up, and Langford opened a letter from the received file.

"There, take a look at that. 'Greatly enjoyed Sydney. Started my journey across the country today on the Great South Pacific Express. It's like the Orient Express down here, and it runs from Sydney's harbor up to Cairns and Port Douglas in North Queensland. It's pretty luxurious...' and so forth."

"How considerate," Hannibal said in an even tone. "Notes from her laptop I assume. How often did she write?"

"Darn near every day," Langford said with a chuckle. "And every few days I got one of these from where she was." Langford drew a picture postcard from a cubbyhole in the computer desk. Hannibal accepted the card, which featured the Sydney Opera House. It was dated August 12th and could have been bought in any souvenir shop on the Australian continent. Of course, it would not be found anyplace else. The message, in a sharp but still feminine hand, read, "Didn't stay for an opera today, but it was well worth stopping just to see this place. Love you always, your Joanie."

And now Hannibal had to wonder how Joan Kitteridge managed to be in two places at once.

-24-

The thick pane of glass was not all that separated Sarge from Fancy. Sarge wore a knit shirt he had chosen, while Fancy wore the coveralls issued by the state of Nevada. Sarge's face reflected a relaxed confidence, while Fancy's betrayed the fear of a man who finally realized just how grim his life could become. Most importantly, when their conversation ended, Sarge could stand up and walk back out into the bright Southwestern sunshine. Fancy desperately wanted to.

"Could I really go up for murder?" Fancy asked, as if Sarge's answer could somehow make a difference to his fate.

"Could be," Sarge said. "People have been sent to the chair on lots less."

Fancy leaned forward on his elbows. "But you know damn well I didn't kill Oscar. If I go up, the real killer gets away."

"Yeah, that's true. And my man Hannibal, he might be able to find the real killer too, which would get you cut loose."

Fancy was good at cutting through the red tape straight to the point. "Okay, I get it. What do you want? I don't know anything useful."

Sarge scratched his chin and looked up at the dim florescent tubes in the ceiling. "Well, now, Hannibal don't agree with that. He called and told me he's got a few too many mysteries going. Wants me to help clear them up. If you can solve one of those mysteries, he'll be one step closer to finding the real killer."

Fancy pressed his palms against the glass. Sarge could smell his desperation right through the dense pane. "But I told you I don't know anything."

Sarge just smiled and nodded his head. "We found out you didn't meet Joan Kitteridge in Vegas, Fancy. In fact, turns out you worked for her for a while."

"Joan tell you that?"

"She's been pretty cooperative with Hannibal," Sarge said. He watched the confusion race across Fancy's face for a few seconds before continuing. "She says you two didn't get off to a very good start. Didn't she fire you for getting into some confidential information?"

"We had a disagreement," Fancy said, waving the issue away with a hand. "I left her company's employ. What else did she tell you?"

"She told us what she knew," Sarge said, leaning forward slightly. "Of course, she doesn't know everything. And what you know could help get you off the hook."

Fancy dropped his face into his hands. "Aww, man! You think I'm a blackmailer or something. Man I don't know anything. I didn't pay any attention to any of that stuff I stole."

"That's no surprise." Fancy looked up, and Sarge could see in his eyes that it was time.

"You're not smart enough to be a blackmailer, Fancy man. So just who were you funneling information to?"

"That won't help you any, you moron," Fancy snapped. "You're looking for a lead to who might have killed Oscar? Idiot, Oscar was who I was finding out stuff for. Think that will help you? Huh?"

Sarge rolled his big shoulders. "I look like a detective to you? I'll just pass that on to the man who might be able to figure this all out."

*   *   *

"Without this, I won't be able to figure this all out," Hannibal said. Quincy Roberts looked from Hannibal's reflective lenses to Cindy's guarded smile and scratched at his thick gray beard. "I'm just not sure this is in Dean's best interest."

"Do you think Dean murdered someone, Doctor?" Cindy asked.

"Of course not."

"Then it seems to me the truth is in his best interest," she said softly.

"But hypnosis," Quincy said, shaking his head. "This sort of thing can be dangerous."

Hannibal looked around the silver and white office, focusing on the series of framed diplomas hanging in perfect straight lines behind Quincy's desk. "Are you saying you're not qualified to perform this technique, doctor?"

Quincy huffed. "More to the point, his current problem is more pressing than his father's murder."

"I don't think we can separate them," Hannibal said patiently. "If Dean remembers enough to clear his mother of the murder we can pretty much clear him of Oscar's murder as well. Also, I have information that seems to indicate that Oscar was involved in some sort of blackmail. What if he found out who really killed Dean's father, wouldn't that be a motive for murder?"

Quincy pushed his glasses up on his nose. "You're shooting in the dark."

"Maybe," Hannibal admitted. "But I might be closer to the target than anyone thinks. All I'm asking is a chance."

"I don't want him badgered," Quincy warned.

"I'll ask the questions," Cindy said. "I've spent enough time with distraught clients to know how to shake the truth loose gently."

*   *   *

The big orange ball hanging on the horizon to his right reminded Hannibal just how full a day it had been. It sometimes seemed that the only time he had to relax was in between stops, like this leisurely drive southward down the tree-lined Beltway. He knew there would be more to it, but he hoped that what he now knew from Sarge, plus what he would learn from Dean would allow him to piece the puzzle together. When Cindy's hand moved across his knee, he realized he did not know for sure where he was going.

"So, when do you think you want to try questioning Dean?" Hannibal asked her.

Cindy faced Hannibal, partially to turn away from the sun. "Actually, I was thinking tonight, right after I make you a nice home-cooked dinner at your place."

"Now that's the nicest invitation I've gotten today. Maybe we can delay the questioning long enough to have some nice dessert..." Hannibal was interrupted by the burr of his phone. Pressing a button on his sun visor allowed him to speak without his hands leaving the wheel.

"Hannibal? You there? This is Monty."

"Yes, I did recognize your voice, Monty," Hannibal said. "What's the latest?"

"Well I'm here with Mister Santiago and he thought I should report in."

"You're with Ray?" Hannibal's brow knit above his dark glasses. "I thought you were watching Mrs. Peters. Did something happen?"

"Hey man, you know me," Monty's young voice came through the speaker. "I been on the lady like white on rice. But she just made the job a little easier by coming over here and Ray wanted to know if maybe you wanted one of us to come in."

Cindy looked at Hannibal quizzically. He shrugged his shoulders in response. "Over where, Monty? Where is here?"

"Here is the Courtyard Marriot in Crystal City," Monty said. "Mrs. Peters came over here and I don't think she's going back. She brought her luggage."

Hannibal smiled in understanding. "Can I assume this is Gil Donner's hotel?"

"That's why Ray's here," Monty said, and Hannibal could feel his head shaking at the other end of the line. "Ray was watching this one and spotted me following the lady. So Ray, he figures you don't need two of us on this one stakeout and wonders if one of us should go home."

Hannibal thought for a moment before answering. "Well, you know, I'm not real happy about you skipping school today. But at this late point in the day, I guess it doesn't matter much. And I do think I'd like you to continue the double coverage. They might separate in a hurry and I've got a feeling it's kind of important to keep close tabs on both our travelers. Cool?"

"Cool with me," Monty said. "Grandma can use the money."

"Okay, buddy," Hannibal said as he pulled into his own block. "Make sure you check in with her, too. She needs to know where you are. And work it out so you and Ray can get something to eat. I've got to get going now. More surprises coming at me. Later."

"Surprises?" Cindy asked, as Hannibal parked in his traditional space. "What's going on?"

Hannibal was all business as he stepped out of the car. "I recognize the guy in the green Ford across the street. He might be trouble, but he also might be carrying a lot of answers I need."

The Ford's driver sat with his elbow sticking out of the window. Hannibal walked over to the car, half expecting Harry Irons to step out to meet him. When that didn't happen, Hannibal just stared curiously into Harry Irons' swarthy Mediterranean face.

"You looking for me, Harry?" he asked. "You could have waited inside."

"Yeah, they told me, I just felt like waiting in the car."

"Well, unless you've got a beef with me, why don't we go in now?"

"I ain't looking for trouble," Harry said, dragging on his cigarette, "but we don't need to go in. I'm just here for Francis." He handed Hannibal a piece of paper that must have been folded over four times.

"This is.....?"

"An address," Harry said, dragging on his cigarette. "Francis, she's kind of laying low right now, but she wants to talk to you. Says she's got things to tell you."

"I take it she told you we were wrong about the young man she was looking for?"

"Her son," Harry nodded. "Yeah, she told me. I should have known she wasn't looking for another man. I was just being..."

"Yeah, I know," Hannibal smiled. "We all get like that when we find a lady who's good to us. Maybe I can help get her out of trouble."

*   *   *

The building at the northern edge of Silver Spring was well maintained, but not new. The grounds were spotless and flowers were nicely placed to offer the feel of a country cottage, despite the fact that this structure was one of collection of five story buildings standing in a semicircle. Parking lines indicated that cars should face the curb, rather than stand beside it. Most of the empty slots were labeled with address numbers but he found one marked "guest" and drove his Volvo into it. The tall maples and pines hugged each other in the center island.

Residents relaxing on their porches seemed less cordial, and Hannibal saw no children in the area. Knocking on the door of the top floor entrance, Hannibal wondered why Francis stayed in the low rent motel she used if this place was an option. He received a partial answer when Francis Edwards opened the door and waved him in without a word. They stood in the center of the wide living room for a moment, just looking at one another. He would expect a woman to move toward the sofa, or the balcony with its view of private woods, or perhaps the kitchen area, which was separated by just an island.

"You're not at home here," Hannibal said. "Whose place is this?"

"Well, I needed a place to go where I could stay out of view of the police for a while," she began. "When I called Walt this morning he didn't want to know where I was. When I told him I wanted to talk to you he suggested I meet you here so you wouldn't know where I was staying either. That way you wouldn't have to lie to the police. When I got here I just found the door unlocked."

Hannibal walked to the kitchen, pulled off his glasses and gloves, and began exploring cabinets. "Walt Young invited you to his condominium? That's certainly different." He wondered what kind of a lawyer was stupid enough to keep a woman who may soon be a murder suspect in his own home, even for a brief time.

"He's done everything he can to help me, Mister Jones," Francis said, still standing and looking lost in the big room. "He knows I haven't killed anyone."

Hannibal's cabinet search was fruitless, but he found a bottle of white wine in the refrigerator and poured two glasses half full. "Tell me, Francis, did you know Walt before you left your husband?"

Francis eased onto one of the stools on the other side of the island and accepted her glass with a nod. "Never saw him until just before the trial. And that's one of the things I wanted to correct, Mister Jones. I never left Grant. He left me."

Hannibal tasted his own wine in order to encourage her to drink hers because he thought she needed something to relax her. "I see. But that's not the reason you wanted to talk to me."

Francis looked down into her glass, drank it nearly dry, then returned to her downward staring posture. "Mister Jones, I want you to know that I haven't killed anyone. Not ten years ago. Not a week ago. But I know what it's like inside and I won't let my son go there. I told Walt that if Dean is in danger of conviction I would confess to last week's murder." She looked up, moisture hanging in her eyes. "He said I should talk to you first."

Hannibal realized now that Young had left his own condominium empty on a Sunday afternoon because he thought only Hannibal could prevent her from making a terrible mistake. He hoped Young was right.

"Ma'am I think offering yourself up like that would help no one. Please just give me a little time to track down the real killers. I know some people might think Dean is a killer. More people think you are."

"I didn't know this boy who died last week," Francis said. "And I could never have hurt Grant."

Hannibal refilled her glass. Up close, her eyes were so clear and blue he didn't think she could hide the truth there. "Even if he was untrue to you?"

To her credit Francis stared right back into his hazel eyes. "I know Grant was... I know he had another woman, Mister Jones. It wasn't hard to figure out from what Dean told me in bits and pieces after Grant and I separated. It hurt, certainly, but not enough to turn my love into hate."

Hannibal's breath stopped in his throat and he held her eyes with his own. It had never occurred to him that she might know. "Francis, did you ever get an idea who that other woman might have been?"

"Of course," Francis said with a smile that he would have called wistful in other circumstances. "I'm not the idiot Grant's family would have me be. It was the young woman who used to baby-sit for us. She was beautiful of course, and probably no more than nineteen or twenty so, I mean who could blame him?"

Hannibal was bursting to fill in the rest, but he did not want to risk planting it in Francis's mind. He closed his eyes and hoped. "Any chance you remember her name?"

"Oh, I'm pretty sure it was Joan. Yes, Joan something or other."

"Yes!" Hannibal realized that his smile must have startled Francis. He upended his wineglass and paced around the kitchen island. "I think I might just have it. Oscar, the victim Dean's accused of murdering, worked for a woman named Joan. I think she might well be the link. If she was the same girl who baby sat for you..."

"You think Grant's girlfriend killed him?"

"Probably not," Hannibal said, pulling his gloves back on. "But I do think she was married at the time. And based on what you just told me, her husband would have had a good, solid motive for killing yours. And if Oscar found out about it somehow, there's a motive for the second killing."

Francis' quiet quickly cooled Hannibal's excitement. He waited for her to tell him what he was missing. When she spoke, it was with well-practiced helplessness.

"No one will believe you. My son testified in court that it was me he saw."

"Well, did he?" Hannibal asked.

"Of course not," Francis said, her fists curling at her sides. "It was that horrid Ursula. She must have badgered him until he thought he saw what she told him to see. But no one will believe him now if he changes his story."

"I think we can change that," Hannibal said, stopping to stand beside her. "We intend to probe Dean's memory tonight. I think what we get will hold up in court and..." Hannibal was interrupted by three sharp knocks.

"That must be Walt," Francis said, moving toward the door. "We can find out right away what will stand up in court."

Hannibal pushed his glasses back into place, prepared to have some words with the lawyer about having his client at his home. He never got to say them. Francis pulled the door open and found herself staring up at the imposing figure of Stan Thompson.

"Good evening Mrs. Edwards," Thompson said. "You're under arrest for murder."

-25-

Francis gasped and fell back, allowing the detective to step through the door. Two uniformed men entered behind him. While one of them produced handcuffs Thompson began reading Francis her rights. Hannibal interrupted him by standing between him and the woman, allowing barely an inch of free space between their chests.

"Mind telling me just what the hell you're doing?"

Thompson breathed liver and onions down into Hannibal's face. "What I'm doing is arresting a suspect. You want to add interfering with an arrest to harboring a fugitive?"

"A fugitive?" Hannibal said. "Since when?"

"Oh, since about a half hour ago," Thompson said. He looked past Hannibal to Francis who was flanked by the other two policemen. He smiled at her the way the winner of a chess game smiles at the loser. "The lab boys finally finished their analysis of the wounds and guess what? Looks like Oscar Peters was killed with the same knife that went into Grant Edwards. Same weapon, same approach, same entry point. That was enough to get me a warrant to come in here. Lucky thing I had a tail on the great detective here."

"Thompson, you son of a bitch, you set me up." Hannibal bared his teeth. Thompson turned his maddening satisfied smile to him.

"A real detective uses all the resources at his disposal, son," Thompson said. "And since I'm in such a grateful mood, I'll invite you to come along peacefully. Or do we need to put the cuffs on you too?"

"Yeah, I think you'd better," Hannibal said. His face relaxed just before he hooked his right fist up into Thompson's midsection. He watched the big detective double over and back away a few steps then turned to face the two uniforms. They stepped away from their prisoner and pulled their clubs into attack position.

"Hold on, boys," Thompson said from behind Hannibal. "No need for violence. I'm sure Mr. Jones will cooperate now that he's gotten that little bit of anger out of his system. Won't you, Mr. Jones?"

Breathing deeply, Hannibal was ready for violence of the worst sort, but he realized that it would not help Dean, or his mother, for him to be locked up for physically abusing a couple of innocent police officers. He gradually slowed his breathing and even more gradually raised his fists straight out in front of him. One of the policemen produced his handcuffs and quickly turned Hannibal around. Hannibal was surprised to see Thompson's smile fade when they heard the click of the cuffs behind him.

*   *   *

Cindy waited until she and Hannibal were out of the police station before she turned and hugged him. He briefly returned her embrace, but his mood would not allow for much affection. He located his car and stepped quickly toward it.

"Thanks for bailing me out, babe," he said. "I knew if I called you everything would be all right. Do you think Walt will be able to get Francis out too?"

"Not likely," Cindy answered. "They've formally charged her with Oscar's murder. And I've got to admit that if I were a judge I'd consider her a flight risk."

When they reached the car, Cindy handed him the keys. It was not until that moment that he realized what had happened.

"Did you drive my car over here?"

"Seemed like the most practical thing to do," she said as they got in. "I didn't think you wanted too many people to have that address you gave me, so I just took a cab over and got it." Hannibal nodded. Knowing Cindy didn't own a car, he wasn't sure she had a current license, and decided not to ask.

"You know the evidence they've got against her?" he asked.

"Yes," Cindy said, "And Walt and I have already asked for copies of all the photos and documentation describing the two knife wounds. But from what I've heard, all the circumstantial evidence points to the same killer in both incidents."

"That doesn't surprise me," Hannibal said, pulling out into traffic. "But I'm more sure than ever that the killer isn't Francis Edwards. Now, if you'll excuse me a minute, I owe somebody a phone call."

Hannibal pushed buttons on the phone hanging on his visor, and three rings later Irma Andrews answered. "Wanted to keep you in the picture," Hannibal said. "They've arrested Francis Edwards for the murder of Oscar Peters. If you're hot you might be able to break the story."

"Appreciate the thought," Irma said, "but our stringer on the police beat already caught it. Did she do it?"

"Not a chance."

"Well, I don't know if this helps, but Joan Kitteridge didn't do it either," Irma said. "I checked out her alibi, and she most definitely was at a Falls Church Chamber of Commerce dinner until a few minutes before we saw her Monday night. Lots of witnesses who have no reason to lie for her. There's no way she could have done the deed."

It was no surprise, but still Hannibal had wished otherwise. "Thanks Irma. I'm on my way now to one place we might get a clue as to who did."

-26-

The scene at Charter was more like some satanic ritual than a cross-examination. Dean lay in his bed at the center of the room, bright ceiling lights giving his face an almost angelic glow which combined with the innocent expression to give him the look of a victim or, perhaps, a sacrifice. An intravenous drip flowed into the inside of his left elbow. Dr. Quincy Roberts sat on his right, holding a small medallion hanging from a short chain. Off to the left, in the dimmest corner of the room, Hannibal sat holding Bea's right hand. Cindy held her left. All eyes were on Dean, all faces strained. The look reminded Hannibal of cult members who knew what they had to do, but felt guilty for being willing participants in a grim sacrifice.

They had listened to Quincy's slow rhythmic speech for ten minutes, while Dean stared at the twirling coin and slowly counted down from ten to zero. Hannibal didn't like hypnosis, was perhaps a little superstitious about it. Or maybe he just didn't like the thought of losing control of his own thoughts.

Finally, Quincy turned to face his audience and said, "He's ready. I've prepared him to answer any question posed by Ms. Santiago."

"You're on, babe," Hannibal said. Cindy sighed, stood, and switched seats with Quincy. She took a couple of deep breaths, then looked up and smiled at Dean. His eyes floated in a nearly closed posture, but he may have seen her.

"Now Dean, I need for you to answer some questions for me," she began. "I need for you to think before you speak, and to tell me the truth when you answer. Don't worry about how you might have answered a question in the past. Don't worry about what I or anyone else might want the answer to be. Just tell me the truth. Can you do that?"

"Yes, ma'am," Dean muttered. Bea sobbed hearing him speak almost as a child. Hannibal squeezed her hand.

"I want you to remember the night your father was killed," Cindy said. She was looking for a reaction, but there was none. "Can you do that for me?" Dean nodded.

"You were at home with your father and someone came to visit you, is that right?" Another nod.

"Who did you see?" Cindy asked.

Dean's brow knit for a moment. "Nobody." Hannibal slid his glasses off and watched Dean's face very closely.

"Now, Dean, I want you to go back there now," Cindy said in her most soothing tones. "I want you to really be there that day. Can you do that?" Dean nodded his head but was otherwise still. "Where are you, Dean?" Cindy asked.

Dean shook his head quickly, as if throwing something off. A lie, perhaps. "I'm on the dining room floor, behind the door. There's yelling. A fight."

"Whose voices?"

"Papa's," Dean said. "Papa and...Mama?"

Cindy leaned closer. "Are you sure it's her voice?"

"I think so. It's a woman, but she's kind of whispering. But Papa's shouting. Really loud."

Hannibal felt Bea shuddering beside him, but his focus was on Dean's face, which showed an inner conflict of some kind.

"After the fighting, tell me what you heard," Cindy said. "Everything you heard. Like you're there right now."

Dean's eyebrows rose without his eyes opening. He cocked his head, as if he could hear those awful sounds again. "They're fighting. Papa yelling, yelling. Then... then the door. Yes, the door opening. Now it's quiet for a second. Then the thump."

"Thump?" Cindy asked after a moment of silence.

"The thump. And now I hear footsteps. Quiet again. I get up to see what's going on now it's quiet." Dean shuddered in his bed, then snapped upright like a puppet whose strings had been yanked hard. "Mama screams really really loud so I run out to see what happened and..."

Everyone jumped when Dean's eyes snapped open. He sat still, and Hannibal could tell he wasn't seeing anything. At least, not anything in the room right now. Perspiration dripped into Dean's eyes, but they did not blink from the horror in his mind. Cindy reached out to cover one of his hands with her own.

"Tell me what you see, Dean," Cindy said. "You have to tell me what you see."

Dean's eyes clamped shut, and big tears dropped from them onto the white sheets. "Mama. Mama is standing over Papa with this huge knife in her hand. Blood's coming off the knife. She's standing in his blood. It's on her shoes. It's all over." Dean's voice rose into hysterics before Quincy pulled Cindy away and took her seat.

"Dean, this is Dr. Roberts. All that you saw is in the past. The distant past. It can't hurt you now."

"Want to bet?" Hannibal said under his breath.

Cindy turned to Hannibal, wrapping her arms around him. She was shaken by her part in this drama, but he could barely bring himself to hold her. He was energized by what he had heard. He stood, pulling her with him, barely able to be quiet while Quincy talked Dean back into a restful sleep.

"If that's the truth it's sure not what he said in court," Hannibal said. "Did you hear it?"

Bea looked up, her brow knit. "I heard him say he caught his mother with the knife, standing over his father. What a horrible thing for a child to see."

"No, no," Hannibal said, breaking away from Cindy and pacing toward the bed. "There was an argument, but he didn't see his mother. Whoever it was left. Remember, the door opening? Then the thump. Surely Grant's body hitting the floor. Then a pause. Then Francis walks in, finds the body..."

"There's a lot of supposition there, don't you think?" Quincy said.

"Well, no I don't," Hannibal said, facing the doctor across Dean's sleeping form. "What's the alternative? She opens the door, stabs him, stands there for a minute to think about it, and THEN screams? No, she came in after the fact and found the body. Wake him up."

Quincy hesitated. "That might not be a good idea."

"There's no time, Doc," Hannibal said. "If you want to save him, wake him up."

-27-

Dean still looked like a child to Hannibal, even after dressing in chinos and a sweatshirt. Bea sat beside him on the edge of the bed and held him for a good five minutes while Hannibal conferred in a corner with Cindy and Quincy. They had agreed to stay away until he felt receptive to questioning.

"I'm ready to talk, Mr. Jones," he called over Bea's shoulder. When she shook her head at him, he added, "I want to find out what really happened. I think you can help me find out."

Hannibal walked in close to Dean, looking closely into his eyes, big like Japanese anime figures, and asked himself one last time if the boy could really understand the truth.

"Okay Dean, what I need now is not what you saw or what you heard. I need to know what you thought. Are you ready to talk about that?"

Dean shrugged and sighed. "I've got nothing to hide, Mr. Jones. I just don't know if I know what I was thinking ten years ago."

"Let's keep this simple," Hannibal said, pulling a chair over to the bed and dropping into it. "You do remember who your baby-sitter was in those days, don't you?"

Dean's eyes widened, then narrowed to slits. He lowered his head to look down at Hannibal's hands. "Yes. It was Joan Kitteridge."

Bea pulled his arm and turned him to herself. "Your boss was your baby-sitter?"

"Coincidence?" Cindy asked, standing behind Hannibal's chair.

Dean shook his head. "I've tried to stay close to her. Thought I could maybe find out.

Something."

"You thought she had something to do with your father's death didn't you?" Hannibal asked. "Maybe it was her voice you heard arguing with your father that night."

"But baby," Bea moaned, pulling his head to her and staring deep into his eyes. "I don't understand. If you suspected Joan enough to follow her for all these years, why did you try to tell people you killed your father? You said you killed him and Oscar. Why?"

Dean seized Bea's arms. It was the first intensity Hannibal had seen out of him. His breath was labored, as if pushing a great weight. Hannibal thought maybe there was a great weight, but it was on his chest.

"Don't you see? At first I thought mother had killed him, because he was with Joan. I'm the one who told mother they were together. If I'd kept my mouth shut, she wouldn't have known, and my father would be alive today. I'm the one responsible. I killed him."

Hannibal stood and started pacing again, rounding the three sides of the bed and turning around to retrace his steps. "Okay, Dean, the little boy in you might believe that, but when you grew up you must have realized there were other possible answers. And you obviously thought Joan Kitteridge knew something, right? That's why you followed her around."

Bea looked at Dean with a different expression now, as if just accepting an unexpected depth in this man she loved. "You followed her?"

"She was my father's girlfriend," Dean said, squeezing Bea with one arm. "She watched me every day. Practically family. But when the trial started up, she was nowhere to be seen. And over the years I started to wonder why. I began to remember that there was another man. I think she had another boyfriend."

"Actually," Hannibal said, "There's good reason to believe she was married at the time."

"Well, that didn't change my guilt," Dean muttered. "If Joan's other man did it, mother must have told him about Joan and my father. Again, if I'd kept my mouth shut, Papa would be alive today."

"Or Joan did it herself," Hannibal put it, "to keep him from confronting her husband."

"Well anyway, I felt like I had to know what really happened. So when I finished school, I tracked her down. I think she gave me a job out of sympathy."

Now Cindy looked at Dean out the corner of her eye. "Now I'm thinking you were close to Oscar, but not for the reason I first thought."

"I know Oscar, er, experimented," Dean said with a grin, "but he and I were never more than friends. We got to talking one day and it turned out we had some background in common. And he told me once that he had something on Joan, some kind of information that might tie in to something bad in her past."

Hannibal almost lunged toward Dean, pushed by the force of a revelation. "Of course! That's why you felt guilty about Oscar. You thought he was killed because of something you told him, maybe just confirming Joan's connection to your father's murder."

"Yes," Dean said, hanging his head again, "So you see, I killed him too."

"Well I don't think so," Hannibal said, laying a hand on Dean's shoulder. "It looks like Oscar was a blackmailer maybe, so lots of people might have had a reason for going after him. Personally, I think your boss Joan is the lead suspect. I'm thinking she did the deed and left. Your mother comes in, sees her husband dead and picks up the knife just like people always do in the movies."

"I'm sorry," Quincy said from the other side of the bed. "Believe me, Joan was just not capable of that sort of a crime."

The whole room seemed to hold its breath as a single thought jumped from Hannibal's mind to everyone else's like a psychic signal. Finally, when he could no longer hold his breath comfortably, Hannibal looked up at the older psychiatrist, forcing calm into his voice.

"And just exactly how would you know that, Doctor?"

-28-

Under the stars Quincy, Roberts' white shirt glowed, making him look like some puffy, gray-bearded angel recently descended from the dark clear sky to a muddled ball of confusion. Cindy and Hannibal faced him as if awaiting the answers to all questions. Hannibal's stomach rumbled, reminding him how the day had gotten away from him. Maybe he should have stopped for a bite, but he was hungry for something else even more than food. He hungered for the truth.

"So she was a nut case way back then," Hannibal said, none too delicately.

Quincy bristled. "Joan Kitteridge was my patient, yes, but she was never violent. In fact, I'd go on record as saying she was incapable of violence. She had serious ego strength issues. I shouldn't be telling you this."

"Us now or the police later," Cindy said. "They'd just subpoena your patient records. It IS a murder investigation."

"It was so long ago it probably doesn't matter now," Quincy said. He drew in a deep breath and puffed it out heavily. "The poor girl was so badly dominated by that man she could hardly breath without his approval. How she survived to be a success in the business world..."

"By that man," Hannibal prodded, "you mean her husband?"

"Well of course," Quincy said. "So young to be married, too. If I could have gotten him to come in to therapy I might have helped her more, but I never even saw the man."

*   *   *

By the time Hannibal got home, he was both ravenous and irritated. At these times, Cindy knew the wise thing to do was keep her distance until he was fed and calmer. It was a good time to be alone, just the two of them, at least until he could regain his perspective. That's why her mouth dropped open in fear and her eyes darted back at Hannibal when they found Anna Ingersoll slumped into his doorway. Hannibal stared at her for a moment, as if he spotted a booby trap set between himself and his long delayed dinner.

"What are you doing here?" he asked between tightened lips.

"I didn't know where else to go," Anna said.

Sensing that Hannibal was about to tell her, Cindy said, "We're about to have a late supper. Some sandwiches and maybe some soup. Why don't you come inside and join us?"

The trio entered Hannibal's railroad apartment and he led them down its length toward the kitchen. At his bedroom, he stopped to lose his suit coat, tie and shoulder holster. In the kitchen, he dropped into a chair and began rolling up his sleeves. Anna sat opposite him but Cindy went straight for the coffeepot. Hannibal smiled when she handed him a steaming mug, the first sign that he might soon return to normal. But knowing the job was only half done, Cindy loaded bread, mayonnaise and lettuce onto the table, then pulled out the half ham she knew was in the refrigerator.

After taking a long slow sip of coffee, Hannibal turned his attention to Anna for the first time. Her short-cropped hair was recently dyed a slightly darker blonde than before, a color that always looked dirty to him.

"What brought you here?"

"He's been following me," Anna said, her body vibrating the way a Chihuahua's does. "Day and night, just won't leave me alone. I need some peace. I knew Nicky would be safe at Monty's so I left him there and took off. Ended up here."

"Well you'll be safe here," Cindy said, carving thin slices off the ham with a butcher knife, "but you can't keep running forever. You need to get a restraining order against that big lug."

Hannibal carefully spread the right amount of stone-ground mustard on a slice of dark rye bread, positioned two slices of the honey baked ham on it, covered them with a slice of extra sharp cheddar cheese and laid on the second slice of bread. His mouth began to water in anticipation as his nose reacted to the sharp scent of the mustard mingled with the sweet aroma of the ham. This was going to be good.

"That's a legal issue," he said, not looking up from his sandwich, "which we can deal with tomorrow." Then he wrapped his mouth around a big bite of the sandwich. His eyes half closed as he chewed. Cindy smiled.

"He'll be okay now," she said. "And I'm betting he'll be fine with you staying over in his office tonight if it will make you feel better."

"Yes," Anna said quietly. "That would be nice. Sometimes I just get so scared. I guess it's the memories. It's like I carry in my head every time he's hit me with those big ugly hands of his."

Anna jumped like a bee-stung child at the thump on the back door. Two more heavy blows followed. Hannibal muttered an obscenity under his breath, put down his sandwich and stood. The pounding was coming from his front door. After one more sip of coffee he walked back through his apartment to open it. He knew who he would find on his doorstep, he just didn't have the patience for it right now.

Standing just inside the door, Hannibal said, "It's late. What do you want?"

"I can't find Anna," Isaac Ingersoll said from the other side of the door.

Hannibal unlocked the door and opened it as far as its safety chain would allow to stare up into Isaac's watery blue eyes. "I am not the missing person's bureau. Besides, if you can't find her it probably means she doesn't want to be found. I don't thinks she wants to see you."

"I don't care," Isaac said, and the beer cloud drifted down into Hannibal's face. "I need her."

"You see, that's your problem," Hannibal said. "You don't care what she wants, but you know, she has the right to do whatever she wants. Now, I think it's time you went home and got some sleep, don't you?"

Hannibal thought he had the situation under control and his mind wandered for just a second to honey-baked ham and coffee. That's when Isaac's eyes left Hannibal's and turned to the darkness behind him and to his left. Hannibal turned his head in time to catch a quick glimpse of Anna's terror-stricken face before she darted back into the darkness.

Before he could turn his head back, the edge of the door slammed into his face. Pain lanced out from his temple to fill his head as he staggered back. Darkness flowed in around him, but a missile shot through that darkness to smash into his chest hard enough to drive all breath from his body. Even as he dropped to his knees, Hannibal knew that missile was Isaac's fist. He felt more than heard heavy footfalls moving away toward the kitchen.

Damn. How could he have been so stupid? To trust that monster to behave rationally was a huge mistake. Self-loathing rose like bile into Hannibal's throat. He was the reason Anna was now in danger. And worse, Cindy was in that same room standing in the path of a human locomotive.

Hannibal forced himself to his feet and staggered forward through a cloud of floating blue dots. His apartment had never seemed so long, but he pressed on toward the light at the end of the tunnel and the human locomotive standing there.

Hannibal was still out of focus when he reached the kitchen. He stepped to the right, moving around Isaac's huge frame to a point where he could lean on the table. Now Isaac stood on his left, with Cindy on the other side of the room facing him, and Anna to his right with her back against the sink. While the husband and wife ignored him, Hannibal gathered his strength to try to deal with Isaac when he finally made his move. Too late he realized he should have stopped on his way through the apartment to pick up his gun. It would have made everything so much easier.

Isaac looked down at his wife cowering against the sink and said, "I need you home. Let's go. Now!"

Hannibal crouched slightly, preparing to leap. He knew Isaac would reach out at any second to grab Anna and drag her out of the room or maybe to slap her a couple of times first to make her more cooperative. Cindy was frozen next to the refrigerator, and he could understand that. Until you share a room with one, you don't realize just how big a professional football lineman is. But Hannibal thought once Isaac took a step he would be off balance enough that a diving man, even one Hannibal's size, might be enough to bowl him over.

Then Isaac's head moved back slightly, his brows lowered in surprise. Something had changed. The air in the room was charged with a different electricity. A glance to his right showed that Anna was standing just a bit straighter. Something had snapped inside her, something wound so tight it had to spring back hard. Her jaw was thrust forward slightly. And her right hand had curled around the handle of his carving knife.

"No," she whispered, then repeated more loudly "No! That's enough. I don't need to take any more of this." Her arm moved slowly around to the side with the knife's blade rising out of the top of her fist. Her breathing deepened, the way a person's does when they're working themselves up for something. Hannibal wondered how many years of rage and frustration she was focusing.

Isaac apparently didn't get it. "What are you going to do now?" he asked with a derisive grin. "Going to cut me?"

His arms opened wide as if in invitation. Shock showed on his face when Anna emitted a low coarse growl, raised the heavy knife overhead and dived toward him. Her rage drove her into the air so that for a brief speck of time her eyes were actually above his. Isaac's mouth dropped open but he didn't move, didn't even raise an arm in defense as the edge of the blade arced downward toward his neck.

Hannibal leaped a split second behind Anna. She was slashing at a forty-five degree angle down and across her body. The blade would lay the right side of Isaac's neck and throat open. Except that Hannibal's back slammed into Isaac's chest and her right wrist smacked into the space between Hannibal's crossed wrists.

They fell to the floor together, Hannibal on his left side, Anna lying on her right. The knife rolled free from her fingers and she lay still. Anna's eyes were glazed over and she gazed at Hannibal as if she couldn't believe what had just happened. He was feeling very vulnerable as he turned to face Isaac, but his concerns appeared groundless. Isaac stared at his wife for a few seconds, then flopped into one of the kitchen chairs. His mouth had not closed in that time.

"You would have cut me. You would have cut me bad. How could you?"

"Oh my God!" Anna screamed. She worked her way to her knees and again lunged for her husband, but this time she held her arms wide. She wrapped her arms around his neck and rested her face in the space between his head and his right shoulder. In her loud sobs, Hannibal could hear hate, fear, anger, frustration, all of the negative emotions pouring out at once. A tiny light appeared in Isaac's eyes, perhaps a light of understanding. Very slowly he raised his huge arms and enfolded Anna in them. Then, at last he said the right thing.

"Oh, God, baby, I am so sorry." Then his eyes filled with tears and he joined his wife in pouring out all the bad.

Sitting on the floor, Hannibal suddenly saw something too. Something obvious that he had missed. He turned to Cindy, sudden excitement brushing away his fatigue.

"Did you see that? Old Doc Roberts was right. Francis didn't kill Dean's father. Or Oscar. Our murderer's a man."

-29-
TUESDAY

Isaac Ingersoll looked up from his plate of half-eaten scrambled eggs and said, "I owe you, Hannibal. Don't think I don't know that."

The aroma of crisply fried bacon still hung in the air and Hannibal suspected it helped everyone's appetite. Anna and Cindy had whipped up quite a feast out of simple ingredients. Hannibal pushed more eggs up on his fork with a slice of toast.

"If you really feel that way, you know how you can pay me back," Hannibal said. "Accept the counseling we talked about and get serious about overcoming your problem."

"I swear I'm turning over a new leaf," Isaac said. "Guess I never realized how much I was making my Anna hate me. I can't stand to think I could lose her forever." As he spoke, he covered her hand and most of her forearm with his palm.

Hannibal had to admit that Anna looked cute in Cindy's robe. The four of them sat around Hannibal's kitchen table enjoying some quiet time. Anna had slept on Hannibal's sofa while her husband stayed across the hall in Hannibal's office. Last night's action seemed to have made an impression on him, and he was docile now.

"I'll be going in to the office a little late," Cindy said. "If you guys will work with me here I'll get on the phone and set up some counseling sessions for you through an agency that won't charge you much. You'll have to live apart for a while, but I think if you can be honest with yourselves and make an effort, the professionals can make your relationship work again."

"Okay, honey why don't you work with these folks in here?" Hannibal said, pushing away from the table. "I want to take a closer look at those pictures you brought me."

"They're out in the living room," Cindy said, already reaching for the wall phone. Hannibal picked up his coffee and a table knife before shuffling off to the front room. Warm and comfortable in his sweat suit he wanted to do some relaxed thinking away from the Ingersolls' problems. Besides, he was expecting company.

Plopping down on the sofa, Hannibal clicked on the television and tuned in CNN. Then he slid a set of 8" X 10" photographs out of the manila envelope Cindy had left on the coffee table. Early sunlight over his shoulder spotlighted the pictures of two men who had never met but were inextricably linked in death. One of those links was the focus of the pictures. Each man had received a single vertical knife wound, just above his collarbone. Forensic scientists had studied these pictures too and told their bosses that they were the same width, the same length and almost certainly the same depth. Made with the same or extremely similar knives. It would not be hard to convict the same person of both murders.

Thinking of his own violence-filled life, Hannibal realized he was glad his mother would never be presented with this view of her son. Considering his violent life, Hannibal fully expected his last photo to be posed by a police forensics scientist examining a knife or gunshot wound. By leaving ahead of him, Hannibal's mother was safe from this shock. It reminded him of a couple of small debts he owed to two mothers he had spoken to in the last week. Francis Edwards, now Irons, had trusted him and was now in jail for that trust. He owed it to her to prove her innocence. And he owed Emma Peters two things. First, the identity of her son's killer. Also, he must return Oscar's high school yearbook to her. He was foolish not to give it to her immediately. It might be her last, most valuable keepsake of her lost son.

This time when a knock came at the door Hannibal just called, "Come in. Coffee's in the kitchen." Sarge stepped in and passed Hannibal, who had already gone back to examining the photos.

When Sarge returned to the room with a big mug, he was crunching on a piece of bacon.

"That's a big boy you got back there," Sarge said. "Now what's up? You want a fuller report of our Vegas vacation?"

"Just glad you got back safe and sound," Hannibal said. "Want you to take a look at these two pictures."

Sarge accepted them as Hannibal stood up. "Nasty business. But effective, that's for sure."

"Yeah," Hannibal said, "and the best clue we have to the murder. Now I've been thinking I had the murderer in my sights, a woman, but what happened here last night changed my mind. That little petite blonde in there went after the big guy with a knife."

"You're kidding?" Sarge grinned big. "Bet he was surprised as hell. Guys like that never expect the worm to turn."

"Yeah, it changed his world view, all right," Hannibal agreed. "But check this out. When she went at him, she held the knife wide, like this, and swung in on him to slash him." Hannibal mimed her actions with the table knife.

"Yeah, that's what I've seen as a bouncer," Sarge said, nodding. "When women get mad they swing at you like that, or backhand, the same way, to get more force." He glanced quickly toward the kitchen to make sure no female ears were tuned to him. Then with his voice lowered he said, "When a woman hates you, she doesn't want to kill you. She wants to hurt you. There's a big difference."

Hannibal nodded, smiling. "Right. That's what I figured. So I thought, got to be a man. But men I've seen in fights generally go for the gut. I mean, who stabs at the throat? You've seen a lot more knife fights than I have in bars and such. How do you get a wound like that?"

Sarge held out a hand and Hannibal surrendered the little knife. Sarge stood facing him and tried a couple of tentative moves toward Hannibal. Then he stopped to think. "Do I have to be facing you?"

That raised one of Hannibal's eyebrows. "Hm. I guess not."

Sarge stepped quickly toward Hannibal but to his right. Sarge's left arm looped quickly around Hannibal's throat as

Sarge stepped around him. The knife in his right fist moved to a position just an inch away from Hannibal's throat. Then he froze and loosened his grip enough for Hannibal to look down.

"Yow," Hannibal said, bent backward by the shorter man's grip. "Yep, that would do it all right."

"That's the way they taught me to take out a sentry in the corps," Sarge said, relaxing and releasing his friend.

Hannibal rolled his shoulders forward. "Sure. Should have been obvious to everyone. Not just a man, but a man who's had military training. He stepped in silently after the argument, but before Francis came in. One quick strike and out. Maybe Dean wasn't so far off after all."

"I'm not sure what all that means," Sarge said, "except I'm pretty sure it means a busy day for you."

"You got that right," Hannibal said, sliding the police photos back into their envelope. "I need to see the man who might be able to tell me where Joan Kitteridge ran off to. I have to return an item to the most recent murder victim's mother. And I guess I need to know a lot more about Joan's ex-husband. I can think of two people who might be able to tell me about him. I'll question one, and I think I can get Cindy to talk to the other."

*   *   *

Each time Hannibal pulled into the Kitteridge driveway, his tension level was a little bit higher. This time he arrived intending to be downright confrontational, and that did not feel good to him. Langford Kitteridge was certainly spry and energetic, but he was still a lonely old man, whose only family was missing and presumed in hiding.

Again Hannibal rang the doorbell in his working suit and tie, glasses and gloves. This time when the door to the big colonial swung open, Langford looked at Hannibal with both familiarity and hopefulness. His face seemed even more deeply lined than before, worry pulling the skin of his face downward.

"Mr. Jones! Please come in. Do you have word of my niece?"

Hannibal stepped inside, but stopped in the cavernous living room in front of the long black leather sofa. "No sir, I haven't been able to turn up anything. I was hoping you could give me some more information that might help."

"Yes, yes. Anything." Langford waved Hannibal down into the couch and lowered himself into the one opposite. They faced each other over the top of a wide glass-topped coffee table. Track lighting softened the older man's face, but not enough to make Hannibal's job any easier.

"Sir, I don't know if Joan is in trouble or not. But if you haven't heard from her in all this time she might be. And if she is, I think it could be some trouble returning from her past. Specifically, trouble being caused by her ex-husband." Not a lie exactly, Hannibal thought. In fact, it could well turn out to be one interpretation of the truth. He watched Langford closely, following his white bushy eyebrows as they rose and lowered.

"I told you, Mr. Jones, Joanie has never been married."

Hannibal sighed. "Yes sir, you did tell me that. But now I know that was a lie. And I was hoping, with her safety in question, you might be willing to now tell me the truth. I think it must have been when she was very young, and I think he must have been a military man."

It happened almost too quickly to follow. The color drained out of Langford's face, then rushed back up into it. He turned away, and his eyes focused on some imaginary spot in the distance. A grandfather clock ticked somewhere in the house, and Hannibal imagined the sound was connected to Langford's mind grinding away. Hannibal reminded himself that Joan Kitteridge had probably learned her calculating ways at this old man's knee. But when Langford turned back to Hannibal, his face was clear and relaxed again. His eyes were hooded, but Hannibal knew that shame could cause that in men old enough to still occasionally feel it.

"She was barely eighteen," Langford said softly. "Had no interest in listening to the old man. Just took off to be with this fellow. I still don't know what the attraction was. For her, anyway. Anybody could see the attraction for him, eh? But it didn't last long. He treated her poorly and she soon understood her mistake."

Hannibal tried to buoy the mood with a small smile. "Young people make mistakes. But sometimes the mistakes don't go away as quickly or as permanently as we think. What can you tell me about the boy?"

"Nothing really," Langford said. "I never cared to know anything about him. Except as you say, he was a soldier."

"All right," Hannibal said. "I guess that's no surprise. How about a description? Can you tell me what he looked like?"

"Back then?" Langford's eyes turned up as he called his memory into play. "Well, let's see. I seem to recall a handsome man, a tall man, on the slim side but well muscled, as a soldier would be. Dark brown hair and eyes. High cheekbones. Not a dark complexion but well tanned I'd say."

"You've a good memory, Mr. Kitteridge," Hannibal said. "It almost sounds like someone I know."

*   *   *

The address was neither hard to find nor a surprise. Standing on the roof of Mark Norton's condominium complex Hannibal could have thrown a football with a reasonable expectation of hitting the building he worked in before the ball hit the ground. He parked his Volvo in the only unmarked space he could find. Almost as an afterthought he grabbed Oscar's yearbook, thinking it might make a useful prop when questioning Mark. Once inside, Hannibal called for an elevator. Mark lived on the 11th floor and just as Hannibal touched that button in the elevator his telephone hummed at him.

"Hannibal? It's Cindy."

Even on the worst of days, it brightened his heart to hear her voice. "I know who it is sweetheart. Have you talked to Francis? What did she think of Dean's theory?

"Well she was sure glad to know her son doesn't think she's a murderer," Cindy said. "But his basic idea is all wrong. She says she didn't know that Joan was married and never met or talked to her husband. She couldn't have told him about her husband and his wife, and she says she wouldn't have told him anyway."

"So Dean's out of the guilt trip area," Hannibal nodded as the elevator smoothly raised him into vertical space. "No way he can be responsible for either of the killings, even by proxy."

"Yes, but where does that leave you for a suspect?"

"I still like the ex-husband," Hannibal said in front of Mark's door. "And I have to say Joan's tastes seem to be consistent. The description of her husband sounds an awful lot like the guy behind this door I'm knocking on right now. Better talk to you later, babe."

Mark Norton answered the door in jeans, tee shirt and white socks. One small lick of his hair stuck up defiantly from the back and he hadn't shaved. He clearly was not on his way anywhere today. Hannibal smiled his small menacing smile and stepped past him into the great room, which reminded Hannibal of Walt Young's place.

"Okay Mark, let's not dance around. Where's Joan?"

Mark didn't bother with bravado. He closed the door and headed for the kitchen area as if Hannibal was an invited guest. "She's not here. Look around if you like. Drink?"

"No thanks," Hannibal said, "but you go ahead." He waited for Mark to gulp down half a bloody mary so that he could have his attention again. "She seems to take off quite a bit, unannounced. You should keep better tabs on your wife."

Mark's answer was a slight surprise. "Joan isn't the type of cat you put a bell on, Mr. Jones."

"So I've learned," Hannibal said. "She's been really hard for her uncle to keep track of. He hasn't seen her in days. And he has no idea she's married you know. How'd you manage to keep such a secret over so many months? And why?"

"So many what? Boy are you confused. We've only been married for two weeks. How about some fruit juice?"

This time Hannibal nodded and moved over to take a seat on one of the stools in front of the counter, keenly aware that his position was now the reverse of what it was when he chatted with Francis Edwards in Walt Young's condo. He decided that he didn't need to play hardball to get answers here. Mark clearly wanted to keep this friendly, and that was fine with Hannibal.

"So, you weren't married when you spent the summer together in Vegas?"

Mark handed over a glass of chilled apple juice. "Now you're fishing, buddy. I've never been to Las Vegas before the day you saw me in the hotel room, and Joanie spent the summer in Australia."

Hannibal sipped his juice and watched Mark's face closely. Leaning on the counter he was completely relaxed, his mind not really centered on the conversation. If he was lying, he was a pro. On the other hand, he might simply feel safe standing behind the truth. That would make him just about the only innocent in this case.

"Yeah, that's what her uncle thought too. Now don't tell me. She e-mailed you every day, right?"

Mark adopted a smug smile and pulled open a kitchen drawer. "Yeah, she did, as a matter of fact. But of course, e-mails can come from anyplace. You'll be more interested in these postmarks."

With the flourish of a stage magician, Mark flipped his wrist and laid a fan of post cards on the counter in front of Hannibal. And like the mark at a carnival, Hannibal spread the postcards out with one hand, pictures toward himself, considering which one to pick out. Except this time he knew it was the magician who had been fooled. There was no longer an ounce of doubt in his mind that Mark had been dodged as easily as Langford Kitteridge had.

Hannibal soon found the card he wanted. Its glossy cover featured a picture of the Sydney Opera House. "Ah, this one's from August 12th," he said blandly. Mark's brows knit as Hannibal raised the card and held it at arm's length with the picture toward himself. He looked over the edge of the card at Mark's now startled face "Didn't stay for an opera today," Hannibal said, as if reading right through the card, "but it was well worth stopping just to see this place. Love you always, your Joanie. Right?"

Mark snatched the postcard out of Hannibal's hand. "How the hell did you do that?" "Sorry, pal," Hannibal said. "She sent the same card to her uncle. On the same day. With the exact same message. But none of that changes the fact that court records show she was in Las Vegas at the time getting a divorce."

"Divorce?" Mark quickly built another bloody mary while he talked. "How can that be? I mean, Joan wasn't married before."

Hannibal enjoyed the sweet aroma of his apple juice before draining the glass. "Don't feel bad. Her uncle missed her getting married twice. I figure she got somebody to send her the postcards from Australia, filled them all out, and sent them back."

Mark swallowed most of his new drink and walked around to the couch. He stood for a while, as if he wasn't sure sitting down was safe. "That would be an awfully elaborate ruse, don't you think? Just to keep me from knowing she was married before? Besides, she doesn't have any friends in Australia."

"Well, maybe a professional contact, or a business associate." Hannibal said, then froze in place staring right past Mark. The word professional had done it. A memory jumped into his mind. The only papers he found in Oscar's bedroom were airline ticket stubs, neatly folded in the table beside his bed. In the last year, he'd flown to Canada, Japan, Russia and yes, Australia.

Hannibal lifted the yearbook onto the counter and stared down at it. "Oscar Peters was there," he said. "Oscar, her employee. She knew him when he was just a kid, way back in Germany."

"Really?" Mark moved back into the kitchen and reached for the refrigerator, but his attention was drawn by the book Hannibal had just put down.

"Yeah, they went back that far. He did this for her, to deceive both you and her uncle about her having been married previously." Hannibal opened the book and began slowly flipping the pages.

"Do you really think that was a secret worth killing for?" Mark asked, sounding uncertain for the first time. "Could she have done such a thing?"

Hannibal kept the pages turning slowly, staring down at a time most of us remember as being more innocent. "He was a real person Mark. A human being, with a past, and hopes and dreams just like the rest of us. It's hard to avoid the fact that Joan is connected with his death." Then he looked up. "Where is she, Mark?"

Hannibal turned the book upside down and Mark stared down into it as hypnotized by the moving pages. Learning so much so quickly about his new bride had drained all the fight out of him. "I heard her say something about going to see Gil Donner today."

Hannibal turned the book back around to face himself. "Wonder how she knows Gil," he said. "Any ideas?" He had fanned past the general crowd scenes and club photos to the glamorously posed senior class photos. Right that minute he hated the world that turned some of those winsome faces into selfish, hate filled or dangerous people. Then his hand fell flat onto the page just under one of the pictures and he drew in a long, deep breath. She was very lovely back then, and now he knew her deep, blood tinged auburn hair was natural. Her skin was still as creamy and clear as it had been in high school, and her eyes were just as dark. As she looked up from the page at him his mind pulled the scattered threads of the case more tightly together around her.

"It would seem that Joan and Oscar go back even farther than I suspected."

-30-

Within fifteen minutes Hannibal was turning off Route One into the hotel and office mini suburb just north of Alexandria called Crystal City. On the way, he had called Cindy to let her know he had the case all figured out. While pulling into the access road behind the Courtyard Marriott, he mentally walked through the likely scenarios of meeting Gil, Emma and Joan together. He tried to predict who would say what, how each would react, and how he could best separate Emma from the other two. He was convinced that Gil and Joan were conspirators involved in the three connected murders. Emma, he thought, was an innocent and he needed to separate her from the rest.

He grabbed the yearbook, dropped change into the meter at the curb and walked around to the front of the hotel. He spotted Ray parked a few yards away. At least no one would go in or out unobserved.

Hannibal brushed past the uniformed doorman into the chrome and steel lobby, complete with conversation groups reminiscent of the gathering of faux living rooms one finds in large furniture stores. The elevators rose up transparent columns on the other side of the lobby, and he stalked purposefully toward them. He had a plan, but just before he reached the elevators, his plan was short-circuited by a woman calling his name.

He spun to see Emma Peters on the nearest sofa. Her soft features beamed at him as if he were a long lost family member. The woman was woefully short of family, he thought, and he couldn't simply walk past her even if he wanted to. Working to raise a smile, he went to her and sat opposite her on the facing couch. For a moment, it was as if he was visiting her in her own living room.

"Mrs. Peters, you're looking well today. But why are you sitting out here in the lobby?"

She touched her bluish hair and Hannibal thought she might be a little embarrassed. "I was here visiting an old acquaintance, but he has company right now."

Hannibal thought it time to cut through some of the smoke screen. "You're here with Gil Donner, ma'am," he said. "You know him because years ago he was Provost Marshall in Berlin and your husband's boss. His visitor is Joan Kitteridge. I now know that she knew your son back in high school." He laid the yearbook on the glass table that separated them. Emma recognized it immediately.

"Where did you find this?" she asked, laying her gnarled hand on the cover as if it were her son's body. "Did you take it from Oscar's home?"

"Actually, your husband gave it to me when I went to Germany," Hannibal said. "I should have given it to you right away, but I thought..."

He wasn't sure how to finish that sentence so she finished it for him. "You thought I'd want to know why Foster would part with it. That was kind of you, but I wouldn't be surprised if you fished it out of our trash. Foster can be a cold man."

Hannibal reached forward to touch a bookmark sticking out just a bit at the top of the book. Emma moved her hand and he opened the yearbook to the designated page. The room was dominated by the sounds of people rushing more than they needed to on their way to their next destination. Over that noise he heard Emma's small gasp.

"Yes, this is the woman upstairs," Hannibal said softly. "Joan Kitteridge. She went to school with Oscar. More recently, she was his boss, at her own software company."

"His boss. Her company." Emma spat out the words. "I knew that little tramp when she was young and dirt poor. Oscar even brought her home once or twice for a meal."

"But then she married young, didn't she?" Hannibal asked.

Emma's face reddened, making a sharp contrast to her blue tinted hair. "In Germany," she said. "She was with him before she was even out of high school. But I understand he died in a training accident."

Hannibal reached out to take the old woman's right hand in both of his own. The hand was cold, but the veins on its back were a road map of the long and twisted trail he had taken through life. There were secrets buried so deep she could barely see them. He thought now was the time to dig them out.

"Mrs. Peters, I need for you to tell me what it is that ties Joan and her ex-husband to your husband and to Gil Donner. What connects them."

Emma released one loud sob and a tidal wave of tears spilled out of her eyes. She faced downward, her sorrow splashing onto Joan Kitteridge's teenage face. "The murder," she said.

Hannibal looked around but none of the travelers stopped to ask about, or even seemed to notice the old woman sobbing in the lobby. Still, he leaned closer to make it clear he was comforting her, and offered her his handkerchief. He couldn't see how Gil Donner or Foster Peters figured in the death of Grant Edwards or Oscar's more recent murder. One possibility remained. "Do you mean Carla Donner?"

Emma nodded, holding the handkerchief to her nose. "Foster covered it all up to protect them. Oh, God, he covered up the murder and somehow, Oscar always suspected. He knew his father had done something wrong. That suspicion drove them apart."

"You said protect them? The murderer and..."

"Gil," she said, forcing words through her crying. "He was afraid if there was a real investigation everyone would know..." Hannibal waited for her to regain her breath. "They'd know she was with another man."

Hannibal was rubbing her hand now, feeling her shake. "And somehow Joan knew about all this?"

This time when Emma's head started nodding it didn't stop. "She must have known. Her husband was having an affair with Carla."

-31 -

Hannibal stopped at the hotel room door to add to his tally of victims. While Foster Peters lived with his own actions, his wife Emma felt such guilt about his actions that it had eaten her alive from the inside out for perhaps twelve years. Hannibal had called Ray inside to keep an eye on Emma while he went upstairs to face the conspirators who were almost certainly working at getting their stories straight in case of trouble. He had just raised his hand to knock when the door opened inward and Joan almost walked into him.

"Where you headed, girl?" Hannibal asked, planting a gloved palm in the center of her chest and shoving her back inside. "This is where it gets interesting."

As Joan fell against the bed Hannibal took the room in at a glance. Donner had decorated his space to look like home. A five or six inch statuette of an infantryman stood guard on the low chest of drawers. What looked like a class photo of men in uniform stood in the center of the round table by the window. Between that table and Hannibal, Gil Donner stood at the writing desk holding the telephone to his ear. As Hannibal stepped past the bathroom door on his left Donner slowly lowered the phone back into its cradle.

"What the hell are you doing here?" Donner asked.

"Giving you a chance to confess and maybe lighten your sentence."

"I have done nothing," Donner said, taking one step forward.

Hannibal pulled his automatic from under his right arm and pointed it at Donner's right knee. "Nothing except perhaps destroying evidence and certainly falsifying reports. Maybe you're just guilty of being a bad cop. Or isn't a provost marshal considered a cop?"

Donner and Joan exchanged a look that seemed more desperate than Hannibal would have expected. Joan sat up on the bed, looking more like a woman than an executive for the first time in Hannibal's experience.

"You don't understand," she said plaintively. "You can't keep me here."

"Then why don't you make me understand," Hannibal said. "While we're waiting here for the police to show up, make me understand why you covered for your ex-husband when he killed Grant Edwards."

Frozen in place, Donner stammered one word. "How?"

"And I'd really like to know why you covered for him when he murdered your wife," Hannibal said, leaning against the wall. He was enjoying the stunned reactions of his two-person audience. "I do think I get why Oscar had to die, but it all goes back to your wife, doesn't it Gil?"

"You can't think Kyle Brooks killed Oscar Peters," Donner said. "He died in a training accident years ago."

"Please," Hannibal said, waving Donner into a chair. "If the man was dead, Joanie here wouldn't have had to sneak off to Las Vegas to get a divorce before she could marry Mark Norton."

"Even if you were right," Joan said, "why would a man I was married to kill Oscar?"

Hannibal pointed Joan to the other side of the bed where she sat very close to Donner. "I figure it this way. Stop me if I go wrong, now. You, Joan, were a witness to Carla Donner's murder. Either that or your hubby came home and told you he did her in. He was sleeping with her in that little second flat the Donners kept for entertaining their extra curricular friends. In any case, you told your good friend Oscar, didn't you?"

"She caught us up there," Joan blurted out.

"Quiet," Donner said. "Don't tell this jerk anything."

Hannibal sat on the low chest of drawers shaking his head. "You and him. Only you weren't married yet. In fact, you were probably underage. Okay, Carla goes to her little hideaway and finds her boyfriend going at it with a high school kid. She flips out. Attacks him. He defends himself a little too robustly and kills her. How am I doing so far?"

"This is silly," Donner said, hands held wide. "Remember this is my wife we're talking about."

"Yes, and I can't figure yet why you would help cover up her murder," Hannibal said. "Joan I understand. He married her, so her testimony would be inadmissible. But that didn't last too long. They moved to the States, she dropped her married name and went back to living with her uncle. You have been a handful for him, haven't you?"

Again Joan and Donner exchanged significant looks. Joan opened her mouth to speak, but Donner cut her off. "His theories only work if all the killings were done by one man, and your husband, Kyle Brooks, died in a training accident in Germany."

"It just doesn't wash, Donner," Hannibal said. "If her ex really had nothing to do with Grant Edwards' death, why were you asking Walt Young about it?" Donner was still cool, but Hannibal could smell Joan's fear. He kept talking, hoping she would fill in whatever pieces were missing. "I figure Grant was murder number two. Brooks slipped into the house just before Francis got there and stabbed him with a bayonet, then slipped out to let Francis take the rap. You see, Joan had moved on to Grant, and our ghost was jealous."

"But jealousy can't be a motive for the final murder," Joan protested. "I was never intimate with Oscar Peters."

"Oh, no, but he had to die, didn't he?" Hannibal asked. "After all, he was blackmailing you wasn't he? I'm thinking when he and Dean put their heads together, he found out about your connection to Grant Edwards' murder. That led him to suspect that your ex-husband was still alive. And that made you a blackmail target. And that made him a target for your murderous ex."

Donner shook his head, but that didn't hide the tiny beads of sweat beginning to appear on his forehcad. "This really is a pretty fanciful group of conjectures, don't you think?"

"What if everything you say is true?" Joan said, her eyes cutting toward the door. "There's still no reason to hold me. I haven't committed any crime. And I really must be going."

For a moment Joan assumed the icy confidence Hannibal was accustomed to. She stood, smoothed down her skirt and moved as if she would walk past Hannibal and out the door. Hannibal pulled his gun in beside his waist and cocked his right fist.

"Him I'll shoot if I have to," Hannibal said. "You I'd just knock down. Remember my job is to save Dean Edwards, and nothing bad happened to him until you moved the knife."

"What?" Donner stared at Joan, as if waiting for her to explain.

"Nobody else went into Dean's apartment over your garage who was in any way connected to the murders. No one was there after Oscar's death who didn't belong there. Somebody would have noticed a strange man lurking around. So you're the only one who could have hidden the murder weapon in Dean's place. You implicated him."

"No!" Joan said, still on her feet. "I like Dean. And you have got to let me go before another man close to me is hurt."

"Another?" Hannibal's mouth dropped open when it came to him. He had been so focused on reconstructing events of the past that he completely forgot about the present. The first killing might have been accidental, and the last may have been to protect old secrets, but the second, Grant Edwards' murder, had surely been about jealousy. He looked up at Joan to find her again staring past him toward the door. She wanted out, and he suddenly realized why.

"Mark," was all he had time to say before the impact to his lower back sent him sprawling across the room. His right arm hit the writing table and his left hit the bed, leaving no way to reduce the impact when his face thumped into the floor. Through the haze of semi-consciousness he could hear Joan's heels clicking out of the room.

-32-

Hannibal felt the gun being pulled from his left hand and braced for the bullet that did not come. Instead he took one hard kick to his midsection. Hannibal felt he deserved it for unforgivable carelessness. Very slowly he turned onto his right side to scan his surroundings.

The cheap carpeting scraped his face when he landed. His breath rasped in his throat. Pain shot up his spine as he moved, but he faced his situation stoically. His sunglasses had flown from his face so he had a very clear view of Cook, Donner's blonde haired escort from the German bar. The man looked even taller standing above Hannibal, pointing Hannibal's own Sig Sauer down at him. He craned his head to find Donner, above and behind him, sitting calmly at the round table, legs crossed, smoking a cigarette.

"Well, this is a spot to be in, eh?" Donner said with a faint smile. His hard blue eyes pushed to a squint. "I am fortunate of course, that Cook returned from his errand when he did. Of course, had he found what he was looking for, this would all be over now."

"I take it Joan's on her way to warn Mark at last?" Hannibal said. "You should have sent Cook with her. In her ex-husband's mind, she's betrayed him. She won't be able to stop him."

Donner smiled, his chin pushing down into the rolls of skin and fat below it. "I think her position is stronger than yours. Policemen will soon be here, yes? And they will find an elite soldier, a ranger, and a veteran visiting from Germany who have been attacked in their hotel room."

"They know your hostage is involved in a murder investigation," Hannibal said as calmly as he could. "And they know that you, Donner, are a part of that investigation."

"Will that justify the private detective pulling a gun on us in our own hotel room without any hard evidence that we were involved in any wrongdoing? Even a policeman would not have been able to walk in here uninvited without a warrant and point a loaded gun at me. Tell me, who are they more likely to believe? You or me?"

From the hall a voice said, "Won't matter what you say."

Hannibal's head spun. First his eyes fixed again on his gun. Then he looked past it to Ray standing in the doorway. The gun began to swing away as Cook's face turned toward Ray. This idiot would kill his friend without a second thought. Hannibal hooked his right foot behind Cook's. Then with a grunt he stamped out with his left. His heel smacked into the side of Cook's knee. There was a subtle snapping sound like a small twig stepped on in the woods.

Cook's mouth dropped open and he made a gasping noise as he went down. Ray hopped forward to stamp down on Cook's wrist, holding the gun down. He reached down to recover the weapon.

Donner leaped from his chair and swung a booted foot forward. Hannibal's legs were tangled up with Cook's, limiting his movement. He barely avoided the main thrust of the kick. The heel grazed his head, but despite the flash of pain, he grasped the heel flying past and pushed hard. Caught off balance, Donner fell backward into the round table. Spurred by his rising anger, Hannibal managed to get to his feet just about when Donner did. The older man cocked back a fist, then seemed to reconsider.

"Please," Hannibal said, leaning back against the low chest of drawers. "Please try."

Donner looked past Hannibal to Ray, who lowered the gun to his side and shrugged his shoulders. Donner looked away, as if he were planning to sit. Then without warning he whipped his fist up, leaning with all his power into a right cross aimed at Hannibal's jaw.

Hannibal's left hand slapped the punch inward. Donner may have even seen Hannibal smile as his gloved right fist slammed up and forward into Donner's midsection. His fist seemed to sink to its wrist in that soft belly, and the air burst out of Donner like the cork from a champagne bottle.

Donner crumpled forward. Hannibal seized his jacket lapels with both hands and swung him around, trying to sit him on the low chest of drawers, but Donner's knees were rubber bands now and he slumped on to the floor.

In that one brief instant, Hannibal had a gut-wrenching picture of the present superimposed against the past. Just behind and to the right of Donner's face was his West Point class photo.

Hannibal recognized Donner in his sharp, crisp uniform primarily by his eyes, the same hard deep blue marbles in the live face beside the photo. But the old picture showed a hard body and a Spartan face with deep cleft cheekbones and a dimple in the chin. Nothing like the sagging cheeks and double chin Hannibal faced in present day real life. What a waste, he thought. Then his eyes were drawn to the man standing beside Donner in the photo. Hannibal's jaw dropped an inch as he matched the photograph to a verbal description he had heard not long ago. This man was taller than Donner, handsome and on the slim side. But beneath that military jacket one could see he was muscular. Dark brown hair and eyes. High cheekbones. Well tanned.

"I'll be damned," Hannibal said. "You went to the academy with him, didn't you?"

Hannibal dropped Donner and grabbed up the photo, searching the lettering beneath the photo for the name.

Seated on the floor, the dazed Donner mumbled, "You won't stop the General. He's too much for you, too much for any man."

"The general?" Hannibal asked. "I get it. The man was your commander I bet, as well as your classmate. But would that cause a man to share his wife and even cover up her murder?" Then Hannibal glanced at those hard blue eyes for a moment, eyes that were beginning to go misty. "Yes, I suppose you would. You'd do anything to protect this man you revered, this general...."

Hannibal hesitated as he searched the names at the bottom of the photo, but when he found Kyle Brooks he was a short, pale, blond-haired blue eyed man. The photo matching the description of Joan's husband went with a different name.

"Oh Jesus," Hannibal said, sucking in a sharp breath. "General Langford Kitteridge."

-33-

When Hannibal turned to rush out of the room he stepped into a cloud of blue uniforms. The police had finally arrived and their first act was to relieve Ray of the pistol he was holding. The incoming wave of police momentarily pressed Hannibal back into the room, until he spotted a familiar face at the back of the crowd.

"Thompson," Hannibal called. "Let me out of here. I need to talk to you now, to prevent another killing."

Stan Thompson waved and the uniformed officers parted to let Hannibal through. In the hall he looked into Thompson's impassive face and realized he had way too much to say and not nearly enough time to say it.

"Look, I'm glad you're here," Hannibal began. "I know what happened now, and I know why. You can get almost the whole story out of the older man in there, Gil Donner. His wife was our killer's first victim, even before Grant Edwards. But right now, he's on his way to scratch vic number four. I need a police escort to get to the scene with lights and sirens or else we'll be too late."

Thompson maintained his bored expression. "You'll have to give me a hell of a lot more than that before I send a car off with you to parts unknown, Jones."

"You don't understand," Hannibal snapped. "There's no time. We may already be too late. And I can't stand here and debate it with you. You don't want to send a car, fine. Then tell them to watch out for the Volvo doing a hundred miles an hour toward Falls Church."

Behind him, Hannibal heard Thompson shout "Halt!" but the sound faded quickly as he dived into the stairwell. Seconds later he burst into the lobby at a dead run. Sprinting across the floor he almost crashed into Irma Andrews at the door. Instead he grabbed her arm and continued out. Despite the surprise on her face, Irma ran with him as best she could.

"Get in my car if you want the whole story," Hannibal told her, panting as he ran. "The police might be after us, but if they don't stop us, you'll get the full story you started on with Dean Edwards at the end of this ride, one way or the other."

Hannibal rammed his car into gear and pulled away from the curb before Irma quite had her seat belt on. He drove south on Route One as fast as the traffic would allow. He knew Mark Norton's place was not far away, but this could well be the longest five miles of his life. Hannibal's senses were turned up to maximum sensitivity and his passenger had the good sense to sit quietly and grit her teeth. He swung right onto Glebe road dodging from one lane to another to gain every possible second's advantage. He raced through one red light a second after it turned, before cross traffic could fill the intersection. Finally he roared with squealing tires up the ramp onto I-395 where he could really open up his engine.

"Are we rushing to capture the murderer?" Irma asked.

"That and prevent another killing," Hannibal said. "What were you doing at the Courtyard, anyway?"

"When I heard on the scanner that you called the police I figured it might have to do with my story."

"If we're in time, this will be the end of it," Hannibal said, swerving to pass a slow moving SUV on the right. "Oscar Peters was this murderer's third victim, and all of the killings revolve around Joan Kitteridge. She'll be there when we get there I think."

"Well then, let me call a camera crew," Irma said, pulling out her cell phone. "Maybe we can get some arrest footage."

Hannibal left the highway for King street, amazed that no police car had spotted him. A handful of seconds later, he slowed to well below the speed limit and pulled to the right hand lane.

"What happened to our hurry?" Irma asked. "Don't we need to head off the murderer?"   "Actually, we almost overtook him," Hannibal said. "Three cars up." He pointed ahead at the low slung midnight blue Lexus they had almost passed. Its license plate read KITYCAR1.

Hannibal hung back as the Lexus turned into the parking lot. He parked on the opposite side of the lot, four cars away from the little red Corvette with the KITTYCAR license plates. He slouched low as the driver of the Lexus got out of his car and headed for the building.

"This is the killer?" Irma asked, skepticism dripping from her voice. Hannibal understood her disbelief. Despite the energy in his step, the gray headed man in Dockers and a corduroy blazer still had to be in his sixties. As he entered the door, Hannibal slid out of his driver's seat.

"We follow at a discreet distance," Hannibal said. "Meanwhile, call the police and tell them you've witnessed an assault at this address in number 604."

In the elevator, Irma asked, "Isn't this dangerous? What if he kills his victim before we get there?"

"Not much chance of that," Hannibal said. "Not with her standing there. In fact, I think he'll be stuck for just what to do."

Standing outside Mark Norton's door, Hannibal felt no such hesitation or confusion. He had determined that enough people had been hurt in the last fifteen years and that it would stop here. Driven more by his own desire for closure than a need for justice, he tried the door. The knob turned in his hand and he stepped inside.

The tableau that greeted him was not quite what he expected. Mark Norton sat on the sofa, beside two suitcases. Langford Kitteridge sat on one of the stools at the breakfast bar. Joan Kitteridge stood in front of the glass doors leading to the balcony. Her eyes widened as Hannibal walked in, her jaw dropped open and she actually stuttered out her first few words.

"Mr. Jones, what are you doing here?"

"Surprised to see me alive, Joan?" Hannibal asked, waving Irma to the couch. She sat and pulled a reporter's notebook out of her bag.

"You're becoming a nuisance," Langford said over his shoulder. "I think you should go."

Hannibal closed the door behind himself and stood between it and the rest of the room's occupants. "I don't think so. Not until I'm sure Mark here knows what he's getting into being involved with Joan. After that he can make a bad choice with his eyes open if he likes."

Mark smirked arrogantly. "We've just told Mr. Kitteridge about our marriage, Jones, and she's explained about her earlier matrimonial mistake. Now what do you think you can tell me about her I don't know?"

Hannibal looked not at Mark but rather into Langford's deeply cleft face when he answered. "Well I wonder if she told you she was an eyewitness to the first murder Langford here committed. And I don't think she told you that he came over today intending to kill you. He would have too, if Joan hadn't gotten here first. Guess you two were packing to escape, eh Joan?"

In all that, Mark had only captured one word. "Murder?" he repeated.

"Yep. He'd do anything to keep Joan for himself."

"Wait a minute," Irma said, scribbling wildly. "Isn't this her uncle?"

"God, I hope not," Hannibal said. "Because they've been lovers since before Joan was of legal age. And when she did reach legal age, they were married. Mark, meet Joan's first husband. You aren't blood relatives, are you?" This last question Hannibal addressed to Langford.

"You're treading on dangerous territory," Langford said, slipping lightly to his feet. "We're not blood and, even if we maintained our privacy, there was nothing illegal or even illicit about our marriage."

"Well, you've always seen the morality thing in shades of gray, haven't you. Langford?" Hannibal asked. "Before you met Joan, you were sleeping with the wife of your good friend Gil Donner."

Langford reddened. "I never sneaked behind his back. Gil and Carla had an open relationship."

"That appears to be true," Hannibal said. "They even had a little love nest apartment where they met their outside interests.

Funny, you'd have expected Carla to be a better sport, about sharing, I mean."

"Okay, I'm lost," Mark said, standing up. "What has all this to do with a murder?"

Hannibal looked at Joan, giving her a chance to speak. She silently shook her head, so Hannibal continued. "As it turns out, Langford here reached the rank of general in the Army over there in Berlin. Having an underage girlfriend would have derailed that career for sure, but he had a safe place to take her. Gil Donner's little love nest. The way I see it, Carla must have caught you two up there, doing the nasty. I don't understand how she could justify being jealous, but I don't think she reacted well. Otherwise, Langford wouldn't have killed her."

All eyes turned to Langford. His eyes cast toward the carpet. "It was an accident."

"Maybe," Hannibal allowed. "But if she was planning to leave Gil for you, she'd have been a terrible security risk after she found out you liked them younger. In any case, she ended up dead, and again a connection to you would have ended your precious career. So you set her up to look like a suicide. Then you convinced your subordinate, Gil Donner, the Provost Marshall, to limit the investigation."

"She was already dead," Langford said, taking a step toward Hannibal. "There was nothing to be gained by exposing my mistake."

"Yes, and Donner was in no hurry to expose his lifestyle. The two of you decided nothing you did would hurt her anymore, but you didn't seem to notice or care about ruining the life of a good MP named Foster Peters. No biggie, right? One thing you learned in your early career in Vietnam was, every enemy action creates a certain amount of acceptable collateral damage."

Mark stepped closer to Joan, hands held wide. "Is this true, baby? You saw him kill a woman? And then you, you married him?" Joan nodded slowly, but could not produce any words.

"Well they wanted to stay together, but now they had no place to go," Hannibal said. "And I think maybe old Langford here was really in love with her. So he took her in, and made up the dead brother story to make it acceptable for her to be in his home.

228

Then, to tie her to him better, he married her. I don't think he knew at the time that Foster Peters' son, Oscar, was one of her young admirers. Did you let it slip that Carla Donner's death was suspicious, Joan?"

"I thought he knew," Joan said, shaking her head. "After all, his father was the investigating officer. I guess I did say too much before I realized he was ignorant."

Hannibal continued, watching Langford's eyes, seeing trouble in them. "Pretty soon after that you moved back to the States, right? I'm guessing here, but I figure the general here got posted to the Pentagon for his last assignment. Were you already looking for a younger man then, Joan?"

Langford dropped to his feet, more lightly than one would expect for a man his age. "Joan would never consider leaving me," He said in a low, deep voice.

Hannibal chuckled. "Please. The age difference and your overwhelming control of her were tearing her apart. You put her in therapy with Dr. Roberts. But it didn't do what you wanted it to, did it? He encouraged her to find someone nearer her own age. Then she met Grant Edwards and got the hots for him."

"He tried to steal my Joan!" Langford bellowed. The women gasped loudly as he pulled a large knife from under his jacket. He flipped into a reverse grip, the point toward his elbow, edge out. Hannibal recognized it as a Ka-bar, the fighting blade favored by Marines since World War II.

"And you killed him with a knife very much like this one," Hannibal said, holding his hands wide and backing away slowly. "When you found out about him and Joan, you started following her. You heard them arguing. As soon as she left, you went to the door. He let you in but he didn't know why you were there. Did he turn his back to you or did you slip around behind him to drive the knife into his throat?"

"He didn't deserve her," Langford said. "He couldn't fight for her."

"Yeah well we don't need to either," Hannibal said, reaching for his holster before he remembered that the police took his gun back at Donner's hotel room.

"No gun?" Langford asked. "Well, I guess you can't stop me. And anyway, Edwards was an adulterer who deserved to die."

Hannibal stepped back in front of the door. "Maybe. But I think he was waiting for his wife to try to work it out that night. That's why he and Joan argued. She showed up soon after you left and found him dead. Did she deserve to spend a decade in jail? Did her son deserve to have his brain warped by the experience? More collateral damage, general. I can't let you leave."

"Then stop me." Langford swung his blade forward, slashing at Hannibal's stomach. Hannibal slammed backward against the door to avoid the attack. There seemed no space for him to dodge a second lunge without moving from the door. Fire in Langford Kitteridge's eyes said he was prepared to kill again to escape.

Mark Norton seemed to awaken from a trance. He stepped forward, shouting. "You crazy old man. No wonder she wanted to get away from you." He lifted a barstool above his head, preparing to swing it like a club at Langford.

"No!" Joan shouted. "Don't hurt him."

Langford swung toward Mark viciously. "You tried to steal her too."

"You moron, he never suspected you had her," Hannibal said. "Just as you never suspected she went to Las Vegas last summer to get a divorce from you."

While Mark held Langford's focus, Hannibal reached out for his right hand but the older man spun back around faster than anyone in the room thought possible. Hannibal hissed as the heavy blade slashed through his jacket. He felt a burning flash of pain as he leaped aside. Joan screamed, and Langford darted through the door. Mark dropped the barstool and rushed to Hannibal's side.

"Are you all right?" Mark asked.

"Barely touched me," Hannibal replied. "Hurts like hell but I'm not really injured. Got to get after him."

Joan started for the door, but Mark grabbed her arm. "That's why you went to Vegas?" Mark asked. His face showed the kind of hurt little boys reflect when disappointed. "You didn't want me to know you'd ever been married to that old coot, so you lied to me and sneaked down there."

Hannibal shouldered past the couple into the hallway. Langford was nowhere in sight, but his options were limited. As he ran to the stairs, Hannibal wondered what kind of connections the old general had around the Beltway. With money and connections it was just possible he could disappear, maybe even get out of the country before anyone tracked him down. That thought drove him down the two flights of stairs, his side pulsing where the tip of a fighting knife had opened him over his right ribs.

Bursting through the lobby door, Hannibal almost allowed himself a smile. Langford was running toward his car but he had put the big knife away. A midnight blue Crown Victoria pulled into the parking lot, subtly blocking anyone from driving out. It was certainly an unmarked police car. But then, without breaking stride, Langford Kitteridge ran right past his own car.

"Damn," Hannibal muttered between clenched teeth. Leaning forward, he sprinted with all he had. By closing his mind to the pain in his side, he closed the distance quickly. A clumsy tackle brought Langford down under him.

A voice in the distance said, "Hey, what the hell? Leave that old man alone." Hannibal knew it had to be a cop, reacting to the present scene with no knowledge of the history. Not so crazy, he thought. Wasn't that why the most recent murder had nearly gone unsolved?

"Give it up," Hannibal said into the old man's ear. "I don't really want to hurt you."

Then shock overwhelmed Hannibal's mind. A solid punch into his injured ribs all but paralyzed him. Another rocked his head. With startling strength, Langford managed to roll Hannibal over. The knife looked bigger raised above his head, but Hannibal raised a hand to grasp Langford's wrist. The steady downward pressure seemed augmented by the power in Langford's eyes.

"A warrior doesn't ever give up, soldier," Langford said.

Another familiar voice said, "Drop the knife." Langford looked up to see Stan Thompson staring at him behind the front sights of his Glock automatic. "Put it down, old man."

Only then did Hannibal see the fear behind the warrior in Langford's eyes. It was that fear, the fear of aging, the fear of losing his edge that was the seed of this man's obsession for a girl barely out of junior high school, an obsession that had only grown as they both had aged. He had to own her, but in a very real way she owned him as well. And he had carried that obsession for all these years not even realizing how it was eating him alive from the inside out. The weight of that obsession was all Hannibal could see now, pressing the old man down on him. That was what he saw when he repeated Thompson's words, only quietly, for only the two of them to hear.

"General Kitteridge. Put it down."

The fight seemed to drain out of Langford's body and Hannibal heard the knife hit the pavement by his ear, point first, then clatter to the ground. Then the weight was lifted off Hannibal as two uniformed men took Langford's arms and raised him to his feet. While Thompson put his gun away, Hannibal stood up and dusted himself off. Only then did he notice the video camera fifty yards away. He smiled at Irma, standing beside the cameraman. Her crew had captured it all, and she had the story she deserved. Another debt paid, he thought. Despite the minor wounds he was more relaxed at that minute than he had been in a week. A long nightmare, reaching back a dozen years, seemed to finally be ending.

"You're probably wondering what's going on here." Hannibal said.

"We got enough out of that Donner guy back in the hotel to put a lot of it together. Can I take it you've got the rest of the story figured out?"

"I think so," Hannibal said. "You just need to get..." He stopped mid-sentence, looking around. He zoomed in on the red Corvette just as it was backing out of its parking space. A new burst of adrenaline flooded his system, shoving him across the parking lot. "Stop that car!" He shouted. "She's in there and she can't get away."

Behind Hannibal, Thompson made subtle hand signals, and another car pulled forward, blocking the Corvette's motion. When Hannibal reached the car he yanked the driver's door open, grabbed Joan Kitteridge's arm and snatched her out of the car. To her credit, she maintained her protective covering of anger and fear.

"Are you crazy?" Joan snapped. "You've just taken my uncle away, after he tried to kill my husband. Don't I deserve some peace?"

Mark got out of the other side of the car but stayed on that side. It told Hannibal all he needed to know about this shaky alliance.

"I see," Hannibal said. "You're going to play innocent. Did you think I forgot all about poor Oscar?"

"Are you accusing me of a crime?" Joan asked. "Do you think I killed him?"

Thompson stood behind Hannibal now, examining the girl with new suspicion. "I thought we only had one murderer here."

"Oh, she didn't kill Oscar Peters, but she sure set him up," Hannibal said. "Of course that was after she used him to cover her trip to Las Vegas for a divorce." Hannibal raised his eyes to Mark across the car's roof. "She fooled you both by sending her new employee, Oscar Peters, to Australia. He sent cards to you both, while she kept in touch by e-mail."

"He was my friend," Joan said. "He did me a favor."

Hannibal almost laughed. "Let's be real, Joan. Oscar wasn't the nice guy everybody thought he was. He did it because it was one more thing he had on you."

"Blackmail?" Thompson asked.

"That's why his friend Fancy was digging through the company records," Hannibal said. "And that's why he got fired. You see, Joan here gave him a job because of what he knew about the first murder, but he couldn't really prove anything and besides, he thought the killer, her husband, was dead. So he kept quiet at first. Then he got to be friends with Dean. They talked about the fact that they both had known her before their present jobs."

Mark walked slowly around the car, but instead of reaching for Joan he stood beside Hannibal. "Poor Dean. If he described his father's killing Oscar surely figured out that there was a connection between you and the two murders. The one in Dean's past and the one in his own."

"Sure," Thompson said, "And the second killing told him this husband of hers was still alive."

"Right," Hannibal said, closing on Joan. "And Oscar used that knowledge to get money out of you, didn't he?"

Joan's protective coating was proving to be a thin veneer. As it cracked, her face seemed to fall, melting like a wax mask "He took advantage of me. I'm the victim here."

"Uh-huh," Hannibal said. "Poor abused Joan. That's why you aimed Uncle Langford at him, just like a loaded gun. Too bad it took him so long to realize he was in danger. But he did. That's why he called Fancy and even tried to get me to protect him. I should have listened."

"Wait a minute," Mark said. "You mean the old man found out she was being blackmailed?"

"Nope," Hannibal said. "But she went to Oscar's house a few times to try to pay him, to threaten him, maybe to just talk him out of taking her dough. Maybe she even tried to seduce him."

"No chance with that swish," Joan muttered. Her fear was slowly transforming into anger.

.   "Anyway, you worked hard to make your meetings public knowledge. To old Langford and most of your employees, it looked like you were going out with him. Poor Oscar, unable to resist the ego boost, even told people the two of you were dating. That didn't bother you, did it? You were counting on Langford to do what he always did when you showed serious interest in a man. And he didn't let you down."

Mark nodded. "I see now why you kept our relationship secret. You were protecting me from him."

"Well that does fall together well," Thompson said. "It would be a snap for the old man to hide the knife in Dean Edward's apartment. But that makes the motive for the actual murder jealousy. Oscar wasn't really killed for what he knew at all. Dean Edwards really had nothing whatever to do with that killing."

Hannibal shook his head. "Nope. Except that he was an awfully convenient scapegoat. An acceptable sacrifice neither of them was concerned with. Not the target, just collateral damage."

-34-
SUNDAY

Oronoco Park, on the shores of the Potomac River in Alexandria, was a world away from Hannibal's backyard in the District. Trees lined the rocky shoreline but not so close together that they obscured his view of the deep blue river or the speedboats bouncing across its mirror surface. Fortunately, their foliage was enough to mute the grating snarl of the boat engines. It was a perfect autumn day, the sun bright enough to warm his bare arms below his golf shirt sleeves, the breeze just strong enough to keep him from reaching the point of perspiration. The breeze also carried the aroma of sizzling barbecue sauce from the bank of portable grills. Hannibal's mouth began to water in anticipation.

Hannibal had attended any number of backyard picnics, park side picnics and company picnics at past jobs. However, this was his first catered picnic, and he was enjoying watching the cooks in their aprons and tall white chef's hats, the scurrying servers and hustling cleanup crew, happy to be left out of the labor force. He was amazed at what Bea Collins had been able to pull together in just five days. He sat on a wooden picnic table, one outside the huge tent-like covering the crew had erected that morning. From his perch, he could see everyone who had attended his own backyard cookout a few days earlier, plus several more folks, all in a party mood. Bea and Dean Edwards sat at the table properly, hand in hand. A few feet away, Francis Edwards and Harry Irons sat side by side in folding chairs. Harry squeezed Francis' hand and spoke around a cigarette.

"That future daughter-in-law of yours sure puts on a spread, don't she?"

"It was the least I could do for all the friends and family who helped see me through the last couple of weeks," Bea said. "And I wanted us to get to know each other a little better before the big ceremony."

Hannibal's gaze wandered beyond Bea to a spot further along the riverside dirt path where Anna Ingersoll sat on a blanket watching Monty and her son Nicky tossing a Frisbee back and forth. Cindy had been talking to her and was just walking away, laughing. She was dressed much as he was, except that her jeans were much tighter. As she approached him and perched on the table, she tilted her face to one side and grinned at him.

"What's this? You holding class today?"

"Oscar wasn't killed because of what I told him at all," Dean said.

"Nope," Bea said, running a hand through Dean's hair. "It all had nothing to do with you, baby."

Hannibal considered how easy it had been for the old man to destroy this boy's life and his mother's. Remembering the Peters, Hannibal knew Langford Kitteridge had managed to destroy two families. But looking at Bea with Dean and his mother, he began to believe that sometimes, broken families can heal.

As if to contradict his last thought, Hannibal's beeper began to vibrate against his waist. He turned it off without looking because he knew who was buzzing him. Across the open field, past the volleyball court, Quaker leaned against Hannibal's car. He stared down the street to his left with his hands held in what most people would call the "time out" sign, although Hannibal knew it meant "trouble."

Hannibal hopped off the bench without losing his smile and sauntered toward Quaker. He didn't want to spoil the party, which is why he didn't tell Bea, Dean, Anna or even Cindy that he was on the alert for trouble. He was prepared to face two different sources of conflict that day and had asked Quaker, Sarge, Ray and Virgil to take turns on informal sentry duty.

By the time Hannibal reached the sidewalk Isaac Ingersoll was about 30 yards away, walking slowly toward the park as if the path was up a steep hill. The way a man walks when part of him doesn't really want to arrive at his destination. Wanting to make it easier for that part of him, Hannibal moved out briskly to meet him halfway.

"Hey Isaac. What's going on?"

Ingersoll stopped just short of walking into Hannibal. "I don't want no trouble. Just want to see Anna. Just for a minute. Tell her how I'm doing. Maybe she could come home?"

Isaac's clothes were clean but rumpled, as if he had taken a nap in them. His voice was softer than Hannibal remembered hearing it in the past. His eyes looked milky, and Hannibal wondered if he was under medication.

"Isaac, you know that if you walk down there into the park that whether you want it or not, there will be trouble."

"I just want to tell her how well I'm doing," Ingersoll said. "I don't want her to give up on me."

Hannibal looked at the ground, hands on his hips. "Isaac, Isaac. You know she doesn't want to see you yet. I know you're trying, man, but she's not ready."

"I'm doing good in the program," Ingersoll said, his voice close to pleading. "I haven't missed a session. Some of the guys in there don't really want to change but I'm not like them. I love her."

"I know all about the batterers' program, Isaac. It's thirty-six weeks long. It's a bit soon to declare victory, don't you think?"

Ingersoll took one tentative step forward, pushing his bulk into Hannibal's personal space. "Counselor says the program's got like a two-thirds success rate. I know I'm already really changed. Just want to tell her."

Hannibal stood his ground, now having to look up to maintain eye contact. "I'll tell her. Isaac, trust me, this is a bad idea. Please, please let's not make this physical. Let's not ruin your chance of her ever opening up to you."

Hannibal hardly reacted when he felt his beeper vibrating again. He knew he had to maintain his focus on the situation at hand. He worked at appearing relaxed while on another level he decided on what his first, second and third strikes would be if Ingersoll pressed the issue. But until he did, Hannibal had to give the big man's recent anger management training the benefit of the doubt.

While Ingersoll showed the muscle-locking tension of a man wrestling with his own demons, Quaker stepped up behind Hannibal and reached out to rest a hand lightly on Ingersoll's shoulder.

"Hey buddy, why don't we go talk somewhere? I'll buy you a beer."

Hannibal could see Ingersoll's shoulders begin to relax. He was standing down. The moment of greatest tension was past. When he spoke again it was one word. "Anna."

"Listen, Isaac, I'll have her call you, okay? Okay?"

Ingersoll nodded, and Quaker took his arm. "Good deal, buddy. Now let's go get that beer."

Hannibal smiled and stepped back slowly. Quaker gently turned Ingersoll with a hand on his arm, and the two men headed down the street. Hannibal figured he owed Quaker a lot more than the cost of however many beers they gulped down that day. Then his mind shifted to the picnic and he jogged slowly back to the group.

In a moment, he walked up behind Ursula Voss, the other disruption he had hoped to avert from ruining this day of quiet celebration. Looking over the graying bun at the back of her head he realized it was too late for him to affect the situation. The conversation had already started. Dean looked startled. Bea seemed distressed by the conflict. Standing behind them, Francis fumed. Harry held her hand tight, as if trying to rein in a lioness who sees her cubs attacked. Ursula faced them, her voice implying that she was the victim here.

"But you can't just leave me out of the ceremony. I'm family. I'm his family."

"How could you think we would welcome you to our ceremony," Bea asked. "Yes, you're family. You're also the woman who vilified his mother to him, falsely, for half his life. The first words out of your mouth when you walked over here should have been I'm sorry. To him, and to her."

"How can you blame me?" Ursula asked. "The evidence..."

"Bullshit!" Francis snapped, her voice flung at Ursula like a coil of razor wire. "Your lies ruined my life, you bitch. I'd already lost my husband, but you needed to hurt me more."

"I didn't do anything," Ursula said. "It was Dean's word." She took a step back, bumping into Hannibal who kept her from falling.

"You put those word into his mouth, you evil woman," Bea said. Francis' words seemed to make her bolder. "You should not even think of being in his life."

Francis said, "I bet you're sorry I ever got out of that place. Well, you better drag your sorry ass out of here before I do it for you." She put a foot on the bench between Dean and Bea and, for a moment, Hannibal thought she might go flying across the table at Ursula. The women were not that far apart in age, but Hannibal was sure that Francis could crush her frail sister-in-law under her wheels like an SUV rolling over an empty soda can.

"No." Dean said it quietly, but with more self-assurance than Hannibal had ever heard from the boy. He stood with one hand on Bea's shoulder while the other took his mother's hand. His blue eyes were suddenly very clear despite the softness of his features.

"Mother, all you've said is true. But it is also true that when I had no place to go, Aunt Ursula took me in. For some of the most important years of my life, she was all the family I had. You can hate her for things she's done, but I can't hate her."

People were wandering toward the tables, but everyone moved around the circle of silent tension bounded by Hannibal on one side and Dean on the other. Bea looked at Dean the way a woman in love should, with pride and warmth. The look between Francis and Ursula was more like that exchanged by a cat and a terrier. Or maybe, Hannibal thought, more like the look between a cobra and a rat. Then Harry Irons moved around to the end of the table where everyone could see him and took a deep pull on his cigarette.

"So, when do they put the food on around here?" Irons asked no one in particular.

"That depends on your answer to my question," Bea said. "Are you and Francis going to join us at the altar? Turn our ceremony into a double wedding?"

Harry grinned and nodded slowly. Francis turned to him, and all the hate drained out of her face, replaced by a smile that threatened to outshine the sun.

Dean turned to his aunt with a total calm that seemed to startle her. "Well, Aunt Ursula, I suppose if you're ready to celebrate my mom's new life, you'll be welcome at our wedding."

Hannibal wasn't sure what was going on in Ursula's mind, but she slowly lowered herself to the picnic table bench opposite Dean.

Cindy, who had stayed quietly on the sidelines, moved in to put an arm around Hannibal's waist. He realized he had just watched the resumption of a conversation that had been interrupted more than ten years ago. His sense was that Ursula would come around, and that eventually she and Francis would reach some sort of peace. He looked at Dean again, strong but relaxed, and realized that once in a while broken people could be healed too. He turned toward the volleyball net, where a few of the other guests were starting a game. Cindy squeezed his hand. The sun felt good on his neck. Life was good.

And they were finally starting to serve those barbecued ribs.

Author's Bio

Austin S. Camacho is a public affairs specialist for the Department of Defense. America's military people overseas know him because for more than a decade his radio and television news reports were transmitted to them daily on the American Forces Network.

He was born in New York City but grew up in Saratoga Springs, New York. He majored in psychology at Union College in Schenectady, New York. Dwindling finances and escalating costs brought his college days to an end after three years. He enlisted in the Army as a weapons repairman but soon moved into a more appropriate field. The Army trained him to be a broadcast journalist. Disc jockey time alternated with news writing, video camera and editing work, public affairs assignments and news anchor duties.

During his years as a soldier, Austin lived in Missouri, California, Maryland, Georgia and Belgium. While enlisted he finished his Bachelor's Degree at night and started his Master's, and rose to the rank of Sergeant First Class. In his spare time, he began writing adventure and mystery novels set in some of the exotic places he'd visited.

After leaving the Army he continued to write military news for the Defense Department as a civilian. Today he handles media relations and writes articles for the DoD's Deployment Health Support Directorate. He has settled in northern Virginia with his wife Dee and teenagers Phillip and Lela.

Austin is a voracious reader of just about any kind of nonfiction, plus mysteries, adventures and thrillers. When he isn't working or reading, he's writing.

Email: ascamacho@hotmail.com
Website: www.ascamacho.com

ALSO BY AUSTIN S. CAMACHO

BLOOD AND BONE

An eighteen-year-old boy lies dying of leukemia. Kyle's only hope is a bone marrow transplant, but no one in his wealthy Virginia family can safely supply it. His last chance lies in finding his father, a man who disappeared before he was born. Police and private investigators can find nothing on a trail eighteen years cold.

Kyle's family has nowhere to turn until they learn of a certain troubleshooter - that self-styled knight errant in dark glasses, Hannibal Jones. He has two weeks to find the missing man, but his search turns up so much more. A woman who might be Kyle's illegitimate sister. The woman who could be her mother. And the chauffeur who may have killed Kyle's father.

Hannibal follows a twisting, winding path of deception, conspiracy and greed, from Washington to Mexico, pursuing his own religion, his holy grail: the truth. But with each step closer to it he gets, the danger grows.

Available now in trade paperback from
Intrigue Books
Order your copy today at
www.ascamacho.com

Rave Reviews for Austin S. Camacho's
COLLATERAL DAMAGE

"Hannibal Jones is a new kind of pulp detective. Larger than life; he is a world traveler. He knows how to use his fists, but he also is a sensitive soul who can relate to his victims. Camacho has done an excellent job of expanding Hannibal's influence in this second novel. The reader has become comfortable with Hannibal's character, his partners, and his way of operating. Camacho has a great thing going with Hannibal Jones, and he should keep cranking out stories."

Midwest Book Review

"In Collateral Damage, Austin Camacho brings back his harder-than-hard troubleshooter, Hannibal Jones, in a teeth-rattling tale of murder and treachery. It's conventional wisdom that the second novel by young writers rarely lives up to the promise of their first book. Camacho turns this old adage upside down with a powerhouse writing performance. I'm holding my breath waiting for Hannibal Jones 3."

Warren Murphy,
Two-time Edgar Award winner
and creator of The Destroyer adventure series.

"Hannibal Jones is a professional problem solver, a hybrid of The Equalizer and Shaft. Collateral Damage is a well-plotted tale where not everything is what it seems, and when the truth comes to light the reader is certain to be satisfied. Author Camacho creates in Jones a likeable protagonist, tough and tender. Fans of suspense will want to call on Jones."

Blether Book Review

"Camacho employs a smooth, professional writing style that makes for easy and pleasurable reading, as does his well fleshed out and unique hero, Hannibal Jones. Multicultural characters, scenarios, and backgrounds provide depth and insight to Hannibal's character, an uncommonly original lead for this missing person tale. Here's hoping for more from both Hannibal and Mr. Camacho!"

Denise's Pieces Book Reviews